CHASING DARKNESS

Ruins of Rima Book One

E. Abraham

DEDICATION

For those who are trapped and terrified of running.
For those who are afraid to trust.
For those who live in doubt.
You are not alone.

Author's Note

Please read this if you have any triggers or have seen the trigger warnings and need more information!

Chasing Darkness is a spin-off of the Shadows of Synd Series. In Under the Shadows (Book one of the Shadows of Synd Series), you're introduced to the Guild. This organization is vile, depraved, and without moral regard. They steal people's lives for profit. They do not see them as humans, but merely a commodity to be bought and sold. They kidnap, rape, and sell these people with no regret. Because of this, it was very difficult to write about them and therefore I did not write about the inner-workings within the organization.

I debated on whether I would ever write Chasing Darkness. However, I knew this story needed to be written. It took some time to gather up the strength to tackle this very dark world. It was emotionally draining, but once I learned more about Aelia's character, I realized her story deserved to be told.

Chasing Darkness delves into the world of the Guild. Dante is ill-prepared and woefully over his head, not understanding the severity of what it will require to bring down this organization. He witnesses many acts that are forced upon the people being held by the Guild. He must play the part—emulating the others around him to fit in. However, Dante does not participate in most of the trigger warnings listed.

While Chasing Darkness is fiction, an estimated 14,500-17,500 people are trafficked each year within the United States. Some of the atrocities within this book is a reality for those who are taken. The National Human Trafficking hotline is open 24-hours a day, seven days a week.

888-373-7888

TRIGGER WARNINGS

Anxiety
Assault (Sexual/Physical)
Blood
Depression
Emotional Abuse
Violence
Kidnapping
Misogyny
Physical Abuse
Sexual Abuse
Poisoning (from food)
Forced Prostitution
Human/Sex Trafficking
PTSD/Panic Attacks
Sexual Harassment
Slut Shaming
Starvation
Torture

Animal abuse (dogfighting)

Content Warnings:

Sexually Explicit Scenes (consensual between MMC/FMC)
Adult Language
Use of a collar/leash (Imperfect BDSM Etiquette)

ONE
Dante

I never thought my life would sink as low as it has. Being the president of a motorcycle club puts me in some precarious situations, but this takes the cake.

The underground club doesn't look like much from the outside. It reminds me of the speakeasies back in the 20s, with a nondescript entrance, complete with a password. Three weeks ago, I was struggling to find my way into one of the Guild's elite parties.

Now I'm giving the password to the man behind the slit in the door. I overheard it at the dogfight I was at two nights ago from a kid who didn't look old enough to drive, but was clearly spending Daddy's money.

When I rushed off to Synd to help Ryker Helms, another MC president, fend off the Guild, I assumed they only had one operation. The deeper I dig into their organization, the more I'm horrified by the things they dirty their hands with. The Trade and the Auction where they sell people are the worst by far. Every other event is just more bullshit piled on top. This gambling ring is mild in comparison.

I straighten my tie, and pull my cuffs over the expensive watch I picked up last week. It's cumbersome and too flashy, but it certainly helps me fit in. I fucking hate it. I'm used to leather jackets and grease on my hands, not fancy suits and clean nails. If I'm going to infiltrate the Guild, though, I must play the part.

The heavy metal door screeches as it opens, revealing a long, dark hallway. Music thuds through the space, pounding in my ears. I'll have a headache by the time the night is over. Hopefully, this venture is more fruitful than the previous ones I've been to.

I'm already a week past when I said I'd be back at Vipers' headquarters. Leaving Maddox in charge isn't the most ideal situation. I can only hope I have a club to come back to when I'm finished gathering information on the Guild. I can't bring them down by myself, but with reinforcements, we might have a chance.

Slipping into another persona, one I don't particularly like, I prowl down the hall toward a black curtain draped across the doorway. A man with a wicked-looking knife hanging from his belt grins as he pulls the fabric back, exposing a den of iniquity.

On the surface, the space looks like any other gambling hall. Round gaming tables are laid out around the space with a bar set up on the side. A stage lines the other wall with scantily dressed women dancing.

On the surface, they look like they're having fun, but as I make my way closer, the outline of bruises flash across their exposed flesh. There's a deadness in their eyes, as if they've been doing this for so long, they no longer register the men reaching out to grope them.

A couple women work the floor, carrying drinks back and forth from the bar. As they pass the men seated around the tables, hard hands snatch at their arms, their hips, their hair—anything to harass them. The women scamper away as soon as possible, only to be subjected to the treatment again when they return with glasses filled with more liquor.

"Would you like something to drink, sir?" a timid woman asks, and I turn.

Makeup cakes her face, hiding whatever atrocities the Guild has visited upon her. Glancing at her hands, I notice a slight tremor as she grips a notepad and pen. My gut tightens as I stare at her blue eyes, fear blowing out her pupils. I may rationally understand what I have to do, but it doesn't make it any easier to pretend to be like every other man in this room. Reminding myself I can't save them all, I clear my throat.

"Whiskey on the rocks," I say, and she nods. Latching onto her arm, I yank her back. "Top shelf."

She shakes in my grasp and I drop my hand. A bitter taste overtakes the back of my throat, but this is the way things must be for now. I track her as she scampers away to the bar. A man, probably not much older than eighteen, if that, brushes past me, taking my attention away from the woman. Gripping his wrist, I stop him, squeezing as he spins around.

"Best not try that here," I growl.

Shaking his lanky brown hair from his face, he nods, a glint of defiance in his eyes. I wonder how he got in here. He's not particularly skilled in pickpocketing. He wasn't even able to unclasp my watch. I doubt the Guild would employ him, especially for this.

"They'll let any riffraff in here, won't they?" a man around the same age as me murmurs from the table a few feet away.

"It's disgusting, really." I push the kid away.

He stumbles, then flips me off before disappearing. Scanning the table, the other men are all younger than me, shooting wary looks at the man who spoke. The dealer hesitates to lay the next card, glancing at the one who is clearly in charge.

"Get to it. I'm here to play cards, not watch you bumble around," he barks out, drawing the attention of the others at the next table. "You joining or are you here for other entertainment?"

He glances up, bright blue eyes piercing me as a smirk pulls up his lips. The serving girl rushes up with my drink, practically running away as soon as the glass is in my hand. The man's hand snakes out, wrapping his around her waist. She winces as his fingers dig into her flesh. My palms itch as he drags her onto his lap and his hand reaches up to grope her chest.

Falling into the chair next to him, I school my face before he can see my disgust. The dealer slaps down the last card, indicating final bids. The man continues his quest on her body as he throws in a handful of chips. Everyone groans as he reveals his hand, several shoving back from the table.

"If you're waiting for an invitation to join, you won't get one," he mutters before planting an open-mouthed kiss on her neck.

"Women shouldn't be allowed at the table," I grunt. It's the only excuse I can think of to get her away from him.

He laughs, shoving her off his lap, and she stumbles away, righting her clothes as she goes. Another man sits down in a vacant seat and pulls out a wad of cash. Taking the money from my pocket, I peel off several bills, laying them down. I don't gamble often, and every den has different rules, but this one seems pretty straightforward.

"What business are you in…" He raises an eyebrow.

"Dante Cruz. And I deal in many things, mostly offshore affairs. You?" There's no way I'm giving out my real last name, but I won't fall into the trap of not answering my first name if I give out a completely false one.

When I was at the dogfight, I had a different story, a different life, a different lie. This environment is higher class. The vaguer I am, the easier it'll be to keep track of hopefully. He nods, peering at his cards.

"Byron Michaels." He holds his hand out, and I shake it firmly. "I keep my businesses closer to home. Easier to dominate the masses when you control their vices."

I grunt in response, a sinking feeling coming over me. It's largely how the Vipers are run, though with more morals. If we control the underbelly, we're able to make sure no one abuses it. Helms runs the Reapers much the same way, but he has the added benefit of aligning with the Kings and Byrns. We've been doing a lot of business with the mafia families in Synd through the Reapers since Helms and I reconnected after my father died.

Hopefully, my half brother Maddox can maintain whatever relationships we have until I can return. He never did get along with Helms despite us all growing up together. Actually, Maddox never seems to get along with anyone he can't control.

"A worthwhile cause," I say with a grin.

Men's voices shout over the music from another game across the room. One takes a swing at another, screaming about cheating, and several men rush in. They're subdued and marched from the room. Their shouts are cut off when the back door slams shut.

A woman screams from the stage when someone leaps up next to her and grabs her arm. Her fingers wrap around the pole, hanging on for dear life as he yanks at her body. Whipping my head around, I search for more security to stop him, but they watch the scene with passive gazes.

He breaks her grip and hauls her through the back curtain, her sobs trailing in her wake. Disgust turns my stomach, but I drop my gaze to my cards. I'm in this for the long haul. Blowing my cover and saving one girl won't help the multitude of others the Guild has stolen away from their lives, no matter how much I wish otherwise.

Byron's hand lands on my shoulder. "Don't worry. He'll have a little fun and she'll be back. Then you can have your turn."

It takes me a beat, but I tip my head. "I'm surprised this place hasn't been shut down yet. Be a damn shame when it is."

He grins, throwing more chips onto the growing pile. "You won't have to worry about that. The Guild runs this place, Cruz. No one would touch them regardless, but we've got quite a few higher ups in our ranks."

"High enough to actually matter? I'd hate for one vigilante to bring them to their knees."

He eyes me, but I keep my concentration on the game. Since I've sat down, several rounds have gone by without my really noticing. Somehow, I've accrued a pile of chips. Mostly I'm just throwing out random bets, more concerned with the information Byron is dropping. I toss more into the middle, and the man to my right curses, throwing his cards on the pile.

"Bold bet putting a thousand in the pot with that river," Byron says.

"What's the point of being meek when you're not? Powerful men don't hesitate, do they, Michaels?"

"Certainly not," he murmurs, a calculating look entering his eyes. "We have a few judges within the fold. Not to mention the mayor of Rima. He has a specific proclivity he can't engage in anywhere else."

"Don't we all?" I say with a smirk, even as my chest tightens.

The dealer pushes the pile of chips in my direction, and I shake my head. Panic crosses the young man's face and he signals one of the bosses. A burly man stomps over, swiping the chips into a bucket before marching to the back.

"Not going to stick around and let me win my money back?" Byron asks, flipping a chip between his fingers.

"I find myself in need of some fresh air and perhaps some other entertainment. If you're still here when I'm done, I'll be sure to stop by," I say, pushing from the chair.

"Be sure that you do."

The boss comes back, handing me a stack of bills. I don't bother to count it, just shove it in my pocket. There's only so much of a place like this I can stand before I'll lose my temper. Plus, with the way Michaels is eyeing me, I'd rather not get into a position I can't get out of.

I nod to the man, then weave my way through the tables, intent on the back door the others were escorted out of. No one stops me as I exit, the spring air washing over me and cooling my heated skin.

The rankness of the dark alley invades my nose and bile builds in my throat. I wonder how many decaying bodies have been tossed in the dumpster, leaving nothing behind but a revolting smell. This would be the perfect time to be a smoker to mask the foul stink.

Most of the traffic has died down this late, with only a few cars passing the entrances of the alley. A dumpster sits several feet away, and I move toward the light filtering through the open mouth of the alley, hoping distance will help with the smell.

Peeking around the corner of the building, I scan the sidewalk. A few men loiter around the front. If this place was closer to the city center where the clubs are, they'd probably fit in, but on the quiet street they stick out.

The door behind me slams open, and Byron steps out, growling into his phone. Prowling back and forth, his face flushes, then he hangs up. I wish I could have overheard his conversation, but he seemed to be listening more than talking by the time he came outside. I'm surprised he hasn't noticed me yet, even though he's buried in his phone.

Someone peers out from behind the dumpster, eyeing Byron. Leaning more into the shadows, I track the kid's movements as he slinks closer to the older man. When he crouches, the light from the streetlamp illuminates his face and I realize it's the same man who tried to lift my watch. My heart pounds in my chest, and I'm torn between warning Byron and letting this play out. He may be my only ticket into the more elite activities the Guild puts on. I can't let this opportunity pass me by.

The kid produces a knife, light glinting off the blade as he steps closer to Byron.

"Wallet," he squeaks, his voice barely reaching me. "Now."

"You have got to be kidding me. You can't honestly think I'll allow you to rob me," Byron sneers, sliding his phone into his pocket.

"Give me your wallet and that fancy watch or I'll stab you."

Byron tips his head back, his laughter echoing between the buildings. "Don't state your intentions, boy. If you're going to do it, don't announce it."

The kid grips the handle, brandishing it in front of him. "Give it up. Last chance."

"How about I teach you how to actually handle a knife?"

Byron steps closer, and the kid lashes out wildly. The knife slices across Byron's arm. He lets out an angry howl and stumbles back. I wait for him to pull his own weapon, but he just glares at the younger man. The thief advances, swinging the blade out, and Byron is forced to retreat until the wall stops his progress.

I slide closer, unsheathing my knife as I go. When the would-be thief lunges, I let the dagger fly. It sinks into his forearm, forcing him to drop his own weapon. He staggers back, tugging it out and letting it clatter across the ground. Wrapping his fingers around the wound, he gapes at the blood seeping through his flesh. Byron whips his head toward me, mouth falling open as the kid takes off for the opposite end of the alley.

"Impressive," Byron grunts, winding a handkerchief around his injury, though it doesn't look deep. In fact, I'm pretty sure it's not even bleeding anymore.

Grabbing my knife, I straighten, wiping the blade on my leg before slipping it back into the sheath with trembling fingers.

"I trust you're not injured?" I ask, keeping my face impassive though my mind still reels.

"I'm fine. You're a man of many talents, it seems, Cruz."

"One can never be too prepared, Michaels. Unfortunate he got away." I gesture to where the man disappeared.

He waves away my words. "Listen, I may have an opportunity for you."

Raising an eyebrow, I tuck my hands in my pockets. Relief floods my body even as my hands curl into fists. This is the in I need, but now that it's here, I have the irrational urge to decline. All these weeks I've been searching, almost hoping I didn't find an opening. A chill chases up my spine until it freezes into an icy grin.

"I'd love to hear it."

Two

Aelia

Another day in hell. Actually, hell would be preferable to this place. At least it would be warm there. I swear I've been cold for years. It's probably because I haven't had a proper meal in that much time. After this long, I should be used to it and yet every morning I go to bed with cold feet and numb fingers. Something so small shouldn't consume so much of my mind, but if I focus on the little things, I won't lose my mind.

Banging on my door has me jolting as I'm pulling on my stiletto heels. Calling it a door is being generous. My room is an old closet with an opening half the size of a normal entrance. I don't even have a mattress, just a pile of blankets on the floor. Getting dressed in such a small space grates on my nerves, but since I have no say over anything in my life, I'm grateful for even this.

"Get up," Grant bellows, hammering on the door one last time before he stomps away.

Sighing, I resign myself to making it through one more day. I peek around the door, checking the hallway for anyone else before slipping out. The building they've claimed is huge, housing most of the organi-zation. I think it was abandoned, but I wasn't brought here until they had the place cleaned up. A couple bedrooms are still covered in dust since they focused on the places they needed for the business.

Entering the office suite attached to a large conference room, I slow when I spot my boss. He's not really my boss, but it's the only way I can think of him without examining the mess my father trapped me in almost ten years ago. Even back then, the Guild had been around for a few decades, passed from one despicable human to the next.

Shuffling around to my makeshift desk, I settle into the chair. It's the most comfortable thing I've had in my life for a while. He only gave it to me to keep up with appearances. Can't have a random whore sitting on the floor with a laptop without inviting questions as to why she's not being sold.

"Begin," Jenkins murmurs, and I grab a notepad and pen.

The laptop is still booting up, but Jenkins won't wait for it. He'll blame me for wasting his time. I shudder, thinking about the last time I fucked up. The small scars still litter my skin, reminding me of my transgressions. The mental ones run deeper.

Grant constantly berates me, telling me how temporary my place is. Although I'm beginning to think he's exaggerating. The threat worked when my father first sold me, but it's watered down now. They'd never sell me. I know too much. They'll have to bury me, which is still on the table.

"Joseph Merrick is requesting another meeting. He wants to bypass the system and be granted full VIP access because of his position. Reynolds told him that wouldn't be a possibility, but he was insistent on speaking with someone higher up."

Jenkins leans back, tapping his finger against his full lips. My eyes keep skipping to him as I pull up the programs I need for the day. Mostly I work with the money side of things. I'm basically a glorified accountant with a little receptionist work thrown in for good measure. When everything is set, I stare at him, wondering where his life went wrong.

This is one of the mind games I play to make the night go faster—how did a relatively attractive and rich man fall into an organization that traffics humans along with a plethora of other dirty businesses thrown in for good measure? Even in his fifties, he's still handsome with his salt and pepper hair and strong cheekbones. Maybe it was a family business and he was merely born into it. Jenkins certainly treats it like a business instead of the hellscape it actually is.

"Set it up. Also, set up something with Dante Cruz."

I almost ask who that is, but bite my tongue. I'm not here to question things, just figure them out.

"Yes, sir," I murmur, and he turns his soulless brown eyes to me.

The corner of his mouth twitches, and I drop my gaze. He's never touched me, but I can see in his eyes that he wants to. He would love to break me, just like he does the other girls who come through here. I'm kept alive and semi-whole because my father said I was good with numbers. Fortuitous timing for me, since the organization was drowning in a sea of debt from their frivolous spending and mismanagement. I'm not happy about the fact that I've made them more money, but this is quite literally life and death.

"You've been around a long time, Aelia," he says, twirling his pen between his fingers.

I refuse to answer. We play this game at least once a week, him baiting me and me resolutely staying quiet.

"I bet you feel comfortable here now, don't you?"

Internally, I snort. As if anyone could be comfortable here when they're the prey. Opening the statements for the offshore accounts, I check the balances. After a certain amount of zeros, it ceases to be money and becomes merely numbers. Jenkins taps his pen on his desk, probably thinking he can annoy me into answering. I tense when he pushes out of his chair, keeping my eyes fixed on the screen as he approaches.

My stomach turns as he sweeps my dark brown hair over my shoulder, fingers brushing against my neck. Clicking on the cameras, I cycle through them. Anything to keep him from seeing my trembling hands. He leans into my back, planting his hands on the desk and boxing me in.

"If I wouldn't be losing a valuable asset, I'd use your body for what it was made for. Since I can't, go down to the Pit and find someone who looks like you—bring her to me. Maybe I'll even let you watch as I break her."

I nod stiffly as his breath ghosts across me, making my skin crawl. Swallowing hard, I wait until he's stepped away before pushing back in my chair. His arm brushes mine as he adjusts himself, and I hurry for the door.

"One more thing, Aelia," he calls, and I freeze as my hand rests on the knob. "You'll be working the floor tonight. Wear something nice."

Smoothing down the excessively short gray pencil skirt I'm currently wearing, I finally make my escape. Grant leers at me from the end of the hall, and I take the back staircase down. As much as I hate going to the Pit, it's better than being stuck in a room with Jenkins.

The deeper I descend into the bowels of the mansion, the darker it gets. I honestly can't remember the last time I've seen the sun. Sometimes I feel as if it no longer exists. Is there a dawn in hell? Probably not. I assume it's mostly fire and brimstone lighting the way. It's early enough in the night I don't pass anyone. Most are still sleeping, waiting for the night's festivities to begin.

The guard at the entrance to the basement nods to me, pity lining his eyes as he keys in the code and pulls the door open. He's one of the few men who feels anything other than contempt for me. Most of them hate the fact that I'm allowed to walk freely. They're constantly fielding off advances from members demanding me for the night. No one takes it well when they're told I'm off-limits. A lone woman in this place only creates problems for the guards, making me a prime target for their ire.

The large space in the basement is lined with makeshift rooms, one step up from cages, really. There are no doors, just open canvas tents to create large bedrooms. Rachel called it fucked-up glamping. Actual cages line the other side, though they're only occupied by men.

No one tries to escape. There's nowhere to go, anyway. Most of them have been broken long before they make it down here.

Heads whip in my direction as my heels click across the stones, following my progress. They all know why I'm here, and they despise me for it. They'll never hate me as much as I hate myself, though. A lot of them have requested to bleach their hair so they no longer resemble me. Even the ones whose light brown strands aren't even close to mine beg to change, fearful they will be chosen next. One girl whose request was denied huddles in the corner of her room with several others around her.

I used to apologize when I came to get them. At that point, I was beyond tears. The woman I chose wasn't. She begged me not to choose her, but the decision was already made. Jenkins came with me those first few times to make sure I did my job correctly. As soon as I had looked at the young woman, his mind was made up. By the time she left his office, the tears had disappeared, along with the light in her eyes.

This isn't the first time I'll be forced to watch. I've listened to their screams, seen their bruises and burns, and scrubbed their blood from too many surfaces. It's not the sex for Jenkins. No, he likes to hear them shatter, both in mind and body. And since he can't do it to me, he'll do it to the others.

"Mistress," Rachel calls. "Out hunting again?"

I grind my teeth, hating the nickname they've given me. Rachel has been here longer than most. She survives on sarcasm and grit. No one knows why they keep her around instead of sending her to the Auction where most of the women go. The VIP members would pay good money for her, but she just stays here in the Pit, taking care of the others.

"Take the bitch. She's getting on my nerves," Benjamin calls from the other side of the room.

Glancing toward the cages housing the men, my heart races. He's been here for a while, too, waiting for his turn. I thought with his classically beautiful looks, he'd be snatched up. He reminds me of Hermes, the Greek god, with his blond hair and the impish tilt to his chin. Resting his arms through the bars, he cocks his head and grins at me.

"They're all bitches to you, Benjamin. You'll have to be more specific," Rachel shouts back with a laugh.

A guard walks by, slamming a baton against the metal bars, but Benjamin doesn't flinch. They used to keep the men and women fully separated, but there isn't as much space in this building. The last area we occupied had a whole acre to house everything. The cold weather forced the Guild south. They never fully set up in Synd, a city several hours to the west.

I stop in a doorway almost at the end of the room. Scanning the space, I spot the woman lounging on the mattress. I knock on the wooden support, and she rolls her head toward me. Her eyes are green, but our facial structures are similar enough. Dark hair, a little lighter than mine, fans across the makeshift pillow. She needs a shower and some new clothes. It's the only kindness I can offer them without giving too much away.

"Who?" she whispers.

Swallowing the bile creeping up my throat, I steel myself. "Jenkins, Ingrid."

She nods, as if she knew the answer all along and just needed the confirmation. "Well, at least I get a shower then, huh?"

"There is that," I murmur.

She heaves up, ribs pronounced even as she slouches. I turn, tipping my chin up as we pass the others who whisper insults under their breath. I'm used to it, but I wish they understood I have no choice. In this place though, I'm the Mistress, doing the bidding of the devil. The world shouldn't be like this. It should be bright and full of potential.

Hell doesn't care about potential. The devil doesn't care how we got here. The only way out is to be fractured beyond repair or dead—and death would be preferable.

THREE

Dante

The mansion looming before me is massive, even bigger than the Kings' place back in Synd. How the Guild acquired it in such a short time is a feat I don't want to examine too closely. I'm pretty sure it was an old embassy or something, left abandoned shortly before I moved to Rima. It's sat ever since, though the mayor promised in his campaign he'd deal with the eyesore. He's as corrupt as they come, so I'm not surprised he sold it to the Guild.

I rarely come this far south since Viper territory sits on the northern edge of the city. When Byron, as he insisted I call him, told me of it, I feigned ignorance. To him, I'm merely an overly wealthy businessman here to secure some mysterious deals with those running the depraved side of Rima. He framed this meeting as an opportunity to network with a little entertainment on the side. As if I couldn't figure out this is actually the seat of the Guild.

If I had enough explosives, I could probably bring the whole place down. They'd probably just pop up in another city, the incident merely a blip on their books. If this mansion—complete with goddamn peacocks wandering around the grounds—is any indication, they could take the hit.

"Cruz, glad you could make it," Byron says as he exits his car.

Another vehicle pulls up behind and the driver hops out to open the back door. I tense, turning my body when I spot familiar black hair peppered with white. Judge Joseph Merrick steps out, and my chest tightens. This is the one test that truly matters. Merrick and I have never crossed paths, but he knows of the Vipers. At least according to my sister Mac's best friend, Willow. I'm inclined to believe her, since he's her stepfather. The question is, will he recognize me?

"Ah, Judge Merrick," Byron booms, holding out his hand. "Finally got that meeting, I see."

Merrick's mouth twitches before he shakes Byron's hand. "Yes, well. Hopefully, they will see the benefit of having someone like me within their ranks."

Byron nods as if this is a simple business transaction instead of dealings with a criminal organization that makes mine look like toddlers playing with BB guns. I plaster on a neutral expression as Byron gestures to me.

"Meet my newest recruit, Dante Cruz."

Tucking my hand in my pocket, I pivot, extending my other hand. I resist the urge to shoot him, opting to squeeze his fingers as hard as he is mine. He tilts his head, narrowing his blue eyes.

"Pleasure," I say.

"Dante, did you say?" Merrick asks, finally releasing my hand.

"Dante Cruz, Judge."

"Are you from Rima, Cruz?"

He eyes my watch before plastering on the politician smile I've seen so many times in the media.

"Ah, no. I have several residences across the country, actually. This is the first time I've been to Rima." I rock back on my heels.

Two more cars pull into the drive and several rich assholes emerge, laughing as they make their way up the stairs to the massive double doors. To the untrained eye, others would assume this is a gala or fundraiser for the elite. When the doors open, revealing the interior, another world appears.

"Well, hopefully your stay in Rima is fruitful. Have a good evening, gentlemen." He turns, striding off without a backward glance.

Byron's hand lands on my shoulder. "Don't worry about him. I've found him a bit uptight, although a good man to have in your back pocket, if you know what I mean."

I nod, following him up the stairs. The guard greets Byron, then raises an eyebrow as Byron explains who I am and vouches for me. He takes the white keycard the man gives him before waving us inside.

"That's your ticket in to some places for the evening. It will be deactivated when the night is over. You'll have to wait for full access." He flashes a black keycard before tucking it back in his pocket.

"And what exactly is this event?" I ask as we make our way down the hallway.

Several doors with card slots line the walls, some with guards outside. They're all beefy and nondescript. The other members' eyes skip over them as they lean against walls and monitor random doors. I'm sure this place is crawling with security.

"Mostly it's a show to highlight what the Guild has to offer, but more of a teaser for another event coming up. Have you heard of the Auction?"

My skin crawls as we come to a massive ballroom. "I have. I was told the guest list is exclusive."

"Oh it is, but don't worry. I'm sure we can find a spot for you," he says, clapping me on the shoulder with a grin.

He leads us to a round table with several men already clustered around it. People mill about, chatting as if this is a fancy charity event, just waiting to bid on ridiculous items none of them need. In essence, that's still true, except they'll be fighting over people as if they're possessions ripe for the picking.

Byron introduces me to the men around us as we settle in our chairs, but I immediately forget their names. I should make more of an effort to learn who is involved. The way Byron is conversing makes me think he's brought them all on, introducing them to a world I wish didn't exist. I assume they are in the same boat as me, not high enough on the ladder to warrant a full invitation to the Auction.

"Cruz here cleaned me out the other day," Byron says with a grin. "Had to see what else he was made of."

"What happened to your hand, Byron? You choose the wrong girl to fuck with and piss off her handler?" The man to my right chuckles, gesturing with his glass to the bandage.

Byron's eyes tighten the slightest bit. "Just a little accident. Nothing to worry about."

He meets my gaze, and I nod with a smirk. He's set the tone for the reasons he invited me, making it clear he wants no one to know what really happened in the alley. I didn't have any intention of revealing his secret, but at least I have a little something to hold over him.

"Drink, sir?" a woman says from beside my elbow.

Glancing up, I freeze, caught in her dark brown eyes. All the others I've seen caught in the Guild's clutches have a deadness in their gazes. Hers are clear—vibrant—with an edge of defiance. Maybe she's new, not yet exposed to the horrors within these walls.

Clearing my throat, I curl my hand into a fist. "Bourbon on the rocks."

She nods sharply before spinning around in impossibly high heels. Her hips sway along with her long brown hair as she navigates her way to the bar. I track her as she expertly avoids all the questing hands reaching out for her. One man even slaps another's in his quest to snag her. He shakes his head at the younger man, glancing around to see if anyone noticed.

"Some of the women are spoken for already, though they aren't usually put on the floor," Byron murmurs, following my gaze.

"How do we know who we can touch, then?"

He waves away my words. "Like I said, they aren't put on the floor. *That one,* though, is untouchable, and the others find out pretty quickly if they cross the line."

"Then why is she working? And why is she off limits?"

Her eyes meet mine as she makes her way back with my drink in hand.

"Works for the big boss and he throws her to the wolves sometimes just to see her squirm is my guess. Believe me, he'll never give her up. Although, with the way she acts, I doubt he's tasted her."

"What do you mean?"

He grins, then licks his lips, and my gut tightens. "Because she's still unbroken."

The lights dim just as she reaches me, setting my drink on the table. The man next to me, who can't be much older than I am, grabs a handful of her ass. He must not have heard Byron's warning. She jolts upright, alarm flashing across her face. He latches onto her wrist as she tries to twist away.

Slipping my switchblade from my pocket, I flick it open before leaning into his space, my shoulder brushing her stomach. He doesn't notice the knife until it rests against his crotch, and he stiffens, still gripping her.

"I suggest you let her go before I take something precious to you," I murmur.

"What the hell? These bitches are free game, so back the fuck off," he snarls, jerking back, but there's nowhere for him to go.

"This one's mine. I won't tell you again." Digging the tip into the fabric of his pants, he sucks in a breath and releases her.

She stares at me for a full ten seconds, but I don't take my eyes off him. Her body trembles and she steps away. Leaning back, I put my knife away, glancing at her from the corner of my eye. I smirk as she whips around. It's all for show, but apparently it works. A chuckle escapes Byron, and he leans into my space.

"I don't know if you just saved him or fucked yourself, but good luck either way."

A lilting sound fills the space, drowning out whatever else he wants to say. I pay more attention to the where the woman has retreated than the people dancing on stage.

Men line the front, scanning the crowd, but it's more subdued than the gambling den from a few nights ago. No one is hollering at them. None of them jump onto the stage. All are seated, calmly watching the show.

It's subtle, the progression from them observing to something more. The dancers on stage are a mix of men and women, different shapes and sizes, all scantily clad. They start to move, some of them more fluid than others. From my position, I spot a man tucked away on the edge of the stage behind the curtain with something in his hands.

It's then that I notice the collars around the dancer's necks. When a short, blonde woman stumbles back toward the curtain, fear radiating from her body, the guard presses the button. She convulses, almost crashing to her knees, but somehow stays upright, using the pole to steady herself. She goes back to dancing, although she's still subdued, eyes darting to the guard every few seconds. Flexing my fingers, I glance over the crowd, trying to push away the unease riding me.

One man lifts his hand and a guard hustles over, leaning to hear what he wants. The guard casually lopes back to the stage, gesturing to a tall, raven-haired woman whose face falls the slightest bit. It hits me that they're actually handlers, keeping the dancing men and women in line. She wobbles on her heels, almost crashing to the ground before righting herself and exiting through the back curtains. When I look back, the man is weaving his way through the tables.

"Some prefer to break them in private. Others take them to an open room. They enjoy putting on a show. All sorts of ways to play with them. Just tell them what you prefer and they can usually make it happen."

Nausea bubbles in my stomach, and I struggle to keep my face impassive. Draining my glass, I set it down gently instead of chucking it at Byron's head like I want. I could really use another one, but I'd rather not raise my hand. I'd probably end up being escorted to one of the playrooms, and like hell am I going that far to infiltrate their ranks. The Guild needs to be taken down but not at the expense of my morals.

I fought long and hard to make the Vipers a better club. Helms and I used to talk for hours about the things we would do differently, starting with how we treated our women. When our fathers ran the Reapers, women were property, little better than trophies.

We're both slowly working toward a better future, with women being our equals, not our subordinates. The Reapers are further along than us, since Helms has a five-year head start on me. My bastard of a father just refused to die, not that I could bring myself to kill him. An invisible disease took him in the end. It was a better death than he deserved. And I've been working ever since to right all the wrongs he sowed into the Vipers.

My half-brother Maddox doesn't help. Mac thinks I don't notice his treatment of her, but I do. I just can't do anything about it yet. She's strong and has been telling me not to fight her battles for her since we were teens. Saving her will only help reenforce the idea that she can't do it herself. Or at least that's what she's told me.

Looking around this ornate room, I'm glad I didn't tell her where I was going. She would have tried to follow and I doubt I'd be able to save her from the same fates as the women locked away in this hell.

Byron leans into my space, pulling me from my past. I raise my eyebrow as I take a sip from my glass. The whiskey is smooth, but in this environment, I'm unable to enjoy it.

"Put in a good word for you. Don't make me look bad when they call you up." He grins, but there's a glint in his eyes.

Byron lifts his hand, practically salivating as he points to a man dancing in the back. I see the exact moment he's shocked, all his muscles tensing, and then he tips his chin up as Byron trips from his chair, gesturing for the man to follow him. One of the handlers holds up a hand to stop Byron, then points to the side exit next to the stage, and he rushes off.

When I glance back at the stage, the young man is gone, and I turn my head to hide the disgust on my face. No one deserves this type of treatment, regardless of who they are.

Someone clears their throat next to me, and I whip my head toward the sound. It's the server from before, although I don't know if "server" is the right label in these circumstances. She twists her fingers in front of her until she notices I'm watching her movements. Tipping her chin up, she stares down her nose at me.

"Sir, your presence is requested." She spins, marching back toward the bar across the room.

I hesitate before pushing to my feet to follow her, weaving around the tables. I could run—straight out the door to freedom. My haphazard plan may unravel before I've even begun.

The audience's eyes are glued to the stage thankfully, but an older man takes notice of her, reaching out to grab her wrist. She dances away, expertly avoiding his groping hands, and I swipe my hand across my face to hide my sigh of relief. A guard hurries over, placating the man, and she slips away.

Whoever this woman is, she clearly isn't like the others, broken and beaten beyond repair. It hits me then, perhaps she's in league with them, so far into a delusion of her importance that she justifies propping up their organization. The only way I'll find out is by talking to her, which requires me to get her on her own.

Sighing, I tuck my hands in my pockets and follow her as she ducks behind another curtain. I'd rather not go down this road, but as a plan takes shape in my mind, I'm afraid I don't have any other options.

FOUR

Aelia

I don't like having Dante Cruz at my back. I can't see what he's doing and that puts me on edge more than the others' wandering hands. None of my choices are my own, though. Jenkins makes my decisions, dictating everything from my clothes to what I eat.

My stomach gurgles when I remember I haven't had any food since I woke up. Sometimes they forget that we're human and still need sustenance to survive. They don't care if we waste away. In fact, a lot of the patrons prefer skin and bones.

"Where are we going?" he says, his voice rolling over me like thunder on a moonless summer night.

"Your presence has been requested." The thumping music has faded enough that I don't have to turn around for him to hear me.

Pivoting, I climb the stairs to the upper levels. They're wide enough I can avoid the other men, but I can't escape the leering glances. I swear I can feel Dante's eyes burning a hole in my back, and I swallow hard to suppress the shiver. I'm sure if this was a normal circumstance, I'd be salivating over him. Though he's exactly who I would have had a crush on when I was a teenager, I'm no longer in a position to lust after anyone.

Glancing back as I reach the top, I catch his chocolate eyes. He brushes his dark hair off his forehead with a tattooed hand, and I whip back around. No denying he's sexy with his sharp cheekbones and full lips.

There's a dangerous edge to him, and only time will tell if he's the danger that sends thrills or terror through me.

Pursing my lips, I dismiss the whole idea from my mind. There were quite a few people who came through in the beginning that I thought I could ask for help. They all betrayed me for a chance at a higher position with the Guild. I stopped trying to find a way out long ago, at least by asking others for aid. I'm biding my time until an opportunity presents to escape this hell. It'll come eventually. I just don't know if I'll be running away or leaving in a body bag. Most likely, it'll be the latter.

"What's your name?" he grunts as we reach another, less used staircase.

My ankles are screaming by the time we reach the top, and I still haven't answered him. Unless I'm commanded to tell him, I won't. Information around here is just as lucrative as the merchandise, as Jenkins calls them. They're people, but he'll never see them as anything other than profit.

As I reach for the handle to the main office, his hand circles my wrist, and I freeze. My breath stutters in my chest, and I wait for the blow or the proposition or the pain. He'll demand I do what he wants, putting me in the position to try to talk my way out of the situation.

Jenkins won't allow him to claim me, too worried about my mental state. For all Jenkins's pomp and circumstance, he knows finding a replacement for me would be disastrous for the Guild. He's already tried once or twice to put me in my place, shoving me into the Pit and installing someone else into my position.

Every time I end up right back where I started, sitting in that chair and making the Guild more money. I still haven't figured out a way to topple them from the inside. There are too many parts I'm not in charge of, and it grates on my nerves.

"Please, just tell me who I'm meeting," he whispers, releasing my arm.

Turning my head slightly, I peer at him, but all I find is calculation in his eyes.

"Jenkins," I breathe before pushing open the door and stepping through.

Shuffling to the side, I allow Dante in before shutting the door. Jenkins, seated at his usual place behind his desk, glances up from his computer. An older man faces him, not bothering to turn around, but that's not surprising.

"Dante Cruz, sir," I say, folding my hands in front of me.

He runs his gaze along my body, and I tip my chin up the slightest bit. I wish I was still in my skirt and blouse. The scraps of lace don't leave much to the imagination. Even though I'm used to it, his perusal still makes my skin crawl.

"Mr. Cruz, pleasure to meet you. I'm Jenkins, though I'm sure you've never heard of me." He says it with such a smarmy smile I almost roll my eyes. "And this is Mr. Drake. He's been with the Guild for quite some time."

Digging my nails into my palms, I struggle to keep my face neutral. I rarely see my father, and his appearance is a punch straight to the gut. He's usually off scouting other locations for the Guild. Based on the few times a year we've seen each other, I've gathered he resents my continued involvement in the organization. It's his fault I'm here in every way, shape, and form.

He sold me without a second thought, expecting them to throw me into the Auction. When they asked him what my attributes were, he fucked up. He told them I was good with numbers, as if that was something they cared about. Apparently, they did and they told me to fix their money issues. The entire thing snowballed into what it is now—a prison with a comfortable chair.

"You may go, Aelia." Anders dismisses me without even giving me the courtesy of looking.

"Actually, she stays," Jenkins counters, leaning back in his chair.

Anders stiffens, finally glancing over his shoulder at me, and he curls his lip. I'm sure my attire is offensive to him. Everything concerning me is offensive to him. He still pushes Jenkins to ship me off to the Auction, but that will never happen.

When Jenkins installed me in his office, my father wasn't happy, but he couldn't say anything. I like to think my presence is a constant reminder of what he did to me and guilt eats away at him. If only that were true. He's pissed he can't control me anymore, yet I just won't disappear.

Eyeing Dante, I wonder if he has a gun. The chances of me getting ahold of it to successfully shoot my father are slim, but I'm willing to try. The Guild doesn't allow weapons on the premises, though, so I doubt he has one.

"Byron told us quite a bit about you, suggested you might be good for the Guild."

Dante's head tilts as he considers Jenkins's words. "I'm surprised. Byron didn't seem to have enough pull to afford me a meeting with someone such as yourself."

Jenkins chuckles, his charm on full display. "He doesn't. However, we have eyes everywhere. We're always on the lookout for fresh blood."

I suppress a shiver as fear races down my spine. The turn of phrase alludes to more than just new clients and members, though I doubt Dante understands that. Then again, maybe he knows exactly what Jenkins is talking about.

Jenkins folds his hands over his stomach. "I'm wondering how much you're willing to invest to achieve a significant place within our ranks."

"Depends on what you're wanting me to invest. I'm particular about where I put my money, as I'm sure you are as well."

Jenkins's eyes find mine, and I nod in acknowledgement. He and I both know the price and it isn't funds. The Guild has been doing quite well financially, thanks to me until the last few months. The thought makes my body clench. At some point, I'll outlive my usefulness. I can only hope I'll be able to bring them down with me.

"We don't usually deal in cash unless it's to pay for the services we provide. Any family, Mr. Cruz?"

Dante straightens his cuffs, hiding an expensive watch much like the one gracing my father's wrist. "I find family only holds one back, Mr. Jenkins. If money isn't what you're after, then perhaps another deal can be made. I, myself, barter mostly in information."

Jenkins nods and Anders turns then, a glint in his eyes. Dante spreads his hand out as if he's offering them all he knows on a silver platter. Jenkins won't take it, though. Unless Dante can procure a loved one to sell to them, thus proving his devotion to the Guild, they won't take it.

"What do you know of Synd?" Jenkins murmurs.

Sucking in a sharp breath, I hide behind my dark hair. Dante's eyes are on me again.

"Quite a bit. When I caught wind of the Guild's operation, you were in Synd. I was...indisposed at the time, though, and therefore unable to catch you while there," he says, and I narrow my eyes at the choice of words he's used. "When I heard you've moved to Rima, I decided to come here."

"That doesn't explain why you would know about Synd, Cruz," Anders sneers.

"Perhaps you haven't grasped how I operate, Drake. I don't do anything halfway. I've been looking into the Guild for quite some time to make sure you're a sound investment and the organization is run to my standards. As Synd was the last major city you tried to infiltrate, I made sure to look into the area and history. Is that a satisfactory enough answer for you?" There's an edge to his voice and a small thrill runs through me at the thought of him taking my father down a peg or two.

"Usually, we'd slow this process down, but as you said, we recently had issues with Synd. We're needing someone who can help us deal with them," Jenkins says, shushing Anders when he tries to interrupt.

Dante stiffens next to me, and I bite my lip, wondering what's going through his mind. In all the years I've been here, I've never seen Jenkins do something like this. There's a system in place, but when they tried to take over Synd, shit went south fast. Jenkins refused to move headquarters there until they'd established a foothold, which meant I was never there. If he would have made the move early, maybe I'd finally be free.

"I know enough about Synd. We don't need him," Anders hisses, leaning across the desk.

Jenkins bares his teeth at him. "This is not up for discussion, Anders. Remember your place."

Anders explodes from the chair, slamming his hands on the desk. "When this blows up in your face, don't come crawling back to me."

He shoves away, marching for the door, and Dante easily sidesteps him. His arm brushes mine, sending a shiver through me. I tell myself it's from the cold and nothing more. There's something about this man that sets him apart from the others in this place. It makes me nervous in a way I'm not used to.

The door slams, rattling the picture behind me. Dante nudges me further into the corner, and I wobble on my heels. His hand curls into a fist, as if he was going to steady me but thought better of it.

"I apologize for his outburst." The words are ripped from Jenkins as if it's physically painful for him to say he's sorry. Typical.

Dante waves his hand, dismissing whatever else Jenkins is going to say. "It's fine. Anders seems to have a personal vendetta against Synd, which isn't surprising."

Jenkins raises an eyebrow. "Is that so?"

The roguish grin Dante sends him seems more natural than anything else he's done so far. It softens his eyes just enough to make him more human. Tucking his hands in his pockets, he rocks back on his heels.

"I believe a relationship could benefit both of us."

"I'm aware of what you have to offer. But what is it you want from us, Cruz?" Jenkins asks, pushing from his chair and rounding the desk.

I stiffen as he approaches, swallowing down the bile his presence elicits within me every time he's close. Dante steps forward until I'm tucked behind him slightly. Narrowing my eyes at his back, my gaze skips over his shoulder to Jenkins. Dante tilts his head as if he's contemplating it, but the tension in his shoulders says he knows exactly what he's going to ask for.

"Her, to begin with," he growls, his voice rolling through the room, a thunder holding the promise of a deadly storm within its depths.

The older man doesn't even bother to glance at me. I'm nothing to him. Nothing more than property he can direct where he wants. He won't give me up, though. Jenkins has never allowed anyone else to touch me. Not out of the goodness of his heart, since he doesn't have any of that left in his body, if he ever had any to begin with, but merely for control. No, he'll tell Dante to pick something else.

"Done." Jenkins holds out his hand, shaking Dante's before retreating back to his desk. "If that's all, we'll plan to meet later in the week. As you can see, we run our operation mostly at night, given our clientèle, but if you prefer another time, let Aelia know. She'll still be needed here, but you're free to do whatever you wish with her outside of her regular duties."

Dante nods, wrapping his hand around my upper arm as Jenkins hands over a black keycard. Ice floods my veins as I stare at Jenkins. Ever since my father sold me, dozens of men and even some women have offered to take me off the leader's hands. Grant, my handler, has tried on more than one occasion to overstep the boundaries Jenkins set up regarding me.

Dante tugs me toward the door, and I stumble. Shock has rendered me useless at this point, and my body trembles. Maybe he doesn't know the rules and he'll take me outside of headquarters. Then I could make my escape, though I'd prefer to not do it in what I'm wearing. Nightmare images flash through my mind of what he has planned for me. I've seen enough within these walls to know it never ends well for those of us who were sold or taken.

"Oh, Cruz, one last thing. Make sure she's still intact when you bring her back. Do whatever you'd like to her body but refrain from breaking her mind. It would be unpleasant to have to find another receptionist."

I shudder, wrapping my free arm around my waist.

"No promises, Jenkins," Dante chuckles and Jenkins joins in.

He yanks me into the hallway as Grant rounds the corner. I shuffle closer to Dante, though I don't expect him to save me.

"Sir, this one is off-limits. Why don't we find you someone more suitable?" Grant says in the suave tone he reserves for clients.

Grant reaches for me, his beefy hand circling my upper arm, then I'm in the middle, stuck in a sick game of tug-of-war. My ankle rolls, my knee gives out, and I tumble into Dante's hard body. He slides his arm around my waist, molding me to him, and my stomach tightens as his hand grips my exposed skin. Grant still refuses to let go, and Dante mutters a curse only I can hear.

He twists, his fist flying out and landing on Grant's jaw with a sickening crack. My handler goes down hard and when he glances at Dante, blood trickles from the corner of his mouth.

"I suggest you speak with Jenkins if you have a problem. This one is mine for the foreseeable future. Please inform the others I don't like others touching my things. Now get the fuck out of here before I put a bullet in you."

Grant's mouth drops open before he scrambles up, giving us a wide berth as he hustles for the office. He'll bellow and complain to Jenkins, who will probably do nothing. And Grant will take all this out on me.

After Dante's little display, I'm sure Grant won't leave bruises, at least for now, but there are other ways to torture a person that don't leave marks. I'm sure the man tugging me toward the stairs won't care, though.

"Where's your room?" he grunts, glancing up and down the hallway before pulling me around a corner.

"There are several places, sir," I whisper to hide the fear I'm sure will come through.

"Your room should be private enough for what I have planned."

I snort, and he jerks to a stop, raising an eyebrow at me. He raises his hand and I flinch, slamming my eyes shut and waiting for the blow. Instead, he brushes my hair behind my ear, fingers trailing along my neck before he leans in, his breath ghosting across my skin.

"Some place with no cameras," he murmurs, and I nod.

He steps back, clearing the way for me to lead, and I force my feet to move. There's no way I'm bringing him to the closet I sleep in. Plus, I'm not entirely sure I'm not watched in there. An entire floor is set aside for his type of request.

Guards line the hallway, waiting for whatever demand someone has. We pass one door as it opens, revealing an elaborate bedroom, a woman cowering in the corner. Two grinning men exit, one slapping the other on the back as they wander off. The guard shuffles into the room, cutting off our view as he kicks the door shut.

Another guard gestures to a vacant room, and I hold out my hand for the keycard Jenkins gave him. Dante steps around me to insert the card, and the guard shoves me inside. Crashing to my knees, I bite my tongue, copper filling my mouth.

Dante growls something at the guard, but I can't make out the words over the roaring in my ears. Each inhale stabs into my chest, sending shards of panic scattering throughout my body. The thud of the lock is a death toll ringing through the room.

My vision blurs, black dots dancing in front of me, and I realize my luck has run out. I'm never getting out of here alive.

FIVE

Dante

"A re you okay?" I ask, crouching to help her to her feet.

Her hand lashes out, trying to shove me back, but her movements are jerky. She plants her hand on the ground again, her gasping breaths rattling out of her. I've seen this before—the erratic actions, the inability to pull in enough air, the rapid blinking. She's having a panic attack, all because of me.

"Just breathe," I murmur, gently rubbing her back, and she shudders until her entire body is shaking. "I'm not going to hurt you."

A humorless squeak leaves her, and she drops her head. She'll never be able to get it together while on her hands and knees, but I'm afraid to grab her. Everyone reacts differently in these types of situations, and I'd rather she not hurt herself because she's trying to get away from me.

"I'm going to pick you up," I say, sliding my arms around her.

She freezes, every joint locking, making it difficult to maneuver around. I stumble toward the bed as she spasms, then curls in on herself. With her back pressed to my chest, she kicks out, connecting with the mattress. I plant my feet so we don't crash to the ground. I practically drop her on the mattress and retreat to the other side of the room.

She scrambles back, wild eyes finding mine, and I hold up my hands. My heart cracks, watching her break down in front of me. I wonder how many other people have been in this exact position within these walls.

The sooner I find out how to topple their empire, the more people I can save.

I realize I'm not a vigilante who can rid the world of this type of evil, but I have an opportunity here, and I won't let it slip away. If Aelia can help me, all the better. With the things Byron said about her, along with the way Jenkins acted, I get the feeling she's more than just another victim.

"I'm not going to hurt you." My words don't seem to register. She has no reason to believe me.

"Who are you?" she rasps, and she dissolves into a coughing fit.

"My name is Dante. And you're Aelia."

She narrows her eyes. "I don't need to be reminded of my own name."

I nod, glancing around the room before settling my gaze on her again. "Are you sure there are no cameras here?"

She tilts her head, pressing further into the headboard before whispering, "None that I know of. These rooms are for VIP clients."

"You don't want to be here." It's a ridiculous thing to say, but until I can fully trust her not to rat me out to Jenkins and blow my cover, I can't reveal anything.

"Of course I don't. Who would want to be used for their body? Broken beyond repair by men who think they're owed something. You're despicable," she spits out.

Her eyes widen as she realizes what she's done. She opens her mouth then snaps it shut, fear flooding her face.

"I'm sorry, sir. I didn't mean that. I'm just surprised, is all. I've never been in this position."

"Never? How long have you been with the Guild?"

She shakes her head, tucking her knees to her chest and wrapping her arms around her legs. Rocking slightly, I realize I won't get anything else out of her. The only reason she said anything was because of her shock at the situation.

"Who was that man with Jenkins before?" I ask, though I already know. I need to get her talking again.

"Anders Drake," she murmurs.

The name taps at the corner of my brain, begging me to remember some deep-buried memory, but it won't unearth itself. If I've heard the name, it wasn't recently. Maybe I knew him when we were in Synd. Ten years is a long time to remember some random person, especially when I was barely an adult.

"Where is he from?"

"Westmont. Down south. But—" She clamps her lips together, dropping her forehead to her knees.

"But?" I prompt when she doesn't continue. "But that's not where he's originally from? But he hasn't been back there in a while? But what?"

"I shouldn't tell you," she mumbles.

"Because they wouldn't want you to?"

She lifts her head, resting her chin on her knees. "Why do you care?"

"I like to know who I'm working with." I cross my arms, digging my nails into the fabric of my shirt. Her eyes dart down, and I forcibly relax my muscles.

"He used to live in Synd, which is why he's upset with Jenkins."

I bite my cheek, eyeing her, judging whether I should take the risk. There's a million ways that this could go wrong and only one way it can go right. I'm relying on my wits and hoping something goes my way.

None of my decisions so far have been calculated moves. Most of them have fallen into my lap and I've taken advantage of them. I should cut my losses, go home, and contact Helms for help. They have a lot to deal with in the aftermath of the Guild coming through and probably can't offer much, but I'm in over my head.

"If you could get out, would you?" I ask, tucking my hands in my pockets.

She stares at me, throat bobbing, and her fingers flex over and over as she contemplates my question. If she doesn't give in, I'll be in deeper shit than before. Jenkins is expecting me to do awful things to her—take her, use her, probably beat her. When she comes back no worse for wear, he might question who I really am.

I've laid the groundwork at least, so if he searches Dante Cruz, an entirely different persona will distract him. I'll never be able to repay Nemesis, the mysterious hacker from Synd. Unless the shit she put in place falls apart. According to Ren, she's the best in the game. I'll have to take his word for it. My life quite literally depends on it.

"Who are you?" she whispers, narrowing her eyes.

"I'm assuming you're not asking for my name again. Answer my question and I'll give you a little insight."

"My entire existence is at the mercy of evil men. I have been stripped of every conceivable human right and forced to entertain on the whims of others. Ask that question to anyone in my position and they'll tell you that the Guild is a necessary evil, and they are grateful to no longer be subjected to the horrors of the outside world. And every single one of them would lie, if only to survive another session, another day, another week, all while knowing they'll never escape. We'll perish within the shadows, unimportant and forgotten. So don't come in here asking questions you already know the answers to, Mr. Cruz."

"Fair point," I mumble, rocking back on my heels.

"Why do you care?"

"You seem different." I clear my throat, realizing I need to retreat behind my persona. "While I'd rather be spending this time doing other things, I have more pressing issues you might be able to help me with."

She peers over my shoulder, refusing to look me in the eye.

"I can't."

"You haven't even heard what I need."

She's shaking her head before I finish. "It doesn't matter. I'm in no position to do anything but hand over my body to you for a time."

She tips her chin up, daring me to deny it. Sighing, I walk to the window, peeking through the curtains into the night. We face the back side of the property. Moonlight dances across the pond, the gentle waves lapping up the beams. They disappear, only to reemerge on the next crest. How something so beautiful can house such evil is beyond the realm of understanding.

I glance at her from the corner of my eye. "Wouldn't you rather help me than what Jenkins would have me do to you?"

Aelia pales as her eyes dart around the room. "What do you want?"

"I'd like to know how the Guild makes its money."

It's not the only reason I want her help, but it's the most plausible one I can come up with on the spot. I've already gone out on a limb here. Up in the office, I wasn't even planning on claiming Aelia. Asking her to be a mole for me only puts her in more danger. She could run straight back to Jenkins and rat me out. I have no idea what she's been through—what trauma she's harboring.

"What else?" she whispers.

"That's all."

She huffs, resting her chin on her knees. "For now."

If there are cameras in here, I need a plausible excuse for asking this of her. And if she does fuck me over, I'll merely look like I'm manipulating her for my own gain. It's a good fallback overall, but I hate having to hurt her in the process. She's clearly been through enough, and I'm about to pile more on top of her. Hopefully one day I can free her from this prison, but it won't be tonight.

"I won't lie. I'm not a good man, come to rescue you from your pathetic existence. I'll use you for my own gain, much like the rest of the men here. However, if you help me, I promise I won't break you as long as you give me what I want." The words burn as they leave me.

Fear floods her eyes and my heart twists. I won't take back the threat, though. As much as I want to protect her, I have to protect myself as well. A single tear rolls down her cheek, and she turns her face away. I wonder how many she's cried living in this place.

"Make the deal, Aelia."

She shakes her head, then buries her face into her arms.

"I can't," she says, her voice muffled.

"Yes, you can. You have the choice. If you choose not to, then we'll have to figure something else out."

Her head whips up and she sneers, "Choice? You're going to lecture me about choices as we sit in a room where you're supposed to be torturing me?"

Her eyes widen, and her breath rasps in her chest. The vein in her neck beats rapidly, and I wonder if I've pushed her too far. When we walk out of here, I need her to be able to play the part, not actually be broken.

"Torturing really isn't my style," I murmur, tucking my hands in my pockets.

She swallows hard, unraveling her arms from her legs. Sliding off the bed, she wraps her arms around her waist.

"I can't," she says.

"Why not?"

"Because I'm more afraid of them than I am of you."

Six

Aelia

My closet bedroom is suffocating in a way it's never been before. Obviously, I wouldn't stay here if I had a choice. I snort as I adjust my thin blanket, thinking back on my conversation with Dante a week ago. His asinine comments about making a deal as if I have any control over my life still float through my head. I haven't seen him since. Not that I'm lamenting the fact he hasn't come to claim me.

Dante's proclamation that I belonged to him didn't deter Jenkins in the slightest. The Guild leader grilled me at every possible opportunity. Throwing questions at me on what Dante did to me, to what his motivations for wanting access to the organization are. I expect tonight to be no different.

I wait until the last possible second before I open my cupboard door, peeking out through the thin gap. Grant is nowhere to be found, and I heave out a sigh of relief.

My heel catches on the lip of the door frame, and I swing my hand around wildly. Strong arms wrap around my waist, yanking me against a hard chest. I bite my tongue to keep the scream inside.

I stiffen and then go limp. There's no use in fighting. Most of the time, it merely gets them harder. I can't stop the trembling, though. For once, I'm hoping Grant will come around the corner and tell them I'm not ripe for the picking. He's an asshole and disgusting, but he keeps the sycophants at bay for the most part.

"I'm not going to hurt you." Dante's whispered voice flows over me, and my breathing evens out.

It isn't until he drags me backward toward my closet that I realize how different I felt for a moment. I can't pinpoint *why* it was different, though. Figuring it out will eat away at me for days.

He told me—warned me—that he'd figure out another way if I chose not to take his ridiculous deal. And now he's cashing in on that promise. There's little I can do since Jenkins essentially signed my body over to him.

Dante's lips brush the shell of my ear, and I shudder. "Are there cameras in your room? Ways for them to listen to us?"

I shake my head, pulling my bottom lip between my teeth and biting down hard. It stings, but it's better than the alternative. Maybe he'll keep his mouth away from mine while he breaks me. I searched for them after last week and didn't find any. I should have lied.

"Good," he grunts.

He pulls me inside, tugging the door shut, cutting off any hope of escape. Not that I had any to begin with. My hope died out so long ago, I wouldn't know the feeling if it slapped me in the face. Dante's arms unwind from me, and I retreat the three feet the small space allows and tuck myself into the corner.

"What the hell is this place?" he hisses, glancing around.

"This is where I sleep."

The horror on his face sends a fresh bolt of embarrassment through me. I shouldn't be ashamed of where I'm sleeping. Hell, the women downstairs would give anything to have this place. I'm safer than they've ever been in the grand scheme of things. I shouldn't care what he thinks, anyway.

His behavior the other night was confusing, but that doesn't mean he isn't hiding a sadistic side. My gut, which I've learned to trust more as the years go by, is telling me he's hiding something. I can't put my finger on what it might be, though. This all could be an elaborate ruse to gain my trust merely to tear me down later, but for some reason, I don't think Dante would. It's a strange sensation to feel comfort in someone who, for all intents and purposes, is trying to gain access to the Guild.

"What are you really here for?" The question pops out before I can stop it.

He perches on the edge of my blanket pile. "I have some more questions for you. You don't have a mattress. Or a sleeping pad. How the hell do you live like this?"

My mouth drops open, but I snap it shut before my words get away from me again. He's acting as if we're old pals, catching up after an extended trip abroad instead of virtual strangers with a major power imbalance. Tilting my head, I track his movements.

Who the hell is this guy? I doubt Jenkins would let me delve into Dante's past. Jenkins may be too wrapped up in moving the rest of headquarters to Rima to even care who this man is, merely out for his money and information.

Searching for details about Dante on my own is a risk I'm not willing to take. I'm monitored like a hawk and punished for any invisible infraction they can find, though it's been a while since that's happened.

Dante looks up, running his fingers through his disheveled, black hair. I didn't realize how dressed down he was tonight, in dark jeans and a dress shirt. The top two buttons are open, revealing the hint of a tattoo.

He raises an eyebrow, glancing at where my eyes are fixed, and I turn away slowly to stare at the door. Grant will be by soon, and I have no idea how he'll react to Dante being in here.

"You shouldn't be here," I say.

"You're mine. Stands to reason whatever belongs to you, now belongs to me." He says it so nonchalantly, I almost miss the words.

I let out a humorless laugh. "Bold of you to assume any of this belongs to me. Also, I'm not yours. That's not how this shit works. If anything, I'm being leased to you until you're bored with me."

He drops his head, fingers flexing as he processes what I've said. The longer we sit here, the more tense I become. Not because of Dante, though. Right now, I'm running the risk of another beating for being late. Or having Jenkins starve me. Or whatever other hell he can think up.

When the silence becomes too much, I push myself up and reach for the door.

"Where are you going?" he asks, exhaustion lining his voice.

"I have to get to work. If I'm late—" I snap my mouth shut. For some reason, whenever I encounter him, I reveal too much.

"Aelia, I saw you last night."

I freeze, then settle back against the wall. Last night I was working the floor again. I have no idea why Jenkins picked now to put me down there. Most of the time he doesn't want me among the clients, calling me his little whore asset, which never made sense since I've only slept with one boy.

Yet every once in a while he decides it's time for me to "know my place." Jenkins delights in others seeing the complete control he has over me. Or maybe he just likes watching me get harassed. I've been waiting almost ten years for him to finally decide to break me. At first, I thought he held off as a psychological tactic. Now, I'm not so sure.

"Surprised you didn't accost me," I murmur.

There goes my mouth again. Peeking from the corner of my eye, I catch his eye roll. When I first got to the Guild, I made the mistake of talking back. I only did it once. I shudder as the memories I bury deep within my mind surface.

"I wanted to make sure no one else touched you," he growls, posses-siveness weaving through his tone.

"Have to protect your investment, I guess," I mutter dejectedly.

He sighs, fixing his dark brown eyes on me. "Tell me what you do for Jenkins and the Guild."

Swallowing hard, I wrap my arms around my legs, resting my chin on my knees. I lace my fingers together to hide the trembling. Whatever he's after, it's clearly not my body. I chalk up the swooping in my stomach to relief instead of disappointment since there's no reason I should feel let down. Apathy is the only way I've survived this long, and he's awakening sensations I've long since buried. I don't like it.

I weigh the repercussions of not answering versus not giving my keeper everything he asks. Gazing at Dante, I realize in the extremely short time we've known each other, I'm beginning to trust him.

Trust might be too strong of a word. And I certainly wouldn't put my life in his hands, but it's enough to feel like he's not going to hurt me. I'm still more afraid of Jenkins, though.

"What are you going to do with the information?" I whisper.

"I won't tell Jenkins, if that's what you're worried about."

"Why should I trust you?"

"Because you don't have any other choice," he says.

Biting my cheek, I tip my head back, staring at the wall over his shoulder.

"Mostly I do computer things."

His brows pull low. "Now is not the time to be vague, angel."

"Accounting, business management, and anything else they throw at me. It's mostly a hodgepodge of things. I never work in one program for long before they switch it up and I'm constantly monitored."

"You've never reached out to anyone outside of the Guild? Family? The authorities? No one?" It's the accusation in his voice that breaks me.

"No, I haven't," I say, eyes unfocused, face a mask of emotionlessness.

It's as if my brain slowly shuts down, flipping off each section that makes up the essential parts of me one by one. It's the only way I've survived thus far. At this point, I'm a shell of my former self. I wouldn't recognize her if she came up and slapped me in the face. I no longer care enough to protect myself beyond what my body does without my say-so, acting instinctively. One of these days I'll shatter into a million pieces and yet I won't care in the slightest.

"Don't shut down on me again. I didn't mean it like that," he murmurs.

Rage blazes up, burning away the apathy. "Yes, you did. I know how it looks. I have all this supposed access, yet I never reached out to the cops. I never tried to escape. I never tried to do anything other than keep my position because while it was terrible, I didn't have to live through the atrocities others have had to go through. You think I'm selfish. Yet you have no idea what I've been through. You can't even fathom what it's like to survive in this world. So, save your judgment for someone who actually fucking cares."

I'm panting by the time I'm done with my tirade. This man makes no sense to me. One minute he's telling me he's not going to hurt me and urging me to make a deal, and the next he's judging me for not trying to save myself from the hell I've been dragged into.

"I don't think you're selfish. Aelia—" He sighs, scrubbing his hands over his face. "I'm taking a risk here. You hold a lot more power than you think."

I snort, glancing away. I'm totally fucked here. The only way I've stayed safe is by toeing the line. There's no way I can fly under the radar, since I'm stuck in the same room as Jenkins, but I do my best. If I don't draw attention to myself, maybe I'll survive another day.

"What risk?"

He eyes me, as if he's staring into my soul, assessing whether I'm worthy. His stony face gives nothing away, which isn't very reassuring.

When he nods, I feel like I've won something. What that is, I don't know, but as he opens his mouth, butterflies erupt in my stomach.

"I'm from Rima."

Pressing my tongue to the roof of my mouth, I try to keep the words inside, but I fail.

"Good for you. Is that all? I really need to get going."

He scowls, rolling his eyes. "I wasn't finished."

"Well, by all means," I say, gesturing for him to go on.

"I'd rather not have the Guild taking over my city," he whispers. "And I'd like your help in bringing them down."

"No." My response is immediate.

I don't care who he is or what he needs, I can't help him. He might be willing to risk his life, but I'm not willing to risk mine. I've lived this long as a shadow of myself. I don't even know who I would be if I was free. My life is merely a series of events, strung together in order for me to survive as long as possible without breaking completely. Nothing will change my circumstances. Especially not a man. Freedom isn't in my future—only death. And to even entertain that hope would send me into a spiral I'd never get out of.

"What do you mean 'no'?"

"No is a complete sentence. I'll hide your secret but keep me out of it."

Seven

Dante

A elia keeps trying to get away from me. I may have failed to tell her she didn't have to go to Jenkins's office tonight. Or the night before. Or the night before that. It hasn't gone over very well, especially when she realized she'd be glued to my side for the foreseeable future. I'd like to spend more time convincing her to help me bring the Guild down, but her handler, Grant, has been annoyingly present.

I'm posted up at a poker table with Aelia secured on my lap, my arm around her waist. Every time she shifts, I tighten my grip. My subtle clues for her to knock it off apparently fly right over her head, because she keeps doing it. Sliding my hand up her body, she tenses. I stay away from her tits, not wanting to spook her more than need be, but the others are watching.

Wrapping my hand around her throat, I guide her head back. I run my nose along her neck. She shudders, and her body relaxes into me.

"Stop squirming or I'm going to have a hard time walking around," I murmur in her ear.

She turns toward me, nuzzling into my neck. "Maybe if your leg wasn't so bony, I wouldn't have to."

"Pretty sure that's your ass, angel."

"Are you going to call or fuck your woman?" another player growls.

Instead of answering, I brush my lips over her cheek. I'd kiss her, but I'm slightly terrified she'll either go catatonic or use my own knife to stab me. Her mood seems to swing between the two. Add in her emotionless mask, and I'm never quite sure which I'm going to get.

"I'll raise," I say into her skin, and her eyes meet mine.

I tip my head, gesturing for her to bid, and her nostrils flare. I'd rather hide away in another room with her, see if I can convince her to take a risk and help me. Byron tipped me off that Jenkins is watching me, though. Or maybe he's tracking Aelia. Either way, I had to put on a show, so here we are.

Aelia tosses a few chips into the middle of the table. It's not as much as I'd bet, but I'm not going to correct her. For the first half hour we were here, she barely breathed. The dealer sets the flop and the rest groan. I flip my cards without even looking.

"Mr. Cruz, your presence is requested," a man says at my elbow. He can't be more than twenty and his eyes keep darting around.

Another guard comes up, murmuring how he'll tally up my winnings and leave them at the counter. I set Aelia on her feet, scanning the faces of the others around the table.

"Gentlemen," I say, smirking.

I've probably made more than a few enemies, but at least I won some money while doing it. I grab Aelia's hand, tugging her after the man. When she jerks away, I whip my head toward her.

She widens her eyes, trying to convey something I don't understand. Glancing around, I catch Grant tracking us from his spot at the bar. When he narrows his eyes, it hits me. I'm being too gentle with her. I seize her wrist and yank her into my body as I paste an annoyed look on my face.

"What the hell am I supposed to do?" I growl.

"Drag me along behind you. Make me crawl. All you have to do is look around and figure it out, genius," she mutters, ducking her head, feigning submission.

She plays this part much better than I do. I'll need to up my game to pull this off. I grip her hip with one hand, sliding the other into her hair. She winces when I yank her head back until her eyes meet mine.

"Remember, I'm not going to hurt you," I snarl, infusing my hatred for the Guild into my tone.

I release her, then tip her over my shoulder. She cries out, struggling to pull her dress down, but I smack her in the ass. Whatever feelings of desire she drummed up in me before has fled. I won't be able to keep up this charade of manhandling her for much longer. When we step into the hall, my feet stutter, not sure whether to stop or keep going. I spot Grant speaking to an older man I haven't met yet, but his eyes find mine.

"Stop fighting me, angel," I mutter and she stills.

"Mr. Cruz, if you'd like to leave her with me, I can make sure she doesn't take off on you," Grant calls as he crossed the foyer.

I freeze, closing my eyes and slowly pulling in a breath to dampen the rage that whips through me. Sliding her from my shoulder, I grip her wrist and tuck her body behind my own. His lascivious grin begs for my fist.

I resign myself to covering my disdain for him and everything he stands for. Right now, I'm the only protection Aelia has, and I won't throw that away to satisfy the beast inside me.

"I suggest you keep your hands off my property, Grant," I sneer, narrowing my eyes, and he flushes.

"I was only offering you my assistance to watch your bit to ensure she didn't engage in prohibited activities while in service to you."

Aelia's small hand brushes my lower back, and I tilt my head as she whispers, "They call us bits when we're claimed."

I step closer to Grant, crowding into his space as I tower over him. His eyes widen, finally understanding how serious I am. Grant needs to learn his place, and it isn't anywhere near Aelia. She's mine now. The sooner he figures that out, the more likely his head will stay attached to his body.

"Sir, we don't want to keep them waiting," the guard says, clearing his throat as his gaze bounces between us.

"We certainly don't. I have quite a few things I'd like to discuss with them," I sneer as I look Grant up and down.

He flushes again, Adam's apple bouncing as he steps back. When he spins, he almost takes out another patron, and Grant snarls at the man. I use the distraction to tug Aelia along after the guard. I'm lost by the third set of stairs, but Aelia's hand brushes against my side when we need to turn.

No matter what she said in her room, she seems willing to help me not get lost. Maybe I can still convince her to help me bring the Guild to its knees. I don't know how true it is, but my gut says she's the one.

I shake my head, swallowing the chuckle in my throat. Thinking of her as "the one" makes it seem like I'm going to whisk her away and marry her—live happily ever after. In reality, she might be the only one who's capable of infiltrating the upper echelons of the Guild enough to destroy them. Everyone else is either too scared or too entrenched. Aelia is the perfect mole.

"In here, Mr. Cruz." He gestures to a closed set of wide double doors, but holds out a hand when I step forward. "The bit has to stay out, sir. They don't allow them into any meetings."

He has the good grace to wince when I turn my glare to him. Aelia tugs, but I keep hold of her wrist. Like hell am I leaving her in a random hallway, especially with Grant lurking around. He's probably hidden in a stairwell, waiting until I disappear so he can snatch her. He doesn't strike me as the smartest man. Or maybe he merely doesn't have any self-preservation. He probably assumes he's untouchable, no matter what he does.

"Who do you suppose will stop me?" I ask, and he blanches.

"It's the rules, Mr. Cruz," he whispers as if afraid to dispute me. Good.

"You'll find I rarely follow the rules. Open the door."

He scrambles to obey, and the tension in my shoulders eases. I'm still strung tight, though. It didn't escape me he never said who I was meeting with. When he pulls on the door, he bows. Aelia snorts quietly, but I don't have time to scold her.

The room easily holds two dozen people, double the size of the Kings' conference room. Only five seats are occupied, though. They're clustered on the opposite side, leaving a massive span of wood between us. Jenkins leans back in his seat, folding his hands over his stomach as he eyes Aelia.

Striding for a chair, I sink down, unbuttoning my jacket as I do. I'd rather Aelia be seated next to me, but I'm sure this is another one of their many tests. I point to the floor next to me and she sinks to her knees, keeping her eyes downcast.

"What can I do for you, gentlemen?" I ask, raising an eyebrow at Jenkins.

It's harder than I thought to ignore the other four, especially since one is Anders, though he's looking a little worse for wear. His eyes are fixed on Aelia, and I make a note to ask her why he seems to be obsessed with her. Maybe Jenkins rejected him only to turn around and give her to me. I'd rather not have him as an adversary, but since everyone in here is technically my enemy, it doesn't really matter.

"Cruz, I've been doing a little research on you," Jenkins says, tapping the manilla folder sitting in front of him. "Based on what we've found, I have a new proposition for you."

"Is that so?"

I hide my tension behind a mask so thick I can barely breathe. I'll suffocate before I give away my identity. I'd not only be putting my life in danger, but my club's, my family, and all those running Synd. My only hope is that Nemesis did her job and did it well.

Glancing down at Aelia, head still bowed, I wonder if she was the one to run the checks on me. Unlikely. They seem to keep her drowning in numbers, though why they give her access to their financials is beyond me. I'll have to ask her about it next time I'm able to get her alone.

"I'm sure you'll find it advantageous to both parties," Jenkins states, then slides a piece of paper toward me.

On it is a number, that's all, with a helluva lot of zeros behind it. I have the money, especially with the funds Nemesis siphoned from fuck knows where. She merely said the ones she fucked over didn't deserve such wealth. Apparently, they were just as bad as the men seated in front of me. The question is whether I want to hand over more to these people—to help fund an operation actively destroying people's lives.

I'm no saint, but we don't use what we earn to sell flesh, to break people beyond repair, to decimate cities before moving on. When we were teenagers, Helms and I agreed we would run our clubs differently than our fathers. They ruled through fear, flooding the streets of Synd, and eventually Rima, with hate and destruction. They didn't care if innocents were harmed in their quest to hold their territories. Helms and I may still run guns and drugs, but we also protect those under us. If we control the supply, we control whose hands those things fall into. It's a balanced system carefully curated to benefit everyone. Most would still label us criminals, but that's fine. I'll gladly wear the label of bad guy if that means keeping nasty shit out of other's control.

"How exactly do I benefit from infusing the Guild with this much capital?" I murmur, setting the paper down.

Jenkins grins, nodding. "While I won't offer you a seat at the head table, I will allow you access to the VIP areas and services. You've already experienced the exclusive rooms. Those are just the tip of the iceberg for our more elite members. Once we've established your commitment to the Guild, we can discuss giving you access to the business side of things. I'm sure we could use your business acumen in some capacity."

He waits while I pretend to consider his offer. I already know I have to accept. It's the only way to gain more access. This doesn't strike me as the way they usually run things, though. Based on Anders's stony expression, I'm sure he's against adding me to their ranks. The other three men at the table have spent the last ten minutes shifting in their chairs, as if this is as uncomfortable for them as it is for me.

An older man to Jenkins's right clears his throat. "It's a generous offer, Mr. Cruz. Not one we make lightly."

And there it is, confirmation that they're making an exception for me. Why, though? Why would they bend the rules for someone they don't know other than what they could dig up on the internet? They're desperate for something, and I intend to find out what, then exploit that weakness.

"Anything else?" I raise my eyebrow at the man, tilting my head when he coughs, eyes practically bugging out of his head.

"Why you little—" Anders snarls and Jenkins hand slashes out.

"You are here as a courtesy, Drake. Nothing more. If you'd like to continue in your current capacity, I suggest you keep your opinions to yourself. Otherwise, we'll see what you can fetch at the Trade." The threat Jenkins spouts is spoken with a calmness I've experienced before.

It's the same way those of us in power address those who have pissed us off enough that we're ready to end them—when the problem becomes more trouble than it's worth. It's the way I spoke to Maddox before I left for Synd with MacKenzie. It's the way Helms delivered orders when we stormed the Depot deep in Byrns territory to free the people the Guild had kidnapped. Shane King used the same tone when someone questioned whether he was fit to lead while he was deep in the shit with a woman. It's ingrained in us as leaders. I hate that I share the trait with someone like Jenkins.

"What else would you request, Cruz?"

I glance down at Aelia and she peeks at me, her brown eyes meeting mine. A slow smile pulls at my lips and she shivers.

"I only have one." I blink slowly, turning back to Jenkins. "Complete control over her, until I deem otherwise."

Jenkins nods, tapping his finger against his thin lips. "That can be arranged. However, I'd like you to see our full selection before you decide on this scrawny whore."

He snaps his fingers and Aelia scrambles to her feet, chin still tucked to her chest. Her fingers tremble until she weaves them together, holding them in front of her—the model form of submission.

"Take him to the Pit and show him his options. I'm sure he'll find something better than he currently has," he sneers at Aelia.

Jenkins smirks as Aelia nods, shuffling toward the door. No matter who she shows me, I won't change my mind. Before the sun rises, she'll wholly and completely be mine.

EIGHT

Aelia

I thought Dante would have been happy to pick someone else to pull into his plan. Based on the scowl currently gracing his face, I was severely mistaken. The nerves swirling in my gut are cycling through my body, waiting for the perfect moment to strike and knock me off guard. The last thing I want to do is bring him down to the Pit. Not only will it show him the darker side of the Guild, but he'll be also exposed to the darker side of me.

The glittering lights and influx of money in the upper rooms hides the horror coating the walls. At least, I always thought it was easier to ignore the atrocities. The Pit, though, holds the stark reality of what they engage in. Up top, I'm untouchable in a sense. I'm protected more since I'm an asset. Down here, I'm reviled. No one wants to join forces with me, get on my good side, or be my friend. I'm a plague, picking them off one at a time. I don't blame them for their hatred. I hate myself too.

Ever since I snapped at Dante in my room, his silent accusation has wormed its way into my brain, slowly infiltrating every corner of my mind. Most people would have spiraled long ago, but not me. Apparently, all it took was someone accusing me of not saving myself—of not saving them.

"Don't say anything." I hold back the "please" begging to escape.

"I'm not choosing one of them," he growls as we approach the door.

Grant loiters down the hall, tracking our movements. I'll pay for the sins Dante committed. Later, though. Grant might leave bruises, but since Dante hasn't done more than put on a show for those around us, I doubt anyone will see them. My handler has always been careful, even with the revealing clothing I'm forced into more often than not these days.

"You might find someone more to your liking," I murmur.

I nod to the guard, someone I don't know, and he opens the door with a flourish. It's for Dante's benefit. No one cares about doing shit like that for me. The dark stairway seems to stretch on forever, as if we're descending into the bowels of hell. I'd imagine the devil is more benevolent than Jenkins.

"There are many decisions I'd like to change, but claiming you isn't one of them, angel."

I don't know what to do with that. Dealing with the emotions he stirs in me—ones I thought long dead after spending so much time in the dark—isn't something I'm able to handle. At least not right now. Maybe later, when I'm tucked away in my closet, I'll extract them one by one, deciphering the meaning behind each. I do the same with his words. Might as well add more.

"This is a test, Dante. One you can't fail," I breathe, glancing at him from the corner of my eye.

The space opens up, but he spins me around, crowding me into the shadows. I gasp when he presses his body into mine. Usually it's fear squeezing the air from my lungs. This time, though, butterflies erupt in my stomach and my heart stutters in my chest.

"Listen very closely, Aelia. No matter who you throw at me, I will reject every single one of them. My choice has already been made. When I'm standing on the other side of this, I fully intend you to be next to me."

He pushes from the wall, striding several steps away as he runs his hand through his hair. Unlocking my muscles, I walk woodenly past him. I have no response to his grand declarations. He's delusional if he thinks he's going to save anyone, much less me.

Dante isn't the first person who's tried to bring down the Guild, if that's truly what he plans to do. I've never encountered them, but I listened to Jenkins rage about them. Eventually, they were discovered and killed. At least, I assume they were, since he stopped screaming into his phone.

"Twice in one week, Mistress? What good fortune," Rachel calls, then chokes, eyes widening when she spots Dante.

She melts into the shadows, leaving her silhouette to haunt us as we walk on. At least Dante listened to one thing I said, keeping his mouth shut. I don't want to be the one who picks for him, and Jenkins never told me I had to. I wish I could disappear with her, letting him go about his business.

"These women are available," I say, trying to keep my voice steady, and I gesture to the makeshift rooms.

Women cower away from his prying eyes, lips clamped together. One even scrambles into the corner, trying to make herself as small as possible. It's rare patrons are brought down here for their "pick of the litter" as Jenkins calls it. This privilege is usually reserved for the elite VIPs. And I have never had to escort someone personally, though Jenkins makes me come along when he brings someone down here.

"If your tastes run toward men, they are kept over here," I say, striding toward the cages.

Benjamin flashes me a sad smile from the floor of his cage. Legs splayed out, he crosses his arms, resting his chin on his chest. It's the only form of resistance he has, refusing the rise for the man who might be here to break him. I always admired his dissent. I wish I had more of whatever flows through his veins—confidence or fortitude or...whatever it is. Despair hammers at my shoulders, weighing me down even further. Benjamin might act like nothing can touch him, but deep down, he's just as scared as the rest of us.

Dante's grand scheme will only end in his death. If I'm standing next to him, I'll be killed too. Maybe it would be better that way. Then I wouldn't have to live in fear, or deal with the guilt eating away at me for not doing more.

"Why are you doing this?" Dante hisses.

The urge to jab him in the stomach with my elbow is ridiculously hard to resist. If he keeps up the commentary, someone is going to hear him. By the look on Benjamin's face, he already has. There's no love lost between him and the guards, so hopefully he'll keep his mouth shut.

I nod to the guard who wanders closer. He eyes me up and down, and I tip my chin up. I haven't met him before, but he has a sadistic gleam to him, almost an oily quality coating the entirety of his existence.

Usually, the handlers have batons to keep the victims in line. Apparently, that wasn't good enough for this one. A Taser hangs from his belt, a whip fisted tight in his grip. It explains the lashes I saw on Ingrid while she was showering.

Glancing at Rachel, she shakes her head subtly, and I track my gaze toward Ingrid's bed in the tent at the end of the row. It's empty, blood speckling the bare mattress. I'm not surprised, and my heart clenches, breath stalling in my lungs. I pinch my leg, using the pain to ground myself to the present so I don't lose it.

Turning to face the back of the room, I sweep my hand out. "There are several others you can indulge in. These are set for the Auction, but I'm sure Jenkins would allow you to peruse the selection for the right price."

Biting my tongue, I fix my eyes on the far wall. The cages in the back are nicer, better equipped with luxuries the men aren't afforded. The people meant for the Auction are considered elite, bordering on priceless. That's not entirely accurate since they're literally sold to the highest bidder. Men who have more money than they know what to do with flock to the Auctions the Guild sets up. Most of the time it's men, though I guess a few women attend too. Vileness knows no gender.

"Tell me what to do to get out of this hellhole," Dante murmurs as he grips my hip, pressing his body into my back.

"If you don't pick one..." I don't know how to finish the sentence.

I can't tell him he'll be stuck with me. I don't know if Jenkins will decide I'm not worthy of Dante's "affections" and punish me for it. Even if Dante does choose someone else, I'll most likely be blamed for it.

I also can't tell him he'll be exiled from the Guild. That would be the typical route, but nothing Jenkins has done with Dante has been normal. I also won't say anything about how much it will hurt if he chooses another. Helping him isn't an option for me, but that doesn't mean I want him to throw me away like used trash.

I straighten my spine and shake my head. I've known this man all of three days. Actually, I have no idea how much time has passed since he waltzed into my life and attempted to turn it upside down.

"Will they be hurt if I refuse?"

I lean into him the slightest bit, not able to help myself. "They'll be hurt either way, Dante."

"What's this? Did Mistress finally get pawned off? Not surprised he's throwing you aside so soon," Rachel cackles.

Dante sucks in a deep breath, fingers digging into my hip. Carefully, I shake my head, hoping he doesn't fuck this up. His hand drops, and I step between him and Rachel.

"Trade or snuffed?" I call and the other women shrink back. Inquiring about Ingrid is the only way I can think to distract Rachel.

Rachel's eyebrow pops up, and she eyes Dante. "Trade, though it was close."

I don't know which is better. Being sold in the Trade at least allows them the opportunity to escape. Dying would free them from this hell, though.

I'm surprised Rachel is telling me anything at all. Jenkins played us against each other by making me select women for him. He made sure we wouldn't join forces. The people trapped here outnumber the ones who rule. If we ever banded together, the Guild would be fucked. Keeping us at each other's throats is only one tactic they employ to keep that from happening. Jenkins uses fear as his ultimate weapon.

"So, who are you going to ruin this time, Mistress?" Rachel asks, lip curling in disgust.

"Let's go," Dante growls, gripping my wrist and tugging me toward the stairs.

Rachel starts cackling, yelling random insults at my back until Benjamin tells her to knock it off. When Dante and I reach the shadows, his hand lands on my lower back, guiding me up the stairs. His touch is gentle, always so gentle, like I'm made of glass. I both loathe and crave his touch. Mostly, I dread the moment he's gone. It's a dangerous position to be in.

Halfway up the stairs, he grips my shirt, and I stop. I gasp when he slips in front of me, pinning me to the wall. He drops his head, breathing me in, and I press my lips together.

"I need to know what the hell is going on," he murmurs, his lips brushing my skin.

"Jenkins wants you to prove your loyalty to the Guild. Focusing on one bit isn't usually done. What are you doing?"

His breath ghosts across my ear, and he whispers, "I don't want anyone to overhear us."

I swallow hard and his hand caresses my hip. "You have to choose someone. Rachel would be best. She's been here a long time and might help you."

He shakes his head, then pulls backs until his eyes meet mine. "I'm not choosing someone else. You're what I need. With a little more time, I'll convince you to help me."

"But Jenkins—"

"Fuck him. I'm pretty sure he needs me a lot more than I need him right now," he mutters, glancing toward the Pit.

"I certainly hope you're right," I murmur.

I wonder if he needs me as well, or if, when the time comes, he'll dismiss me just as quickly.

NINE

Dante

The last week I've been living in a perpetual state of anxiety. Every time I've stepped foot in any establishment the Guild controls, I expect to be summoned. I keep waiting for Jenkins to make his move, accusing me of being a fraud, yet every night is another round of nothing.

I've kept Aelia by my side as much as possible, especially since she seems to deteriorate a little more each night. Dark circles surround her drooping eyes, and she's even more pale than when I first met her. Trying to talk to her about what's going on is pointless. Her blank stare is the only answer I receive.

"Going to explain this little excursion?" I mutter in Aelia's ear as she leads me through the halls.

"You need to stop acting like we're a couple," she hisses, but I don't know if she's annoyed with me or if I hurt her.

She's been wincing on and off all night. I'm about to take her into one of the private rooms and demand she tell me what the hell is wrong. If someone touched her...

"Why are we here, Aelia? And why do you keep shying away from me?"

"If you act like we're a couple, people are going to get suspicious."

I step in front of her, pressing her against the wall. The room is smaller than the others I've been in, with tiny tables taking up most of the space. A dark stage spans the back, and low voices from the people, mostly men, fill the air. Several doors line the sides, and I reach around her body, opening the one behind her. It's even darker inside, but I guide her back until I can shut the door.

"What the hell are you doing?"

"We need somewhere to talk, and I can't do that in a room full of people. Does this room have cameras?" I whisper.

She sighs, clutching my hand. "We're in a storage room, Dante. Only the mop bucket can hear us."

"What is this event?" I ask, skimming my hand up her side until I reach her neck.

It's so dark in here, I can't even see her outline. The lack of light only heightens my other senses. I pull her closer until our breaths mingle, and she shivers.

"It's a smaller version of the Auction. For locals only," she whispers. "Jenkins insisted you come since you didn't even look at the people in the Pit."

"How do I call a meeting with him?"

"Why?" she asks, her tone all jagged edges and annoyance.

"I'd like to tell him exactly where he can shove his suggestions I find someone else," I growl.

She huffs, turning her head. "I can't help you."

"You can but choose not to. I respect that decision, Aelia, but don't call it something else. You made your choice and I've made mine."

The silence presses in on us, both smothering my senses and sealing us into a bubble of false security. No one can touch us in here. No one threatening to intrude. It's just us, dealing with the push and pull.

"Why me?" Her words are barely a whisper, as if ripped from her soul.

"Because you're worth it."

"You barely know me," she says harshly.

I sigh, resting my forehead on hers. I can't explain why she means so much to me. It goes beyond how much she could help me with the Guild. It's something bubbling inside my chest, wrapping around my heart, and squeezing. The idea that she's stuck here, abused and forgotten by everyone outside of these walls, eats at me every day. It hits me harder now that I know her.

"This isn't exactly my ideal way of getting to know someone." I chuckle, slipping an arm around her waist.

"What, you've never hidden in a supply closet with someone and asked them their favorite color? I thought everyone did that."

I press my lips together, holding back my laughter. Tipping my head back, my eyes dart around the darkness, seeking any bit of light. It's disconcerting to be surrounded by nothing but blackness.

There's a sense of security in here, as though I could spill every single secret and no one would know. Trusting Aelia fully is a risk I'm quickly realizing I will need to take. If I'm going to convince her to help me, I have to give her more.

"I don't want to see those girls up there being auctioned off to the highest bidder. I can't handle it without going on a rampage. I'd burn this entire place to the ground right now if I could."

"I'm sure they wouldn't care," she breathes, body tensing.

I snort, even as much stomach turns. "Jenkins would. Probably wouldn't stop him from setting up shop somewhere else."

"I meant the others. The ones in the Pit. Those in the cages. Women forced to dance for men who only see them as possessions to be used and discarded. Men made to strip and then beaten for the enjoyment of others who like to break people's spirits for fun. I doubt any of them would care if you blew them up. Death is better than living this existence."

"Aelia, help me. I know it's not fair what I'm asking you to do. There's a good chance neither of us will make it out alive, but at least we tried. Isn't trying better than living half a life?"

I wish I could see her—read what she's thinking on her face. Every other time I've tried, though, she's a blank mask. She'd never give herself away. It's too dangerous in a place like this.

"You haven't even told me how I could help," she murmurs, leaning away from me, and I drop my hands.

"You have access. That's enough. I have people who might be able to step in later, but they need access to the system."

"Dante, I don't have that kind of clearance. I'm allowed a sliver of information at any given time. After a while, they switch to something else. I don't even know how to explain it. There's like three programs I'm allowed access to at once. Then, after a couple of weeks, they change to new ones. I never see the full picture. I'm not some silver bullet you can use to bring them down." Her voice cracks, then she stops as if she's revealed too much.

I'm not equipped for this. I'm in a fucking MC, not some operative who can bring down a criminal enterprise. I didn't think this through, and now I'm in too deep. And I dragged Aelia into it as well. Cutting her loose now would do more harm than good. Jenkins assumes I've been using her body, probably beating her as well. Who knows what advantages he'd take with her, thinking she's already sullied. As long as she's with me, at least there's the illusion of safety.

"Are they beating you?" The question slips out before I can change my mind.

She gasps, then something clatters to the floor, and bounces into my leg. Aelia mutters a string of curses as her small hands pat my legs.

"What the hell are you doing?" I whisper, crouching down.

Our hands collide and I lace our fingers together. I try to stand, pulling her with me, but my foot connects with something that sends me crashing to the ground. A gasp leaves her as she tumbles on top of me, and I wrap my arm around her back.

"Are you okay?"

"Yeah, are you?" she asks, resting her forehead on my chest.

"Course, but someone definitely heard that. We should..."

She lifts her head, breath ghosting over my lips. "Get out of here."

"I don't want to see that shit," I admit.

She sighs, muscles relaxing the longer I hold her. The last thing I should do is skim my palm along her side. I shouldn't dig my fingers into her hip. And for fuck's sake, I shouldn't close the distance between our lips. Devouring her isn't in the plan.

The unhinged, completely fucked up strategy I've concocted is chaotic enough without adding extra layers. Throw in the fact she's been forced to live in this cesspit, surrounded by men who wouldn't understand consent if it slapped them in the face. It would be exceptionally bad.

She takes the choice away from me, leaning closer, and her lips brush against mine. I ache as I hold myself still, letting her take the reins. She sighs again, sending a shudder through me. Her tongue darts out, licking along my lip, and I slide my hand to her cheek. I jolt when her nails dig into my chest, and she jerks back.

"Sorry," she gasps, scrambling off me and knocking over a bottle in her haste.

I slowly push to my feet, reaching toward where I think she is. My hand grazes her arm, and she whimpers.

"I'm sorry. I didn't mean..."

"Didn't mean to kiss me? Aelia, it's okay. Let's just get out of here. We'll go somewhere else."

The only way I'll be able to calm her down is if I get her out of this damn closet. If her previous actions are any indication, she'll spiral before long. I trip forward, trying not to crash into her. I don't know what I'm kicking out of my way, but I no longer care about someone hearing us.

A heavy beat seeps under the door now, so I doubt anyone will bust in on us. We could hide out here all night if need be. I'd rather take her some place that has at least a little light.

"Somewhere else," she says under her breath as if she's dissecting each syllable—rolling it around her tongue to decipher any hidden meanings within the words.

"We're in a fucking closet full of cleaning shit," I growl.

Shuffling forward, I press my body closer to hers. She stiffens, and I open my mouth to reassure her. I don't want to crowd her, but not being able to tell where she is freaks me out. The door bursts open, and I curl my body over hers. She lets out a muffled sob as my arms wrap around her.

"Mr. Cruz, sorry to interrupt, but there are other rooms available to you," Grant says, condescension dripping from his tone.

I scowl as I glance up, scanning Aelia's tear-streaked face. She swallows hard, then shakes her head subtly. Pursing my lips, I narrow my eyes. Fuck Grant and all he's put her through. I'm done tiptoeing around him.

I spin, keeping Aelia hidden behind me. "What I do with my bit doesn't concern you. Close the fucking door, Grant."

"She's my—"

"She's your fucking nothing. She's mine. If you continue to interfere with what's mine, we're going to have a repeat of the other night."

"If that's the way you'd like to play it," he mutters, pivoting before marching off.

Aelia's trembling hand rests against my lower back, but then she rips it away. Snaking my hand back, I tug her in front of me. She squeaks, her head whipping toward the door and back to me. A heavyset man wanders past and spots us. I expect him to hurry along, giving us the privacy we obviously want, but he stops. Leaning in, he leers at Aelia's back, taking his time as he scans her up and down.

"When you're done—"

I pull my gun from behind my back, pointing it at his head. He trips over his feet, almost falling over as he sputters.

"Stay away from her or I'll put a bullet in your head," I growl.

He flees, knocking over a chair in his haste to get away from my threat.

"You're making it worse," Aelia whispers harshly. "And you're not supposed to have a weapon in here."

I grab her wrist and drag her from the closet. Some man is announcing the start of the event, and I hurry her along. There's no way I'm staying in that room to watch people be auctioned off. I'd end up shooting more than one of the men waiting for their turn to break their victims. If it's anything like the previous event I was at, some of them would probably do it in the open.

Leading her through the twisting hallways and up several flights of stairs, we finally find our way to the VIP rooms. I assume they aren't bugged since no one's come after me. The last time I took a risk, and I was on high alert for days after. Slamming the door once Aelia is inside, I drop my hold on her and pace the room.

"What has Grant been doing to you?" I demand, planting my hands on my hips and glaring at her.

She twists her fingers in front of her, eyes bouncing around the room. "Nothing more than usual."

"Liar."

Her head whips up at my harsh tone, but I can't help it. I left it alone when she said she didn't want to help me. I kept her close, hoping my presence would keep her safe. It's a naïve thought, but I cling to it.

She'll never be safe. Not until I get her out. It's my new mission. If I fail to bring down the Guild, at the very least, I'll set Aelia free. Hopefully I'll take out Jenkins too.

"He doesn't think you'll care," she murmurs, still refusing to look me in the eye.

"However, I made myself perfectly clear. No one touches you."

"Except you," she hisses, finally meeting my gaze.

Fire burns in her eyes, threatening to send me to the depths of hell. I grin, basking in the strength within her. Through all these years it's still there, burning beneath the surface. Even if it is directed at me.

I nod, the grin sliding from my face. "Except me."

"Excuse me if I don't think that's any better. No matter what bullshit you've fed me about your plans."

"You think I'm lying?"

"I think it doesn't matter either way. Either your *claim* is going to get me killed or *you* will. Or this is an elaborate ruse to fuck with me before you—" She swallows hard, then sets her jaw. "Break me."

"I am many things, Aelia. There's a lot of things you can accuse me of, but cruelty is not one of them." My nostrils flare as I pull in a deep breath.

"Go to hell," she spits out.

She spins, stomping out the door. I let her go, wondering all the while if I'm making the right decision.

TEN

Aelia

"**A**bout time you showed up," Jenkins says as I step into the office.

My feet stutter, but I keep my head down. I'm not late. I'm never late. Grant usually makes sure I know exactly what time it is, but he's been suspiciously erratic with his movements since his run-in with Dante almost a week ago. Grant hasn't been escorting me anywhere. Instead, he's taken to popping up randomly, putting me in my place, then disappearing again.

It's both a blessing and a curse. Every morning I go to bed tense, sleep becoming an elusive thing chasing the sun across the sky in its daily commute to sunset. Anxiety is my constant companion, dogging my steps as I work event after event.

I imagined Dante would show up the next night after the incident in the supply closet, but he's been missing, too. I shouldn't have said anything. I shouldn't have told him what I did. I certainly shouldn't have kissed him. It only blurs the lines more. A momentary lapse in judgment might cost me my life.

Living in this hell has taught me that lesson well, but I forgot. Complacency took the place of panic. After so many years, I wonder if I'll welcome death with open arms. It might be just the reprieve I've been looking for.

"Where's your handler?" Jenkins bites out.

Swallowing hard, I sink into my chair before answering. "Grant hasn't been escorting me anywhere, sir."

Peeking at Jenkins seated behind his desk, I watch his face morph from annoyed to rage to a blank mask. I tense, waiting for the explosion. He's usually eerily calm, only adopting the charismatic leader persona when in front of clients. In this room, he doesn't play a part, but his nonchalance is an act all the same. It took me a while to figure out his moods, to decipher the beast swimming under the surface.

"I wasn't asking about Grant," he says in a low voice.

He pushes from his chair, rounding on me as my lungs forget how to function. The bruises Grant left behind haven't fully healed. I'd rather not add more on top of them. Hiding them from Dante was hard, but then he disappeared. He's probably long gone by now, abandoning me to this cesspit. I don't blame him. I'd run too if I could.

It probably makes me selfish, willing to desert the people in the Pit, the women working the various events, everyone in the Trade. Even thinking about it makes me sick to my stomach, but I know I'd do it. I'd flee as fast and as far as I could in a heartbeat—constantly worried the next beat would be my last. And they would too.

"Answer me," Jenkins whispers harshly in my ear, leaning his body over mine.

"I don't know where he is," I gasp, then silently curse myself.

Any sign of weakness and he'll only seek to punish me further. Showing him I'm afraid triggers something within him, and the only way to avoid the beast lurking under his expensive suit is to pretend I don't exist. In this moment of time, I'm nothing but a wisp of matter, a ghost haunting the halls of this bastardized company.

"At some point, you're going to have to give in, Aelia. Mr. Cruz will throw you aside, done playing the long game of almost breaking you, and then what will we do with you?"

I hold perfectly still, eyes fixed on the door as my muscles tense more with each passing second. I don't even care who walks in. Even Grant would be a blessing. At least I can anticipate his blows.

Jenkins slithers through the grass, striking when I least expect. I'd take the bruises over this any day. Dark marks fade, but the psychological warfare Jenkins engages in has broken me in ways I'll never reveal to him.

His hand slides down my arm, then seizes my wrist in a bruising hold. He twists his fingers and I swallow hard. When he bends my own hand back, I bite my tongue, blood coating my mouth in my quest to keep the cry of pain inside. I can't help the jolt though, and the move presses my stomach into the desk. His hot breath sends strands of my hair fluttering across my neck and a tremor of fear rolls through me.

I jerk at the loud knock on the door, banging my knee on the underside of my desk, and I yelp. Jenkins doesn't move for a good ten seconds, then retreats, sinking into his chair before calling for whoever it is to enter. I drop my shoulders, curling my body as I attempt to get a grip on my breathing.

Peeking from behind my curtain of hair, I suck in a quick breath, holding it as Dante steps inside. He doesn't even spare me a glance as he approaches Jenkins. My fear transitions into a blinding rage. I want to scream at him, throw shit, demand answers. I do nothing, though. Instead, I sit perfectly still, letting my wrath simmer just below the surface, allowing it to burn away the last vestiges of terror, and slowly sink into what's left of my soul. He can rot in hell for all I care. The problem with that is I'm rotting right alongside him. Even here, I'm unable to escape him.

I mentally shake myself, placing my hands lightly on the keyboard, and sign in as I check back into reality. Dante leans his fists on Jenkins's desk, his shirt stretching taut across his back, accentuating the prominent muscles lining his body. A shiver rolls through me, and I pull my eyes away.

"I thought I made myself clear," Dante hisses. "No one touches her but me. And yet here I find that he's been using her as a punching bag."

"Is that a problem, Mr. Cruz?" Jenkins asks, raising an eyebrow as he leans back in his chair, crossing his arms over his chest.

Dante shifts, and I catch the menacing glower on his face. "She's mine to do with what I please, and he's fucking up my plans for her."

"Is that so?"

Dante is walking a razor-thin wire. I wish I could warn him. Biting my lip, I focus on the screen again. I don't owe him anything. He abandoned me for the past five days, leaving me to Grant's special brand of discipline. It doesn't matter that he's chewing Jenkins ass for it.

None of this would have happened had he stuck around, though Grant's been randomly beating me for years for his own pleasure. The minute reprieve I had when Dante claimed me slowly wore off. If I hazarded a guess, my handler is worried I'll slip from his control.

Dante straightens, adjusting his sleeves. Where his usual suit coat went, I have no idea. In fact, I don't think I've ever seen him without it other than the one time. Even in just his crisp white shirt he exudes a magnetism that's hard to ignore.

"Clearly, you're not in need of my support as much as you let on. I'm afraid we'll have to part ways, if that's the case."

With the gauntlet thrown, I expect him to wait for Jenkins to fold. He won't. The leader of an organization like the Guild doesn't get in that position by giving in. He'll let Dante walk away, writing him off before he even makes it out the door. Dante doesn't hesitate. Instead, the man who's supposed to own me right now pivots on his heels and stalks for the exit. My mouth drops open and my eyes dart to Jenkins, then back to my computer as I press my lips into a thin line.

Dante's hand hits the handle before Jenkins clears his throat.

"Wait," Jenkins calls, voice rough as he grunts again.

Dante spins, crossing his arms. "Better start talking, Jenkins. I'm not a patient man when it comes to business."

Jenkins's nostrils flare as his gaze darts to me, and I avert my eyes. The numbers swim across the page, making it hard to pretend I'm ignoring them, which is what I'm supposed to be doing. Jenkins expects me to be invisible until he's ready to harass me or demand shit from me.

"Grant is used to a certain amount of control over her. Upsetting the status quo has...thrown him. He won't be an issue any longer."

"And you expect me to believe that? I've already addressed it with him, yet he's still touching what's mine," Dante growls, and a shiver rolls through me.

I've never wanted to be owned. Living with the Guild for so many years has shown me how that goes for the others. Which doesn't explain the buzz that courses through my body when he says I'm his. Reminding myself that this is all an act on his part does nothing to dispel the tingles curling in my belly.

"He'll be taken care of," Jenkins grunts, pushing from his chair, but goes no further.

"You mean *I'll* take care of it," Dante says, brows pulling low as he challenges Jenkins.

I gasp softly when Jenkins nods curtly. Dante approaches the desk, settling in the chair across from him, and they start to talk softly—too low for me to hear. I give up trying to eavesdrop and focus on the screen.

It's still a mess of numbers. Different shell company names jump out at me. Like every other time I've looked at this program, I mentally catalog each one, then move money from one to another.

An alert pops up on the bottom of my screen. A doom clock, counting down the time I have left to finish whatever Jenkins wants me to accomplish. With Dante busting in, I've wasted so much time I doubt I'll get it all done, and goosebumps march up my arms. My palms become slick, fingers sliding across the keys in my haste. I know the consequences of not finishing. I'd be a fool to think whatever protection Dante has afforded me from Grant's wrath extends to Jenkins as well.

The leader rarely hits me anymore, but these situations are an exception. Panic floods me as the sound of his belt whipping through the air echoes in my ears. The image in front of me blurs, but not from tears. I'm long past crying over something I can't change. That well dried up long ago.

No, this is my body, shutting down and no matter how I fight it, I can't stop what's coming. Shadows dance along the edge of my vision, promising a reprieve from the horrors that stalk me through the night.

Someone's hand falls on my shoulder, squeezing, and I explode, shoving away from my desk violently. Stumbling from my chair, I'm tipped in the air, thrown over their shoulder. My stomach rolls, but Dante's scent swirls around me, and I clamp my lips together to stop from puking all over his back. He strides from the room, smacking my ass when I stop struggling.

"Don't stop. He's still watching," Dante hisses, and I renew my efforts.

I'm not a great actress, but I pull at the vestiges of fear still licking at the corners of my consciousness, using it to fuel my performance. Grant's harsh voice follows us as Dante stomps through the halls, his hand gripping me tightly around my thighs.

I'm frozen, unable to deal with another altercation. The anxiety from the last few days has finally boiled over into a numb acceptance of my future. I feel like I'm right back where I started when my father first sold me to the Guild.

Over the years, I've learned to shut myself off, protecting the most precious parts of who I am deep within. With Dante's arrival, he's turned my life upside down, throwing me into a void, then leaving me to deal with the fallout alone.

"Get the fuck out of my way, asshole. Unless you'd like another demonstration on how far I can go when someone fucks with me," Dante says, coming to a halt.

"You think you're such an asset to the Guild. You may have Jenkins fooled, but I know there's more to you than meets the eye. I'm going to figure out what you're hiding. Then we'll see who's really in danger." The smirk in Grant's tone comes through loud and clear.

Dante laughs sharply, his thumb drawing small circles on my skin, and I shiver. Fear wars with desire, meshing together until I no longer know where one ends and the other begins. I am so fucked.

"We'll see about that. I believe Jenkins would like to speak with you. Better crawl, little worm."

Dante pushes past him, slamming his other shoulder into Grant as we pass. I lift my head, and Grant's dark gaze tracks us until Dante slips around the corner. Trotting down the stairs, my stomach slams into his hard shoulder, and I'm definitely in danger of throwing up now.

"Dante, you have to put me down," I wheeze, and he digs his fingers into my flesh.

"Just a little farther. Don't piss on me," he mutters.

"What the hell. I'm more likely to puke on you, not pee. Though now that you mention it…"

He slides me from his shoulder, and my legs almost give out. A group of men pass, their raucous laughter booming through the air. Dante grabs my wrist, pulling me behind his body. I stumble after him, only pretending a little. My legs are barely holding me up. He stalks into a room, kicking the door shut behind us.

He spins to face me, trapping me against the wood with his arms. I tense, not able to school my face into anything other than shock. Narrowing his eyes, he leans in close.

"Start talking."

ELEVEN

Dante

I don't like that she's cowering, still looking a little green. If she throws up, I might, too. It's one of those flaws I was never able to get under control, much to my father's dismay. I need answers, though. She's hiding shit from me, and I hate having to deal with others to find out what's happening with her.

"I don't know what you want me to say," she whispers.

"I leave for five fucking days and you've got nothing for me?" I snarl.

Her mouth drops open, then snaps shut as her eyes skip away from mine. I want her to look at me, but I'm afraid I'm too wired and I might hurt her. She clearly has injuries she hasn't revealed to me. Our relationship is precarious enough as it is. If I put my hands on her, I might never let go.

"I told you before, I'm not joining your crusade," she spits out.

"What the fuck, Aelia. That's not what I'm talking about."

"Well, you're demanding answers but not actually asking any questions, so I don't know what the hell you want from me." Her hands curl into fists, and her eyes snap to mine, glaring.

I drop my head and sigh. After all the shit I've seen the last week, I'm tapped out. I don't blame Aelia for checking out and hiding behind a blank mask. It's the only way she knows how to survive. Doesn't change the fact that I need her help if I'm going to get anywhere with dismantling the Guild. Tipping my head up, I lean my forehead against hers.

"What's Grant been doing to you?" I whisper.

"Oh," she breathes, closing her eyes.

I suspected before, but her reaction is all the confirmation I need. He's been beating her, maybe more. I'm going to kill him, torture him slowly by replicating every injury he's ever inflicted upon her. Telling her that would be a mistake, though. I don't want her to think I'm as much of a monster as the men who have terrorized her for years. At least not right now. She'll find out soon enough, which will always be before I want. I'd rather she never discover the dark marks on my soul.

"It's nothing more than usual."

I push off the door, pacing around the bedroom. It's the same one we came to just a couple weeks before, when she was afraid of me. And here I am, terrorizing her again.

"That doesn't make it any better," I say.

"Well, that's my reality. So if you're going to freak out every time something like this happens, maybe you should *pick someone else.*"

"No."

"No? No?" Her voice ticks up until she's practically yelling. "What the hell do you mean, no?"

"I mean no. I picked you for a reason."

"Because of the information I can feed you? Fine. I'll tell you everything I've learned over the last seven fucking years. Settle in, because it's a fuck ton, so we'll be here a while. Then you can go along your merry way and leave me alone." Her voice breaks on the last word, as if the thought of me leaving is physically painful.

She marches over to the bed, plopping down, then propping herself against the headboard. Raising an eyebrow, she crosses her arms, and I sigh. Part of me screams to take her up on the offer—at least the first part. There's another part of me, a louder voice drowning out everything else.

I sit next to her, running my hands along the comforter, then think better of it and rest my palm on my leg. Who knows what kind of shit is in this fabric.

"Aelia, I'm not leaving you. I picked you because..." I search for words I don't have.

"You don't have a reason, do you?" she says ruefully.

I sigh, tipping my head back. I don't have the words to explain to her why she's important. It's something in my bones, in the air between us, in the ache in my chest. When I walked into the head office for the first time, I just knew I needed her. She's important, not only to the half-ass plan, but to me. For some reason, she's important *to me*. Putting that into words, though, isn't easy.

"I can't explain it."

"Because it's part of your grand scheme to bring down the Guild?" she scoffs, shaking her head.

"I would be lying if I said no, but that doesn't mean it's the full answer. You need to tell me about Grant."

She throws her hands up, rolling toward the edge of the bed. I grasp her fingers, hauling her back to me.

"You can't throw me around when we're alone just because you think you're all big and tough." Contrary to her words, though, she still settles next to me again.

"I'll do it if you insist on running away from telling me shit," I say gruffly.

"Possessive asshole," she mutters.

"Tell me what happened and we can move on."

"And what are you going to do with the information?" Tilting her head, she raises an eyebrow.

"It won't change what happens to him."

She presses her lips together, staring at the opposite wall as she avoids my eyes. I resign myself to waiting. I've got all night, though Jenkins did say she was supposed to be doing something in the Pit.

Telling him he no longer dictated her whereabouts other than in his office was a risk, but I needed him to know how serious I was. I transferred enough money into their coffers he should set me up in my own wing of this place. The calculating look in his eye is something I'll have to address at some point, but not tonight.

I sigh, brushing my hand down her arm until I reach her palm, intertwining our fingers. She twitches but doesn't pull away.

"Are you going to kill him?" she whispers, voice trembling.

"Do you want me to?"

"Would you make him suffer?"

"Yes."

"How much?" she asks, finally meeting my eyes.

"As much as you want him to."

Leaving Aelia in the VIP bedroom wasn't my first choice, but I didn't want her seeing this. The apprehension in her eyes as I left solidified I was making the right choice. She's witnessed enough atrocities in her life without adding more. She already doesn't have a stellar opinion of me, but she trusts me. At least enough for now.

Once she peeks behind the curtain and sees who I really am, I'm sure that will change. I wish I could stop that eventuality. It's our inevitable future if the plans forming in my mind come to fruition.

"Ah, Grant. How nice of you to join me," I murmur as the stocky man steps into the alley.

He jolts, spinning around to face me as I lean against the bricks next to the door he just exited. The cigarette dangling from his mouth bobs, his hand holding a lighter still halfway to his mouth. He seems to shake himself, stepping further away from me. He's trying to appear nonchalant but failing. Miserably.

"What do you want, Cruz? Here to rough me up again?" He chuckles and I tense, tucking my hands in my pockets so I don't beat him to death. At least not yet.

A car speeds past the mouth of the alley, and Grant steps further into the shadows. I tilt my head, wondering who he's hiding from. I was under the impression he was higher in the food chain and therefore had the protection of the Guild. Grant hiding from someone is curious but doesn't change what I'm going to do.

"Are you going to stand there pretending to be intimidating? Because you don't scare me," he scoffs, sucking in a long drag.

The smoke curls through the air, tainting the space between us. Pressing my lips together, I tuck my chin to my chest. He'll reveal more if I keep quiet, but I don't particularly care what he has to say. My palms itch and I roll my head, neck cracking in the process. Aelia may have convinced me not to kill him yet, but that doesn't mean I can't maim him.

"I knew you were a little pissant. Jenkins may have given you that bit for now, but she'll never be yours."

I smirk, finally meeting his eye. "What's your last name, Grant?"

He barks out a sharp laugh. "Going to track down my family? Try to dig up dirt on me? Don't bother. No family to threaten and we all have dirty hands, Cruz. Why don't you go back inside and enjoy your bit one last time, hmm?"

"Tell me, Grant. What else have you done over the years to her? As she belongs to me now, for much longer than you assume, I might add, I'd like to know."

"So you can figure out how much she's worth? I can tell you—it's nothing." His nonchalant attitude wears on my nerves, and I can't wait to wipe the smug look off his face.

I push from the wall and leisurely approach him, noting his body tensing at my nearness. Behind all his feigned bluster, he's afraid of me. He should be. He's not nearly terrified enough for my liking, though. I lean in close, ignoring the stinging in my eyes as the smoke from his cigarette wafts across my face.

"I'd like to know so I can inflict the same torture upon you," I murmur.

"You won't. Men like you are all the same, huffing and puffing and throwing out a random fist. But they all find out in the end how valuable I am to the Guild. You'd do well to remember how much Jenkins values my worth."

I snort. "Worth? Men like you have no worth. And Jenkins is the one who gave me permission to do whatever I wanted. Even gave me access to the crimson chambers. Care to take a walk?"

He blanches at the mention of the soundproof rooms tucked away in the basement in the wing opposite the Pit. Aelia was gracious enough to tell me all about them and what others do down there.

I almost puked when she described the metal walls, disinfected not for the victims, but for their tormentors. Can't have the clientèle getting sick. Then they won't be able to pay the exorbitant fees the Guild charges.

He gathers himself, throwing his shoulders back. "As if I'm just going to take your word for it."

I grin, stepping to the side and sweeping my hand out. Letting him talk to Jenkins won't hurt. Either he'll shut Grant down and we'll be free to continue this dance. Or I'll find out more about Jenkins and whether he keeps his word. I wouldn't be surprised either way. Jenkins isn't exactly an upstanding character. I am surprised Grant has stayed alive this long if this is how he treats members. Maybe I'm just lucky he reserves his shittiness for me.

I raise an eyebrow when Grant doesn't move. "You're welcome to ask him. In fact, I encourage it."

He glances from me to the door several times, weighing his options. He shuffles around me, then stomps toward the door. Shaking my head, I pull the gun from my back and the click of the hammer rings through the alley. Grant jumps, spinning around as his hands shake. I'm already leaning against the wall, weapon tucked away. I give him a little wave, smirking, and he scowls.

He mutters under his breath, disappearing through the door. It slams shut behind him and I tip my head back. The sliver of sky above reveals muted stars, wisps of clouds covering some of them. I should go back in, find Aelia, and make sure she's still where I left her. No one saw me leave, but that doesn't mean she stayed put or someone didn't come into the room. This isn't exactly a safe situation.

"Where's the body?" Aelia's voice echoes from the darkness at the dead end of the alley.

"Did you walk through the wall or something?" I ask, tucking my hands in my pockets again. No need for her to see them trembling with rage.

"There's a hidden door." She gestures toward the dark.

"You were supposed to stay put."

"Well, there was a point in time I had trouble following orders." She smirks, leaning next to me and crossing her arms. "Where's Grant? Let me guess. You let him go."

She shakes her head, pursing her lips. Tucking my chin to my chest, I pull in a deep breath. I can't seem to figure her out. One minute she's cowering in the corner and the next she's snapping at me. I doubt she'd be able to explain what goes on in her head. The shit she's been through has obviously masked who she would have been. I want to peel back the layers she's wrapped around herself one by one and learn who that person is. The one clinging on for dear fucking life deep inside.

"He's checking with Jenkins whether I have the authority to wipe his existence from the planet."

"That's a weird way to say you let him get away."

I chuckle, then sigh. "When was the last time you were outside?"

Her body tenses, arm brushing mine. I'm surprised she's not shivering. She's not exactly dressed for the weather. Summer may be coming, but the nights are still cool. Maybe she's used to it since she's not allowed to wear normal clothes. Half the time I don't even know how she gets into the clothes they force her to wear. There are so many strings and straps.

"It's been a minute," she mutters.

Instead of looking at the sky like I expect, she hides behind her hair. My hand stalls when I reach to tuck the strands behind her ear. We're in a weird stalemate, neither of us willing to give in. Yet I can't walk away.

Jenkins made it clear what will happen when I move on to another bit. I can't leave her to that fate. He'll break her beyond repair. Although, then he'll have to find someone else to do the busywork for the business.

She clears her throat and my hand drops to my side. "I found something."

"What's that?"

"Something that might help you."

"Thought you weren't going to engage in my extracurricular activities?"

Her head snaps up and she glares at me. "Do you want to know or not?"

"We should go back inside before you start dropping intel."

"The minute we step back into that building, I'm going back to not engaging in whatever asinine plan you have to bring down a huge organization like the Guild. One with massive amounts of money and more members than you can imagine. Not to mention a ton of officials in their pocket."

"I'm well aware."

"Are you? Just because you saw them scuttle out of Synd with their tail between their legs doesn't mean shit. That was a fluke, an anomaly that's never happened before, and I doubt will happen again. It's not as simple as finding where they get their funds from and cutting them off. It's not like you can just blow up this building and the whole thing will crumble. Shooting Jenkins won't do shit. It's a hydra, able to grow two more heads in his place."

"Actually, I meant I'm aware of the support from men who should be on the other side of the law. Judge Merrick and I have dealings."

She rears away from me, and it hits me what that sounded like to her. I open my mouth to explain, but she shakes her head, holding her hand up as if to ward me off.

"I'm not going to hurt you, Aelia. And the fact you still don't seem to know what I'm willing to do to keep you safe is a little insulting," I snap, running my hand through my hair.

"Then what dealings do you have with Joseph Merrick? What about Anders Drake? Any connection to him?"

I tilt my head, watching as the blood drains from her face and her breathing ticks up. We're standing at a precipice, staring into a void neither one of us can fully understand. I'll have to tell her who I am. She'll learn how I'm connected to the others in Synd. Handing over that information could put my sister, my club, my friends in danger. She swallows hard, taking another step back.

"Don't run. I'll tell you, but..." I pull in a shaky breath, nerves rolling in my stomach.

"I'm not going to go spouting about it. I'm not a fucking spy," she spits out, but she's still pale and her eyes are darting around the alley as if she's searching for the lies she thinks I'm going to spew.

"I trust you," I say, surprising even myself with the conviction in my words. "That doesn't mean they can't force it from you."

"You think they'll torture me?" she whispers, her eyes staring over my shoulder, mind a million miles away. Or rather, in the crimson chambers one floor below. "Sorry, that was a stupid question. Of course they would. That's okay."

"What the fuck do you mean, that's okay?" I snarl, advancing on her, and her eyes widen.

"I have a plan. If they try to get me down there, I mean."

My mouth drops open, and I'm suddenly at a loss for words. What the fuck does that even mean? She can't have some grand plan to escape. If she did, she'd be racing out of the alley right now. I glance behind me, wondering why she didn't take off when she first came out here. In fact, if she's known about this exit all this time, why didn't she use it before now?

"What did you find out?" I ask as I lean my shoulder against the stone.

She tilts her chin up, blue eyes narrowing the tiniest bit. "There are some discrepancies within the accounts."

"You're going to have to be a little more specific," I drawl, examining my nails, feigning disinterest.

"They're moving money around, but it's the same money. Nothing new is coming in. I think that's why Jenkins was so eager to make a deal with you. Usually you have to give up—" She covers her mouth, coughing. "You have to sell someone."

"Who? A loved one?"

She scoffs, glancing away. "None of these men know how to love. They have to give up the closest thing they have to love, I suppose."

"To just get in the club?"

"To get on the board. To be a VIP."

Aelia gives me a small smile, but it's soulless. Whatever snark she walked into the alley with has fled now that reality has flooded back in.

"Aelia, who sold you?"

"Why my illustrious father, Anders Drake."

I'm not surprised, yet completely taken aback. The Drake name pings a dormant memory within that won't fully form. The fact Aelia still has to work with her father after he handed her over to the Guild sends white-hot rage coursing through me. It's bad enough she was sold. Then to continue to see the man who didn't care whether she lived or died? To have that man be her father is despicable. I mentally add his name to the list of people I plan on killing before this whole thing is over.

I won't make Aelia any promises. She's barely starting to trust me and I'm not willing to jeopardize that tentative bond between us. Perhaps later I can give her the opportunity to do it herself. It's the only solace I have for now.

TWELVE

Aelia

Dante doesn't understand. I can tell he's not putting two and two together. He probably thinks I'm lying. As soon as I mentioned my father's name, his entire demeanor changed. Combine that with his statement about Merrick and I'm not entirely sure he's been truthful with me. In fact, I know he hasn't. I don't expect him to be. He doesn't know if I'm a spy or not, playing the part of a damsel in distress just waiting for a white knight to come and save her.

I take a deep breath, hoping to at least explain who my father is. "He's the one who—"

"I know who he is. Just...stop talking."

He paces away, running his fingers through his hair. I shuffle back another step as the cool spring air wraps around me, leaving goosebumps in its wake. Rubbing my palms up and down my arms, I suck in a deep breath, steeling myself to walk away from him. A couple weeks isn't enough to get attached to someone. That'd be ridiculous. So why does it feel like I'm leaving the last of my hope splattered across the stone at his feet?

Just as I turn to flee, his feet scuffle against the ground, then his fingers tangle with mine. I freeze, staring at the door. Even though half of me is screaming at me to pull away—run as fast as I can—the other half wants to hear his explanation. I *want* him to talk me out of running.

"He sold you."

It's a statement, not a question, but I answer him anyway. "I was almost nineteen."

"How did you..."

He doesn't finish, probably wondering what the hell to even ask. I've never had this conversation with anyone. No one cared enough to ask or they already knew. I tug, slowly spinning around to face him, wrapping my arms around my middle. The devastation on his face is almost too much to bear. He's going to have to wipe away his emotions if he wants the story. Maybe I shouldn't even tell him.

"What dealings do you have with Judge Merrick?"

He scowls, gripping the back of his neck. "Dealings was the wrong word. I just know who he is. I've dealt with his fucked up way of doing things in the courtroom."

"And Anders?" I hold my breath, hoping he's never heard of my father.

He stomps away, then back toward me. I don't know what's going through his head, but his erratic behavior puts me on edge. I set my hand on the handle behind me, keeping my gaze fixed on him. Do I think he's going to attack me? No. But I'm also not sure what he's going to tell me, and I'd rather have an exit.

"Listen, this is a bigger conversation than we have time for. Jenkins told me you had some tasks you had to take care of tonight."

I rear back, smacking my head on the metal. Rubbing the bump already forming, I wince. Dante's fingers slide into my hair, his face inches from mine. My body tenses when he brushes the wound and his touch becomes a whisper. His other hand skims from my shoulder to my neck before cupping my cheek.

"You okay?" he whispers.

"I'm fine. I just forgot." My eyes fall closed, and I lean into his palm as his heat wraps around me.

"Forgot what?"

"When I'm with you, I forget everything else. Even when we're talking about *them,* I feel like I'm not—"

I swallow hard, wondering if I should take the leap. Voicing my inner thoughts isn't something I'm used to. When my father brought me to the Guild, I screamed until I was hoarse. I ran multiple times, never fully succeeding in my escape attempts. I spent the better part of a year fighting tooth and nail to break free.

It wasn't until he told me my brother was dead that I stopped fighting. What was the point of running when I no longer had someone to run to? My brother was the only reason I had any hope, and it died with him.

"Not alone," he finishes, resting his forehead against mine.

"I have to go dance."

I try to force my body to move, but there's nowhere to go. He's so close, blocking out everything else. Giving in to whatever I'm feeling will only end in heartbreak. He doesn't understand who I am, who I've tried to hide from this twisted world.

Even if he succeeds and we both make it out alive, I'm too broken. I've tried to deny it, ignore every sign that points to my fractured reality, but after a decade of holding the shadows at bay, I'm tired.

"You're not dancing. I've seen what they do to the people on stage. I won't stand by and allow someone to drag you away and—" He shakes his head, jaw clenching.

"You don't have a choice. Besides, it's not like that. This is an exclusive event."

I want to ask him to come. Even if he can only sit in the crowd and watch, I'll feel better knowing he's there. Whether he'd handle me being up there, though, is another story. He can't protect me from their gazes. I bite my lip, leaning away, and his hands drop to his sides. What the hell is wrong with me? I can't rely on him one minute and the next wonder if he's going to betray me.

"You might not have a choice, but I do. I told Jenkins you were mine and I wasn't giving you up. How would it look if I just allowed him to dictate your time?"

"Like you knew who was in charge?"

Jenkins is in control of this whole organization. He's not going to let someone like Dante come in and take over.

"Except he needs me. Or rather my money, among other things. It's why he didn't make me pay the usual price of joining. You said the money isn't new? What did you mean?" He steps away, taking the warmth with him, and I shiver.

"I don't understand it fully since I only see a portion of their assets, but the accounts I'm moving money to and from don't have an influx of cash anymore. Before Synd, I could barely keep up. We had subsidiaries all over the country. Now it's concentrated in Rima. Last month, I closed two offshore accounts. Usually he'd open new ones, you know, to throw off anyone figuring out what the Guild does, but Jenkins told me not to worry about it."

"Maybe he did it himself. Or asked someone else to do it."

I let out a sharp laugh, rubbing my hand up my arm. I told myself I was done feeding him information when we went back inside, but I might not make it much longer before I become a human popsicle. He strips off his coat, settling it around my shoulders before starting to pace, fingers running through his hair over and over. He does it a lot, but only when we're alone.

"He doesn't know how. Until I came along, he had his lawyer doing all the books."

His head whips up. "He has a lawyer?"

"Dirty lawyer, obviously. Keeps the law off his back. Helps with a judge in your ranks, but Morrison is the one who decides when we need to move headquarters. Apparently, we should be able to stay a long time in Rima, at least until the merchandise dries up."

He scowls, confirming my suspicions that he wasn't lying when he said he was from Rima. No one with a vendetta against the Guild wants them moving into their city. They take over and infect everything. Once they've picked over all the people they can sell or the law gets too close, whichever comes first, they move on.

"I haven't met him," he mutters, pulling a phone from his pocket, and I tense.

He must catch the movement, since he gazes at me, raising an eyebrow.

"You can't call anyone. The police here won't help." My heart skips a beat when I take decide to take a small risk. "You know that."

I expect him to interrogate me, accuse me of being a spy or something, but he grins. "Figured it out then, did you?"

I tense, wide eyes still fixed on him. "What exactly have I figured out?"

"That I didn't lie about being from Rima. Which is why I would know the police and shitty judges like Merrick are fucking useless."

"You going to tell me who you really are, then?" I ask, tipping my chin up, and he shakes his head slowly. "Because you don't trust me? Good choice. You can't trust anyone."

He prowls toward me, and I shrink into his coat, his scent wafting over me. His forearm lands above my head as he stoops until we're eye to eye.

"If you were going to snitch you would have done it last week when I disappeared. I'm going to do everything in my power to protect you, but I can't be everywhere at once. If they take you down to the crimson chambers, I'd rather you not have anything to tell them."

"They wouldn't believe me either way. Lie to me. Tell me some random name I can give them."

He chuckles, running his nose along my jaw and my breath catches in my throat. His hand dips down, brushing my hip and skimming along the hem of my shirt until his palm presses against my back. My body sways of its own accord and my fingers curl around the fabric of his coat.

"The only name you need is Dante."

"Why?" I whisper, my voice trembling with need.

"Because it's the one you'll be screaming when I finally make you mine."

His lips brush against mine, a gentle promise at war with his words. I tip my head back and he groans, covering my mouth with his own. He melds my body to his, pressing my back into the cold metal door.

Sliding my hands up his chest, I latch onto his neck. It's the only thing grounding me when his tongue sweeps into my mouth, devouring me. I tense, eyes flying open, then fluttering shut again.

I'm not exactly inexperienced, but it's been a long time since I've done anything like this. Years have passed since a fire last erupted in my gut, spread through my body, and settled between my legs. I don't even touch myself anymore, too afraid Grant will burst into my makeshift room and discover me.

All that suppression falls away, flooding my senses with everything that is this man. Dante's hand slides into my hair, gripping the strands and angling my head to deepen the kiss. I give in to the sensations he awakens. If this is the only moment I have from now until I meet my end, it'll be enough. I'll convince myself it will be enough.

I may not fully trust him, but he's the only person who's treated me like this—like I'm human. If I pushed him away, he'd let me go. Sighing, I melt a little more into him, and his hand cups my cheek. Everything hits me at once and a tear slips free. He leans back and I mourn the loss, my chin quivering with the weight of my emotions.

His thumb brushes away the tear just as another one tracks down my cheek. The concern splashed across his face is almost too much and I try to pull away, but he holds me close.

"I'm sorry," he breathes, resting his forehead against mine.

"No, I'm..." I gasp, scolding myself for losing it. "It's not you. I mean, it is, but it's not. I'm sorry. We'll just pretend this didn't happen."

Leaning back, he scans my face, probably searching for answers I can't give him. When I turn away, he grips my chin, forcing me to meet his gaze.

"Tell me what's wrong," he demands, and I shake my head. "Please."

The gentleness in his voice is too much and I lose it. Crushing my face to his chest, I break down. His arms surround me, holding me close. I wonder for what feels like the millionth time if he's regretting his decision to ask me for help. If I were him, I'd be running for the hills. Any other man would be begging for the chance to get rid of a weepy woman who can't even tell him why they're soaking his shirt with her tears.

I suck in a deep breath, searching for my dignity somewhere around our feet. It's disappeared, probably washed away by my tears.

"You should talk to Rachel," I murmur, tugging from his grasp and keeping my head tucked to my chest.

He guides my gaze back to his and I tip my chin up.

"Why is that?"

"She won't fall apart in your arms just because you kissed her."

"Except I wouldn't be kissing her," he says gently, causing my breath to hitch.

"Well, she could help you more."

He sighs, wiping the wetness from my cheeks, and I let him, even though I should pull away. The more comfort I find in his arms, the harder it will be when it's gone.

"Aelia," he sighs, eyes falling closed. "When was the last time someone took care of you?"

I shake my head, eyes filling again. "When I was sixteen."

"Who?"

I can't talk about Roman. I won't open that door, especially for someone who might drop me the first chance he gets. I swallow hard, realizing how unfair I'm being. Dante has done nothing but protect me as best he can, given the current situation. I still can't tell him, though. I shake my head again and he nods, understanding swimming in his eyes.

"I won't kiss you again." His hands drop from my face and an ache forms in my chest. "Unless you ask."

THIRTEEN

Dante

Clouds gather overhead, threatening to dump more rain on the city. I lean against the window of a blacked-out SUV, hoping the deluge holds off a little longer. I shouldn't even be here scouting Viper territory. If someone recognizes me, my cover within the Guild might be blown, and that will leave Aelia vulnerable. They'll kill her and I can't live with that, especially if it's my fault.

"Sir, it's nine p.m. Would you like to go home before the club?" the driver asks, eyeing me in the rearview mirror.

"No. I'd rather not be late."

I glance once more at the tattered flag stamped with a rearing snake that hangs from a nearby fence. The fabric whips up as wind gusts through the streets, and I sigh. I haven't been able to contact anyone.

Maddox better be keeping his shit together or I'm going to have a mess to clean up after I deal with the Guild. MacKenzie wasn't exactly happy when we left Synd. I suspect that had more to do with Ryker Helms than me, though.

As we pull away from my territory, I wonder if I should have told them more. Informing them I was taking care of something and would be back in two weeks wasn't exactly smart. My sister can hold her own, but I still worry. I can't turn it off.

I sigh again, trying to focus on the next step of infiltrating the Guild. My mind keeps wandering back to my MC. We were in the middle of dealing with the Night Slayers, a rival motorcycle club attempting to take over Rima. If Maddox does keep his shit together, he'll be able to stave them off until I return and deal with them once and for all.

"We need to stop by their headquarters first," I say, leaning forward slightly when the driver attempts to turn off the main drag.

"Yes, sir," he mumbles.

I don't know him, but Nemesis gave me the company name, stating they were discreet. I'm banking a lot on the hacker being fully committed to the leaders in Synd. Helms said he uses her, so I assume she's on their payroll. She snorted when I asked her not to tell anyone what I was asking for, as if I'd insulted her. I don't like putting that kind of control in someone else's hands, but I didn't have a choice.

Getting into the Guild the usual way would have taken too long. The hacker may have built an entire persona for me, but she couldn't manifest a family member for me to sell to the Guild. Not that I would have asked her to. I've already had to make sacrifices I'm uncomfortable with to weasel my way in. A shiver rolls through me at the thought of MacKenzie being subjected to the shit the Guild does. For as strong as she is, she wouldn't survive. My soul wouldn't survive.

"Stay here and wait for me."

I wait until he nods before I climb from the backseat, straightening the cuffs on a suit I rarely wear. The guards at the main doors avert their eyes as I approach, pulling them open, and I stride through.

Several men attempt to stop me, but I'm moving too quickly for them to catch my attention. The last thing I want to do is sit around and make small talk. Especially because their version of small talk is distasteful at best. Their perversions turn my stomach, leaving me want to burn the building down with them inside.

As I reach the top of the third staircase, I turn the corner, relief washing over me when I spot Aelia's door. Then Grant slips into view, approaching her door, and I quicken my pace. His hand wraps around the doorknob seconds before my body slams into his, crushing him into the wall. Gripping his wrist, I wrench his arm behind his back, and he cries out.

"Can I help you with something, Grant?" I snarl in his ear, and his face drains of the ruddy color usually staining his cheeks.

"I was sent to wake the bit," he snaps, but fear laces his tone, and I revel in it.

"I suggest you let me take care of what's mine," I growl.

I grip his hair, smashing his head into the wall before I push back. He groans, knees giving out, and I sneer in disgust as he rights himself. Kicking him in the knee would be a good reminder, but I need him terrified.

Once Aelia convinced me not to kill him, I started thinking about how I could use him. Grant has been with the Guild for a long time. If he's terrified of me, he might let something slip. Or I can force information from him.

"Grant," I call when he's almost around the corner. "Did you happen to speak with Jenkins?"

He scuttles away, his body tense as he checks over his shoulder several times, then disappears. I glance the other way, making sure the hallway is clear before I lift my hand to knock. Aelia's voice rings in my ears, hissing at me for being polite. Instead, I rip open the door, and she shrieks. Stepping inside, I slam it shut behind me.

"Was that believable? The yell? Because it sounded a bit flat to me," she says as she pulls on her high heel.

"Your voice was a little high, but I'm sure on a camera they won't be able to tell."

I lean against the wood, my head brushing the ceiling, and scowl.

"What's got you in such a bad mood?"

"This room is a shithole. I'm getting you out of here as soon as I secure a room of my own."

Her eyebrows crawl up her forehead, then she smirks, throwing me off. Since the kiss in the alley a week ago, she's changed. It's as if she left all her insecurities next to the door, sloughing them off as we went back inside. I wish she could be like this all the time. If I get my way, she'll have the chance. Even if I don't succeed in dismantling the Guild, I'm getting her out.

"Only men with council seats are afforded private rooms. I doubt Jenkins will give you a spot, no matter how much money you throw at him."

She stands, teetering on her tall heels. With the sloped ceiling, she has to duck, but it doesn't hide the outfit she's wearing. It's gaudy and two sizes too small. I swear the back has tassels, though what the purpose is, I don't know. Every time she shifts, I'm blinded by the light bouncing from the sequins covering what little material there is.

"You can't wear that," I grunt, crossing my arms.

"You realize they pick my clothes, right? It's not like I have a walk-in closet attached to the actual closet I sleep in."

I scoop up a skirt, slightly longer than the shit she's wearing. Tossing it at her feet, I search the small space for a regular shirt, finding only a ratty tank top she must wear to bed. Finally, I spot a blouse, if it could even be classified as one, tucked under her blankets.

"Wear this," I say, handing it to her.

"That's for when I serve. I'm pretty sure someone spilled beer on it."

"We're going outside. You need to—"

"Did you get permission?"

I shake my head, trying to follow the switch in conversation. "Permission? I don't ask for permission."

"Except from me." It's a statement she's been making over the last week in various forms. I can't tell if she's reminding me or testing my resolve.

Her eyes skip away from mine, but not before I catch a gleam in them. "I can't leave the premises without permission, which Jenkins has never given me. Ever. The most I see is a sliver of the world before I'm stuffed in the back of a van with a bag shoved over my head."

"Guess we'll find out what happens when I don't ask."

Her head whips up, and she holds her hands out as if to fend me off. She blanches, doubling over as her breath comes in gasps. My first instinct is to pull her into me, but I don't want her to spiral more. I drop to my knees, wrapping my fingers gently around her arms. Goosebumps scatter across her skin, and she shivers.

"Tell me," I demand, my tone harsher than I intend.

"*I'll* find out. *I'll* be punished. Not a damn thing will happen to *you*," she spits, ripping from my grasp.

She stumbles over her blankets, falling onto her ass. I reach for her, but she slaps my hand away. Huffing, I run my hand through my hair. I can't even fault her. Her reaction is entirely warranted. I know what these people are like, yet I dismissed the risk she'd be taking.

"We don't have to—" My phone buzzes, cutting off my pathetic attempt to apologize.

Pulling it from my pocket, I find a text message from an unknown source. No one has this number except Byron, the man who brought me into the Guild. I read it three times before I fully register what it says and who it's from.

"How would you like to sleep in a real bed?" I murmur, glancing at her.

She jerks back, head knocking against the wall as hope wars with terror in her dark eyes.

"How?" she whispers.

I hold the phone out to her and she hesitates, then takes it with trembling fingers. Her lips purse as she reads the screen. I glance away, not wanting to fall into the memories I've been swimming in for the last week.

Licking my lips, I swear I can still taste her sweetness. My cock swells as I remember how she melted in my arms, giving into whatever emotions were rolling through her.

She shakes her head. "This is a trap."

"Doubt it. With the steps I've been taking over the last week, I'm surprised it took him this long."

"What does that mean?" she asks, handing my phone back.

I send a quick reply—demands, really—to Jenkins. We're both testing, seeing how far we can push the other. I doubt he'd approve of my plan to bring Aelia, but I won't be asking. Leaving headquarters might be pushing it, though, based on her reaction. She might not even be ready to be back in the real world, even if it's only to another Guild establishment.

"Why didn't you run when we were in the alley?"

"Are you going to answer my question?" she snaps, wrapping her arms around her legs. It reminds me of the first time I was here.

"I can't tell you right now. Later, when we're settled in the room."

She huffs, resting her forehead on her knees. Her voice is muffled when she says, "I was scared I'd get caught."

"No one was there except for us. You could have even asked me to help you."

"I knew you wouldn't." She glares at me before dropping her head again.

"I might have. I could have gotten you out at least. Dealt with the fallout," I say, knowing it's a lie.

Letting her run when it would have derailed everything I was working for would have been hard. I'd probably be dead right now. It hits me that there may have been cameras in the alley, catching everything we were saying. I checked before Grant stumbled out for a cigarette, but that doesn't mean much.

"They'll put cameras in your room."

"They won't unless he's willing to risk it. Be pretty fucking stupid, though. Is there anything you need from here?" I sweep my hand out, gesturing at the space.

"None of it is mine. Grant has my clothes, but I don't know where," she mutters, refusing to meet my gaze.

"You won't need them. Let's go," I say gruffly.

Grabbing my phone, I send a text to the driver with a list of things for him to pick up. I didn't want to hand out this number, but I need help. They're not technically a shopping service, but with the amount of money I'm paying them, they'll hopefully expand their services for me. He responds almost immediately, and the tension in my shoulders eases.

I tug open her door, stepping out, but she doesn't follow. Instead, she's scanning the closet, a forlorn look on her face. I tilt my head, peeking around the corner.

"What's wrong?" I murmur, glancing down the hallway to make sure no one is about to ambush us.

She shakes her head, finally coming to my side. I wrap my arm around her waist, tugging the door closed. She sways, and I tighten my grip to steady her. The room I've been given is one floor down. I start for the staircase I came up, but she tugs me down the hall. I've never been this way, though that's not surprising.

This place is enormous, with more twisting hallways and back ways than even the Kings' mansion. Being an old embassy, I suppose they needed a lot of space for whatever embassies do.

"I'll need clothes," she says under her breath.

"Like I said, already covered. Are there cameras in the alley?"

She stumbles on the last step and I pull her against my body. Once she's steady, I grab her hand and take the lead. I may not know where these stairs will come out, but I can't keep following her once we're in the main hallways.

I hate having to adjust every instinct I have. I hate having to second guess every word I say. Most of all, I hate being here. I'd rather be back at Vipers' headquarters, showing Aelia my world. With the amount of work it will take to dismantle the Guild, I don't think that'll happen anytime soon.

"They haven't put cameras up in the back alleys yet. At least that I know of. Grant probably would have retaliated if he caught me, but he's been reserved since you threatened him."

Finally standing in front of my new door, I glance at Aelia.

"Get inside and don't open the door for anyone but me."

Her brows pull low as she nibbles on her lower lip, dragging my eyes down to the motion.

"I'll search for cameras," she whispers, dropping her head in submission, probably for the benefit of whoever monitors the hallway.

"No. You'll get on the bed and wait for me. Lock the door."

I drop her wrist, stepping back. Crossing my arms, I wait until she's disappeared inside, the lock thudding between us before I stride away. My thoughts stay fixed on her long after I've left.

Fourteen

Aelia

I hate this room. I hate it almost as much as I hated that little closet I've been in for the last several months. At least I didn't have to share that small space. Now I feel like I'm a prisoner—a pretty bird kept in a gilded cage. As if the opulence can cover the lies rampant throughout the room. They coat the walls, drip from the chandelier, and skew the view of the dark lawn outside the window. I swear they hang in the air, threatening to suffocate me.

The lock clicks, and my eyes snap to the handle as it slowly moves. My fingers inches toward the heavy lamp on the nightstand. I drop my hand back on my lap. Whoever has a key to that door has control over every aspect of my life, whether I want them to or not. Even Dante dictates where I go and what I do.

My chest still seizes, lungs forgetting how to work. A tingling pain shoots up my arm, rendering my limbs useless. Gasping, I press my fist to my chest.

Ever since Dante showed up, I haven't been able to keep my composure. The blank nothingness I existed in before wasn't healthy, I'm sure, but at least I could function. Now, it feels as if every other hour I'm panicking, losing my ability to wade through this world.

"Fuck." Dante's voice filters through my foggy brain.

My lungs remember how to do their job, and I suck in a deep breath. His hand lands on my neck, pushing my head between my legs. Spots dance in my vision, and I slam them shut. His fingers massage the tense muscles, and they ease bit by bit.

He's not going to hurt you. You're as safe as you can be in hell.

After several minutes, I push back and my head thumps against the ornate headboard. When I glance at him, my eyes catch on the rings welded into the posts, and I shudder. I'm sure someone somewhere would see this setup and be turned on. I've never had the opportunity to explore anything like it, though. Being chained to a bed—hell, being chained to anything—still sends my mind spinning down a very dark rabbit hole.

"I wish I could have learned more," I murmur, my tongue feeling too large for my mouth.

"About what?" he asks, his rough voice brushing against my skin and leaving goosebumps in its wake.

"Life. Sex. The world. Take your pick," I say bitterly.

He strides to the door, gathering a dozen paper shopping bags I didn't notice before. He checks the closet before dropping them inside.

"I thought you said you weren't a virgin." His muffled voice floats from the space, and I wonder how large it is.

"I'm not, but missionary with a fumbling sixteen-year-old isn't exactly learning much about what I like. And this place clearly doesn't celebrate a woman's pleasure. Unless the client is a woman, of course."

I hate that every conversation I have with him revolves around the Guild. It's all I know, though. I can't even talk about the weather most of the time. It's night whenever I'm awake. Snow on the ground or rain pounding against the windows is the closest I get to experiencing the elements. As if the clouds heard my thoughts, rain starts pinging against the window next to the bed.

I swallow, remembering the alley. The fresh air was exhilarating, even though it was tainted with a metallic smell. It's probably why I ended up making out with Dante. Do people even say making out anymore? I'm so out of touch, only learning things from Jenkins or the conversations I overhear while serving.

Peeking at Dante as he strides from the closet, I shiver. I lied to him and it makes me want to throw up. I *did* think about running when I stepped into the alley. And then I froze, unable to function. Ultimately, I wouldn't have made it very far. The Guild has perfected infiltrating a city, hiding their men in plain sight. I'm sure their men are stationed at most of the exits from the city.

"Is there an airport in Rima?" I ask. Not that I could take a plane out of here. I don't even have clothes of my own, much less money for a ticket.

"No, though there were talks of building one near Synd. The mafia leaders shut that down pretty quickly." He waves something through the air, covering each wall methodically.

"They're that powerful?"

He snorts, glancing over his shoulder at me and smirking. "You have no idea. Nothing happens in that city without them knowing."

"Except when the Guild came through," I murmur, picking at the comforter.

He nods, then sighs, turning to me. "But they pushed them out. The Guild is vulnerable because of them, Aelia."

I huff, tucking my knees close to my chest and wrapping my arms around them. He finishes whatever his task is and collapses next to me, throwing an arm over his eyes.

"How do you stay awake all night? This shit is killing me," he mumbles.

"I've been doing this since I was nineteen, Dante. You get used to it. I haven't seen the sun past it rising and setting for almost a decade and that's if I'm lucky to walk past a window that isn't covered. I'm surprised the sun hasn't blown up yet."

He rolls on his side, propping his head in his hand. "Is that a real concern for you?"

"Ember read something about solar flares like a week before I went to Synd. Guess it just stuck with me." I shrug, kicking myself.

I'm not as worried about him betraying me anymore but talking about my best friend has my head spinning.

"You're pale," he murmurs, brushing a finger along my jaw. "So I'll ask you two questions and you only have to answer one. Who is Ember, and why were you going to Synd?"

Biting my lip, I contemplate which one will inflict the least amount of heartache. I study him, wishing I could just reveal everything and not have to deal with the aftermath of it all. I open my mouth, then snap it shut, shaking my head.

"Ember was my best friend when we moved to Westmont. Her parents weren't exactly involved in her life. In fact, I'm pretty sure they forgot they had a kid after a while." I take a deep breath, forging on. "And I went to Synd for a boy. Which was not the smartest decision since it eventually landed me here."

Confusion lines his eyes, but he merely nods and rolls onto his back once more. I expected more questions, but he doesn't pry. Part of me wishes he'd keep asking and the other is grateful he doesn't push me.

I gesture toward the machine he left on the nightstand, though his eyes are covered again. "What exactly were you doing with that device?"

"It detects cameras and microphones. This room is secure. Probably not soundproof, but at least they haven't bugged the place. I threatened Jenkins if he tried to pull something like that, but we both know we can't trust him to keep his word."

I gnaw on my lip, wondering what else I'm supposed to do. I'm never allowed a day off. Free time is not in my vocabulary these days. If I'm not in the office, I'm working one of the floors, or dancing, or any number of other things that make my skin crawl. Dante seems content to just be, and I don't know what to do with that.

"What else do you want to learn about?" he says, voice tinged with sleep.

"I don't know."

He peeks at me from under his arm. "Yes, you do."

"Everything, I guess. Seeing the world through the eyes of a teenager is probably a lot different from when you're an adult."

"Not really. Not with how we grew up anyway," he mumbles.

"You grew up with a father who was the head of the mafia and then faked his own death after trying to overtake a city because he was jilted by the other ruling families who forced him to flee, then you were sold to an ultra-exclusive sex trade organization too? My, my, however did you survive with those ruggedly good looks?" Pressing my lips into a thin line, I focus my gaze on the comforter.

Dante pushes up, leaning against the headboard. "Well, shit. Do you really think I'm ruggedly good looking?"

I burst out laughing, then slap my hand over my mouth. When I look at him, his mouth is parted, not a smirk in sight. If I didn't know any better, I'd say wonder dances in his dark eyes. He reaches out, tugging on my wrist, then tangling our fingers together.

"Wait, Anders Drake was jilted by the families in Synd?"

I shrug as my eyes keep darting to our interlocked fingers. "I guess so. All I know is I lived in Synd until I was like eight, then we moved to Westmont. Father set up a new scheme there, but he was never truly invested. He was focused on his revenge. My brother kept most of it from me—protected me as best he could. Then Father decided to go to Synd. I thought it was a business trip."

"But it wasn't," he murmurs, his thumb drawing circles on my skin.

"No, it wasn't. My boyfriend at the time—"

"The bumbling sixteen-year-old who didn't know how to make you come?"

I cough, wiping the smile from my face. "Don't start making comments about how you could be the one to teach me."

He grins, licking his bottom lip. "I'm a really good teacher."

I roll my eyes, trying to remember what we were originally talking about. If I let him go any further, I'll end up kissing him again. Since I still don't know how to navigate that with everything else going on, I can't risk it.

"So, Chad—"

"Of course his name was Chad," he mutters.

"Are you going to keep interrupting me?" I raise an eyebrow at him and he nods for me to continue. "So, *Chad* was my first boyfriend. Seeing as how most of the boys at school ignored me or were afraid of my brother, I was a little too taken with him. I thought he was...different. When my father commanded that he come with him to Synd, I was livid. I didn't even know Chad worked for my father. He was too young, and I didn't even think my father knew who he was. At least not who he was to me."

I sigh, closing my eyes. Images of a night that started with such youthful rebelliousness flash behind my eyes. Ember's twinkling green eyes as she slid over the hood of a car she'd borrowed from someone. Singing along to the radio at the top of my lungs as I drove all those hours to Synd. Laughing as I called Ember to tell her I'd made it. Promising her I wouldn't do anything stupid.

"I didn't realize I was walking into a war zone. The rants Father had been spouting all those years weren't just the ramblings of a disgruntled man. He actually wanted to take down those men. I found Chad, because of course I did." I roll my eyes, trying to lighten the mood.

"Let me guess, he wasn't happy to see you," Dante says, brushing a lock of hair behind my ear.

"Nope. In fact, he screamed at me, then dragged me straight to my father. I thought he was worried about my safety. I mean, there were a lot of guns around. Nope. He tried to use me to manipulate Father into giving him his empire. Said he'd defiled me, so therefore he should be Father's heir. Chad thought Father would kill Roman and name him as his successor. Instead, he got a bullet in his chest."

I tug my fingers from his and scrub them against the comforter. My palms itch, and I swear I can still feel his blood coating my hands after all these years. Dante kneels in front of me, loosely holding my wrists. He rests his forehead on my legs.

"I'm fine," I whisper. "It wasn't fun. Then Father locked me in a storage room in a dingy store. When he came back, he was alone and covered in blood, and he made me stitch him up. Have you ever had to push a needle through flesh?"

He clears his throat, resting his chin on my knees. "Actually, I have."

"Then you know how disgusting it is. We skipped from place to place for a while, then he found the Guild."

He sits back, rubbing his chin. "Why do you think he didn't kill you? After he faked his own death?"

"You'd have to ask him. It's not like he took care of me while we were bouncing around. For a while, I thought he'd let me go. Then he told me my brother died and I just...shut down. I guess I was useful to him in the end," I say bitterly.

"We'll just have to make him regret it, then."

He rolls off the bed, walking to another door. I can't see where it leads to, but I don't even care right now. Maybe later I'll explore. Or I'll just freeze up again. I shimmy down, curling on my side with my back to the rest of the room. Emotionally, I'm spent. It's been a long time since I've thought about my past.

I don't know how I feel about Dante walking away. I expected more questions, more comments, something other than him just leaving the room. Having to relive it more and dissecting my father's motives might be too much, though. Right now, I just feel empty. Unfortunately, that's not much different from every other day.

Fifteen

Dante

"I fail to see how any of this is my problem," Jenkins says, leaning back in his chair.

I've been here almost an hour, leaning against the wall, and studiously ignoring Aelia working at her desk. My shoulders are starting to cramp, but I don't want to attract Anders's attention. The moment he looks at me, I'm afraid I'll end up beating him to death.

Since last week, when Aelia told me how she got here, there's been a vibration in my chest. The fact that she blames herself makes it worse. She thinks she's the reason she's here, no matter how much she hates her father.

"I feel Synd is ripe for the picking. We should swoop in while we have the advantage," Anders says.

"Except you told us that before and look where it landed us. Here. In this shithole of a city." Jenkins spreads his hands, gesturing around the room. He's trying to come off as calm, but a vein in his forehead pulses.

"Rima is preferable for headquarters, anyway. Draining Synd dry is a better plan."

"Because it's your plan."

Anders finally sees how close to the edge he is. He sputters, backtracking harder than I've ever seen before. I smirk, tucking my chin to my chest. Aelia clears her throat softly, and I glance at her from the corner of my eye. She's gnawing on her lip, staring at the computer screen, but not really moving. The sooner I can convince Jenkins to get rid of Anders, the safer she'll be.

I've been at a loss with how to take down the Guild. I never thought I'd get this far, and it only makes shit harder. It's been easier to get information from Aelia since we're staying in the same room.

I press my lips together, remembering the pillow wall she formed between us. When I asked why she thought it was necessary, she told me I migrate in my sleep. Since I woke up clutching those same pillows, I suppose she was right.

I've learned a lot about the inner-workings and finally have a more solid plan. If I can get close enough to Jenkins, isolate him from the others, he'll become dependent upon me. It's the only way forward at this point. At least until I can get Aelia on board. She has a vast amount of information at her fingertips, but the risk might not be worth the reward.

"Is there a reason *he's* here?" Anders spits out, glaring at me.

"Because I don't need to ask your permission who I have in my office, Drake. Now, if you'll excuse me, I have other things to attend to." Jenkins dismisses him, shuffling papers on his desk.

"What about Synd?"

Fuck, he's a dog with a bone. Jenkins slams his fists on his desk and Aelia jolts, knocking over her pen cup. They scatter across the carpet, and she scrambles to pick them up. Neither Jenkins nor Anders pay her any mind, too focused on glaring at each other.

Jenkins pushes to his feet, leaning on his fists. "Get out. Now."

Anders flushes, nodding once before making his way to the exit. He sneers at me as he passes, and I smirk. At least he has the good sense to not slam the door. Jenkins has already composed himself, busying himself by signing a few of the papers. I saunter over, taking the seat Anders vacated, and cross my ankle over my knee.

"Something I can do for you, Cruz?"

"Perhaps allowing Drake to explore the possibilities in Synd would be beneficial."

Jenkins grits his teeth, meeting my eyes. "And why is that?"

At least he's not throwing my ass out. Every step I take is a risk and I'm constantly on edge, wondering if this move will be the one that gets me killed.

"Well, Anders seems to feel very strongly about this. If he occupies his time finding a way in, he might not bother you with it anymore. Plus, he seems quite headstrong. I imagine he'd like to tackle that...project on his own. Sending him alone to spearhead it might be the best option."

I brush a sequin from my knee. I'm sure it came from Aelia's ridiculous clothes. Grant was kind enough to drop off a different outfit every night, regardless of whether I refused them or not.

"And what exactly would that accomplish? Anders going to Synd, that is." Jenkins folds his hands over his stomach as the shirt buttons strain to do their job.

"Either he'll succeed with minimal effort and an insignificant loss of men on the Guild's side. Then you're able to take over and do what you choose with him. Or he'll fail, and you're in the same position you were in before, minus one distraction."

He taps his finger against his stomach, contemplating my proposition.

"I'll consider it. However, we have other issues that are more pressing. If you want to be involved with the Guild as much as you've said—" He gives me a pointed look. "Then you'll need to be more engaged in other things. Spending your money in the gambling rooms and such is all well and good, but we require more."

I nod for him to continue. At least I expected this, all thanks to Aelia. If I secure a place on the council, I might be able to dismantle them enough to take them down.

"What exactly are you asking?"

He chuckles at my word choice. We're still in a delicate dance of pushing the other. It's annoying as fuck.

"There's a motorcycle club within Rima," he says, glancing at his computer screen.

I tense, scrambling to appear composed. In no way will I betray the Vipers. Not even to bring down the Guild. I'll simply have to find another way.

He clears his throat. "The problem is the president. He's a certified psychopath."

"I didn't realize they allowed for that type of diagnosis," I murmur, relief flooding through me. There are many ways to describe me, but that is not one of them, even by my enemies.

"His words, obviously." He waves away my statement. "The Night Slayers could have been an asset, but they're becoming more of a nuisance now. Some feud is happening, and I'd rather not deal with them."

"What exactly would you have me do about it?" I ask, raising an eyebrow.

The rival between the Night Slayers and the Vipers hadn't escalated to the point of needing interference before I left for Synd. Hopefully Maddox has dealt with them. They've been trying to take more territory and steal our product. It's annoying, but nothing we can't handle. I never met their president, but if he's sadistic, I wish I would have done more.

"I'm not entirely sure as of yet. You're not exactly the biker type, so I doubt you'd be able to be a mole." He smirks, and it takes me a beat, but I chuckle.

"Certainly not," I say, but even I can hear the tightness in my voice. "I don't have many contacts in Rima, but I can reach out to the few I have. What about that judge?"

"Merrick? No. He's useless. Great at manipulating the legal system, but not much else. Although, if the rumors are true, he offed his wife with no one the wiser." He cackles as if that's the grandest plan he's heard to date.

"Is Merrick not high within the organization?"

Jenkins's eyes narrow on me, and I wonder if I've pushed too far. The few men at the meeting before couldn't have been all there are on the council. Giving out that information might be too much for Jenkins.

"He's not. He hasn't come up with the requirements to become a VIP, much less sit on the council."

"Hmm. Too bad," I murmur, glancing out the window. Moonlight filters through the sheer curtains, lost in the bright overhead lights.

"And why is that, Cruz?"

"I'd rather not overstep my bounds, Nolan."

He flinches at the use of his given name. He hides his unease well, but not well enough. There is no loyalty, not truly, within the Guild. Once their shared purpose is dismantled, they'll turn on each other like lions tearing into a carcass.

Jenkins needs to believe I'm like them, willing to do anything in order to protect myself and my assets. It's the only way the Guild has survived this long.

"Perhaps another time then."

"Of course. Once I've settled more." I push from my chair, buttoning my suit before nodding to him.

I stride for the door, spinning at the last minute and snapping my fingers. "One more thing, Jenkins."

Annoyance flashes in his eyes before his mask slips back into place.

"What is it, Cruz?"

"I'm taking her"—I point at Aelia but keep my eyes on the older man—"to the fight this evening. I need a means to...wrangle her, should anyone try to interfere with what's mine."

His eyes dart to Aelia, who's frozen in her seat, if her lack of typing is any indication. Approval has replaced the annoyance when he looks back.

"I'll have something delivered to your room. I hope the toys I sent before have been useful in breaking her."

"I like to take my time. Patience is key when dismantling intricate things."

He shifts in his chair, making my skin crawl. When I finally kill him, I'm cutting off his dick first. Maybe I'll let him live afterward. Make him live out the rest of his days without his favorite torture device. I smirk, hiding my murderous thoughts.

"True. I tend to go through them a little too quickly. Perhaps I should take your approach with the next one. In fact..." He looks at Aelia again, and my chest tightens.

"It's an acquired skill. Don't be hard on yourself if it takes some practice," I say, stalking over to Aelia.

I seize her upper arm, and she cries out, then cuts the sound off. This time, I'm not entirely sure she's acting. Jenkins opens his mouth, as if he's going to demand she stay, or tell me to go find him another woman to rape. I don't give him the opportunity, dragging her to the door.

"We leave in an hour, Jenkins. Tell them to leave your gift outside the door. I'll be busy until then," I call over my shoulder.

I don't wait for an answer, pulling her into the hallway and around the corner quickly. I loosen my grip when we're far enough away. Peeking at her pale face, I spot tears in her eyes and curse softly. The bedroom they stuck us in is in the opposite wing. We pass several guards, and they rush out of the way when they see me. Most don't even spare Aelia a glance.

Our room appears after several minutes of walking, and I breathe a sigh of relief. Unlocking the door, I shove it open as the pile of clothes Aelia stacked on the floor slowly slides out of the way. I push her inside, then kick the wood shut, locking it again.

"There has to be a better way to figure out if people are coming into the room," I say, as she wraps her arms around her stomach and paces to her side of the bed.

The fact that in my mind she has a specific side after only a week isn't lost on me. I'm studiously ignoring it for now. No use going down the rabbit hole, wondering if years from now she'll still be sleeping on the left side of our bed. Because there's no guarantee we'll live that long, or that she would stay with me if we did. I shake my head, heading for the closet to change.

"If you have an idea, I'm all ears. For now, piling your pants behind the door is the way we'll go."

I stand in the closet, staring at the mixture of clothes surrounding me. Mine hang next to the ones I bought Aelia. I stuffed the shit Grant brought in the back of the bottom drawer. Aelia keeps telling me she has to wear them, but I refuse. I'll use the power I currently have to make that stop.

I sigh, running my hands through my hair. I've only been here a month and yet I feel drained. The world outside doesn't seem to exist anymore, though I'm sure life is still going on for them. I can only hope it's still there when I finally get us out.

SixTEEN

Aelia

I shiver, following Dante out the front doors. The stairs in front of us are massive. Glancing back, I'm hit with how large the place is. It's probably something I should have noticed, but being locked away inside the building for six months gave me a skewed perspective.

Dante tugs on the leash, and I whip around, the collar around my throat pinching the skin on the back of my neck. He apologized as I buckled it on, but for some reason, it doesn't bother me. In fact, the whole setup makes me feel safer. At least this way, no one will question who I'm with. No random men will grab my ass, or try to drag me into a closet. I clearly belong to Dante.

My father passes us, sneering at me. Then his eyes fall on the collar and he flushes. Normal people would be incensed that their child was being led around like a dog, but not Anders Drake. He's probably upset I'm being allowed to leave headquarters.

"Problem, Drake?" Dante asks, his hand landing possessively on my neck.

"Does Jenkins know you're taking your bit off property?" he bites out, still staring at me.

"That's none of your business. I'd be careful if I were you. Thin ice is easily cracked."

"What the hell is that supposed to mean?"

Dante shrugs, then directs me toward the blacked-out SUV. Jenkins graciously offered Dante the use of a Guild car, though I'm sure it was so he wouldn't take me and run. Dante wasn't happy, but I wasn't surprised.

I wonder how he was able to gain so much freedom within so little time. I've watched several men clamor for years to have a seat on the council. Hell, a lot of them are merely wanting VIP status and they never make it. And here Dante is, swooping in and breaking all the rules. He has to be supplying information the Guild needs, but I can't imagine what it entails. The money isn't enough to convince Jenkins to give Dante such a high status.

When I asked Dante what he told Jenkins, Dante told me not to worry about it. It took me an hour to realize I just let him brush me to the side. It hit me how much I trust him to not fuck me over. Eventually, I'll demand answers since I can't ferret out Jenkins's secrets without revealing myself.

Dante settles in the seat, pulling me onto his lap even though there's space next to him. He nods to the man who slides in the other side. The man grins, eyes undressing me as he scans my body. Part of me wishes I could have just stolen some of Dante's clothes, but I'm used to being leered at. I lay my head against Dante's shoulder, feigning submission.

I subtly try to smell him. There's a hint of exhaust under a woodsy aftershave. I can't place it and it's been driving me nuts. Sleeping next to him every night, I'm surrounded by it. Eventually, it'll seep into my pores, into my bones, refusing to leave me be. Soon I'll forget what it was like to not have him around.

"Any way you're willing to share?" the man asks, and I tense.

"No, Byron, I'm not," Dante growls, running a hand from my knee to my thigh.

His fingers dig into my hip, but I don't mind. I didn't think I'd ever feel safe while still owned by the Guild. Somehow in such a short amount of time, he's convinced my body he's a haven. I burrow deeper into him, wondering why my mind is still holding out.

After his conversation with Jenkins, I'm starting to understand what he's trying to do. He won't succeed without me. I have access to the financials. Granted, they're limited and I'm monitored, but I could feed him information at the very least. Especially with us staying in the same bedroom, it should be easy to work together.

Fear slices through me, sending tingles down my arms. I've spent so long toeing the line, the thought of things changing terrifies me. Digging my nails into my palms, I bite my lip, hoping the pain will center me. It doesn't.

I can't afford to lose my shit here with other people present. Even if Byron, whoever he is, doesn't say something, the two guards riding in the front will.

The leash jingles as Dante swings it around my body, gripping it with the hand on my hip. He turns his head, lips brushing against my ear, and I shudder.

"I'm right here," he murmurs, barely moving his lips.

I swallow hard as the edges of my vision darken. I've spent too much time in my own mind lately. Dante is turning my entire world upside down, forcing me to examine my place within it. I've spent so long trying to melt into the shadows, I wonder if I should have been chasing the darkness instead. My entire body trembles and I gasp into the crook of his neck.

"Bite me," he says under his breath.

I don't have time to second guess him. My teeth sink into his flesh and he shudders. My breathing evens out and my muscles slowly ease. I focus on the feel of his skin underneath my lips. Slowly, I release him, then press a kiss to the mark I've left. His breath hitches, and I wonder if I did something wrong.

When I try to pull away, his arm locks around my back and he rests his chin on top of my head. Sighing, I close my eyes, waiting for the feeling to come back to my hands. I don't know if I fall asleep or if my brain just shuts down, but the SUV comes to a stop inside an old warehouse several minutes later. Dante tenses, gripping me tightly, and I jerk away from the pain.

Byron hops out first, holding his hands up as if Dante will hand me over to him. Our door opens, and Dante sets me on my feet, then climbs out, gripping the leash in one hand and my waist with the other. Byron's laughter echoes around the space, rising over the muffled bass of music from deeper within the building.

"Stay close to me. MMA fights are usually packed."

"Not to mention everyone is drunk off more than just adrenaline," I mutter, then drop my head.

His chuckle rumbles through his chest, reverberating into me. I didn't think he'd hear me over the noise. Following Byron down a dark hallway, the temperature rises along with the noise level with each step. By the time we enter the open space with an octagon set up in the middle, I'm sweating and there's a buzzing in my ears.

The crowd screams as two men, already bloody, circle each other in the ring. I've never been to one of these events. It brings in a good amount of cash for the Guild, but like the dogfights, it's too much to launder safely. Usually they just infuse the funds into the gambling factions, letting the patrons clean the money for them.

We walk right past a man collecting money who nods at Byron. When I glance back, he's wide-eyed, gaze focused on Dante's back. Hopefully, the man didn't recognize him. Or maybe Dante has already made a name for himself within the lower levels of the Guild.

The crowd parts for Byron, and I wonder how often he comes here. The two bouncers blocking the stairs step aside when we approach, and Dante drops his arm from my waist, urging me in front of him. It would be a nice gesture if we were anywhere else. In this instance though, he merely looks like he's protecting his property.

I swallow hard, trying to keep some distance between Byron and me. He keeps slowing down, trying to brush against me. Dante growls and Byron acts like he's been shocked. I don't know what his goal is, since Dante said he wouldn't share. Seems like he's asking for a bullet in the head.

When we reach the top, I lean into Dante, standing on my tiptoes to whisper in his ear.

"I think he's fucking with you."

Dante smirks, tucking his head into my neck. "He's about to lose a limb if he keeps it up. Remember the plan."

He tugs on the leash, forcing me to follow him into a room overlooking the ring. The crowd is muted up here, but a dull roar vibrates the windows when one of the men below straddles the other, pounding his fist into his opponent's face. It's a bloody mess already, but he doesn't stop. After another minute, two bouncers climb over the ropes and pull him off the limp body. I'm pretty sure he's dead.

The winner raises his fist in the air, panting as sweat and blood drip down his face. He stumbles against the barrier, sliding to the floor. I grimace when he swipes his finger through the mess on the mat, gathering up the crimson and dragging it across his lips.

Dante settles in a chair behind me, and I sink to my knees at his feet. Byron sits next to him, chuckling again. It's getting annoying.

He reaches over, patting me on the head. "Good dog" he says, laughter in his voice.

Dante stiffens, ready to make good on his earlier promise. I glare at Byron, baring my teeth at him, and growl. A startled look floats across his face before he flushes.

"Careful, Michaels. She bites." Dante's hand circles my throat above the collar, pulling me back between his legs.

He tips my chin up and runs his thumb over my bottom lip and I nip him. Heat flashes through my body, settling in my stomach, then sinking lower.

"Be good," he murmurs, gripping my chin.

Dante told me this would be hard. I'd have to pretend to be docile, which isn't that difficult since it's not much different than striving to be invisible. I'd have to play the role of his bit, though. That's the hard part. I'm used to fending off men on the floor, not welcoming someone's advances.

When Dante told me to be sexy, I blanched. When he told me to act enamored with him, I winced. I don't know how to do either of those things. Freezing when shit goes down? I've got that down pat. Actually pretending like I'm happy and grateful he owns me? Not a chance. I've opted for submission and invisibility. Those two things I can do.

The hour before we left, he dressed me and gave me pointers. It was humiliating. As a twenty-six-year-old, I should know enough to act like I'm infatuated with him. Honestly, I don't even know if that's how I'm supposed to be. I'm just emulating what I saw in a movie Ember forced me to go to.

His fingers trail along my jaw and into my hair. He grips the strands hard, forcing my head down before letting go. A bouncer throws a bucket of water across the octagon and another squeegees it away. The people closest to the ring get splashed, but they don't seem to notice. I lock my eyes on them, waiting for the next round to start.

Dante called this an MMA event, but I'm pretty sure it's a fight to the death, at least if the last round was any indication. They weren't holding back and there was no referee. Scanning the crowd, I search for a familiar face. None of the guards from headquarters are here that I can see. One woman catches my eye, and I realize she's from the Pit. A collar encircles her throat too, the leash held by a large, middle-aged man. He has a sadistic side, if the rumors floating around are true. Which they usually are.

"Why don't you send your bit to get us some drinks?" Byron yells, though it's not loud enough in here for that.

"Because she's not your fucking piece. You want a drink, flag down one of the actual servers," Dante says.

He tightens his grip on the leash, and the collar digs into my throat. His knee knocks into my shoulder gently, a silent apology.

The next two men jump into the ring, circling each other. There's no gong, no announcer. Only last-minute bets and the screaming crowd.

I fix my eyes on the two men grappling with each other. Fists and legs and blood flies with little regard to where they land. It's brutal and inhumane, yet I can't look away, like a car crash or an execution.

My father didn't insist I attend as many of the disciplinary meetings as my brother, but he forced me to watch a couple. They were exactly like this, systematic and messy all at the same time. I hated them more because they were exhilarating in a way I didn't want to examine too closely.

I wonder if my upbringing broke me in a fundamental way. Normal people don't live like I did. Add in my time at the Guild and I'm pretty sure the only world I'd be able to function in is the criminal world. I understand the mafia. I get how it works. And no one there would blink an eye at the brutal darkness I hide deep within.

Dante tugs me up, and I trail behind him as he approaches the makeshift bar they've set up on the side of the room. He orders, leaning against the counter as he surveys the fight. I sink to my knees, but he grabs my arm, hauling me close to his side. His fingers dig into my hip and I jolt, falling into him. He massages the spot. I tuck my leg between his, turning my face into his chest. Hiding is the only way I'll get through this night.

SEVENTEEN

Dante

"Relax, Aelia," I whisper in her ear.

She shivers, then her leg slides along mine, and my cock twitches. This was a bad idea. A very fucking bad idea. I needed to be here tonight, though, and leaving her behind wasn't an option. I caught Grant sneaking around our door, being suspicious as fuck. I'm not about to let him get his hands on her.

Jenkins's "gift" isn't what I would have chosen. When Aelia ripped it from my hands after I told her we'd find another way, I thought she'd toss it out of the window. Instead, she slipped it around her throat. I had to walk away so I wouldn't devour her. My cock has been hard ever since. I don't know if it's the collar or the fact she took control that makes me want her even more.

Her grinding against me isn't helping the situation either. My hand slips down to her ass of its own accord. When I squeeze the firm flesh, her breath hitches. I nip at the soft skin of her neck right above the collar. Her hands grip my belt, tugging me closer. Not that there's much space between our bodies.

She gasps, sliding her cunt along my thigh, seeking friction wherever she can get it. I should stop this before it goes any further, but she feels too good in my arms. The bartender sets my drink at my elbow, not even batting an eye at us. It's enough to wake me up, though.

Clearly, Aelia needs to ease the tension swirling through her. It's something I can help her with when there's so little I can do for her on the whole. I'd rather Byron and the other men trickling into the room not watch her come.

Grabbing the drink, I slam the whole thing back, then grip her ass to pick her up, and her legs wrap around my waist. When she lifts her head, she tenses. Stalking from the room, I head straight for a storage closet tucked away in the back. It's a better option than the bathroom. These types of places pop up in the grimiest parts of the city, and the facilities within them leave something to be desired.

Kicking the door shut behind me, I lower her slowly. As her body slides against mine, I grit my teeth. She's not ready for me to fuck her. My cock doesn't really care, but I can take care of myself in the shower later.

I lean against the door since there's no lock and mold her body to mine. Sliding my hand into her hair, I tip her head back. Desire drips down her face, darkening her brown eyes to almost black. I dip my other hand under her flimsy tank top, caressing her soft skin. She arches her back, pressing her tits into my chest.

"Dante," she whimpers, then bites her lip.

"Take what you need," I murmur, running my thumb across her lips.

"I...I need..." she stutters, and her tongue darts out.

I rest my forehead on hers as I slip my hand back to her ass and push my thigh against her weeping cunt. My cock strains against my zipper and I grunt, trying to focus on her pleasure. I've never met a woman who can drive me to the edge this quickly. Especially when I'm not even inside of her.

She grinds on me, panting in time with her movements. I slide both hands to her hips, holding her up as her knees shake. Needy noises fall from her as her breath ghosts across my cheek. When her tongue darts out again, she runs it along my bottom lip.

Her eyes find mine and she leans in, biting the soft flesh. I groan, and she presses her mouth to mine. Wrapping my hand around the back of her neck, I angle her head, deepening the kiss and swallowing the delicious sounds coming from her.

She pulls away, gasping. A cry of frustration leaves her, and she stops. She shakes her head, trying to pull from my arms.

"I'm sorry," she whispers shakily.

I cling to her, not ready to let her go. "You just need a little help."

I spin her around and tuck her back to my chest. She tenses, clutching at my arm, and I freeze. After a minute, she guides my hand under her shirt, and I suck in a shuddering breath. Her soft skin is too much for my cock, and it pushes against her ass, seeking her warmth.

"Let me help, Aelia," I breathe. "Tell me to help you."

She nods, her own hand reaching back and gripping my thigh. The leash hangs between her tits, the cold chain brushing my arm.

"Oh no, angel. I'm going to need words."

"Shouldn't we be watching the fight?" she asks quietly.

"Everyone assumes I'm fucking what's mine. Besides, you need this more than I need to be out there. I'd rather be right here with you."

"Dante?"

I nuzzle her neck, nibbling at the soft skin behind her ear. "Hmm?"

"Teach me. Please."

Keeping one hand on her stomach, I grab hers with the other and guide it down her leg. Her short skirt doesn't have far to travel before her thong is exposed. She grips the hem and I wait for her to yank it back down, but she tugs it up more until her bare ass presses against me.

"Keep your hand there," I murmur, then grab the elastic and slide her underwear down.

She leans forward, and I slowly sink down, first running my lips along her ass. I keep going until her thong sits at her ankles. I have every intention of keeping it there, and I stand again. Aelia glances down, a shiver running through her. She steps out of her panties, teetering on the heels she insisted on wearing.

When she bends down to grab them, shoving her ass into me, I grip her hips and rub my cock against her. She pushes into me, and an image of me deep inside her while I fuck her in only those heels flashes through my mind. I close my eyes, tipping my head back to get my shit together. The shower later might have to be a cold one.

"Don't push me, Aelia, or we'll be having a very different lesson."

She giggles and the sound fills my chest, singing a song to my soul I didn't know it needed. I could spend the rest of my life chasing the high of hearing that laugh come from her.

She straightens, clutching her thong, and the spell is broken. This isn't about me or the future. It's about her pleasure, her taking back control. And I'm going to help her do it. The fact she trusts me enough to do this fills me with a satisfaction I haven't felt since I took over the Vipers.

"What do I do now?" she asks.

I grab the thong, already damp, and tuck it into my pocket. My hand slides back to her stomach, and I grab her fingers. Her body trembles as I guide them to her cunt. She's soaked, coating our fingers as we stroke her together. She whimpers when we reach her clit and slowly circle it.

"That's it, angel. You're so fucking wet. Your cunt knows exactly what she wants."

I push her fingers to her core and they dip in. Resting my hand on her inner thigh, I watch as she fucks herself, bringing her closer to the edge. Her legs quake, the muscles under my palm quivering.

"I can't..." she gasps. "Dante, please."

"Where do you want me, Aelia? Show me."

She seizes my hand and shoves my fingers into her cunt. I groan, tipping my head back. Her own fingers go back to her clit, rubbing faster than before. I stroke her as her cunt pulses, her climax shimmering along her skin. She pants, curling her body over my arm, and I hold her up as I push deeper.

She straightens suddenly, tipping her head to kiss my jaw. I glance down at her, never slowing, and she bites her lip. Her eyes darken, desire swimming within their depths. I swallow hard as my palm presses into her hand still rubbing her clit.

"I'm going to...kiss me."

I swoop down, covering her mouth with mine and devouring her. I curl my fingers deep inside her cunt, and she cascades over the edge. She spasms, crying out, and I drink in the sounds of her pleasure. Our tongues duel as she shudders out her release, sagging in my arms.

She rips her mouth from mine, panting as she drops her gaze to my hand between her legs, still stroking her as she comes down from her high. My cock twitches and she grinds her ass into me, making me groan again. Pulling my fingers from her, I pop them in my mouth and lick them clean.

"Why would you do that?" she asks, still breathless from her orgasm.

"Because I knew you'd taste fucking delicious," I say, kissing her damp temple as she tugs the hem of her skirt down. "Are you sure you don't need another before we rejoin?"

"I don't think I'd be able to," she mutters, wiggling as she fixes her clothes.

I chuckle, trailing my fingers along her stomach. "Careful, Aelia. That sounds like a challenge."

"Maybe it is." She says it so softly, I almost miss her words as she pulls from my arms.

I grip my cock through my pants, hoping to gain some relief. It does nothing but have me imagine her hand wrapped around me instead.

Closing my eyes, I drop my head and breathe steadily. I jolt when her hands slide up my arms to rest on my shoulders and her body melts into mine.

"What are you doing, Aelia?" I ask even as I grip her hips.

"I want to thank you."

"Watching you come was thanks enough. Plus, as much as I want you to ride my cock, angel, you're not ready."

She blushes, pushing away from me. I let her go, though I want nothing more than to hold her for as long as I can. Before she turns her head, I catch a fleeting look of regret on her face and understanding flows through me. Grabbing her wrist, I stop her from spinning away from me. She shouldn't hide herself away.

"Seeking pleasure isn't a bad thing, Aelia. Asking for more isn't either."

She huffs as she looks up, cheeks still flushed from pleasure. Or maybe she's embarrassed.

"Fuck you, Dante," she snarls, and I drop her hand.

Definitely not embarrassed. Clearly pissed. I lean against the door, crossing my arms. If she wants to yell at me, so be it, though this might not be the best place to do it. The crowd might drown out a lot, but if she's starts screaming, someone is sure to come wandering by.

They'll probably assume they're in for a good show since all the men in the VIP area are a bunch of sick fucks. Once close enough to hear whatever she yells, though, and we'll be fucked.

"Perhaps you should save the tirade for when we're back at headquarters. In a soundproof room."

Her mouth drops open and she stumbles back. I run over my words in my mind, wondering what I could have possibly said to elicit her response. She glances away, chest stuttering in an attempt to even out her breath.

"I didn't realize that's where you thought your *lesson* was headed." Fear laces her tone, though there's a bite behind it.

"Fuck, Aelia. I meant when a bunch of fuckers couldn't overhear you." I sweep out my hand, gesturing toward the door. "For fuck's sake, I have no intention of using one of those rooms with you."

"Tirade," she whispers. "You said tirade, and all I heard was soundproof room."

I sigh, running my hands through my hair. "This isn't going to be easy."

"I shouldn't have...I don't...goddammit. I fucking hate this. I hate feeling like this. I hate that I'm trapped here. I hate that you're stuck with me, like some fucked-up white knight who has a savior complex. I fucking hate this." She's panting by the time she's done, tears falling down her face.

I gather her in my arms as she chokes back a sob, murmuring, "Me too. I hate that you're stuck here. I hate that we have to do this. And I really fucking hate that I can't fix this."

"Fix me, you mean."

"You're a lot less broken than you think, Aelia. And I'll take as long as you need to prove that to you."

EIGHTEEN

Aelia

Two showers in a day seems like an appropriate amount. Three feels excessive.

I've taken five. I don't know what that says about me. It's literally the only thing to do. I tried looking out the window and counting the trees far in the distance, but that got boring. So did staring at the ceiling. I can't exactly have a dance party, though that's what Ember and I used to do to pass the time. I haven't danced for fun in a long time. I ended up wallowing in self-pity for my lost youth, my lost best friend, my dead brother. Everything crashed into me at once.

That was around the time I took the third shower. The first two were just to pass the time since there's nothing to fucking do in this room. The last two excursions into the bathroom were to convince myself it was boredom sending me in there and not anxiety. I didn't even bother to brush my hair the last time I washed up, which will probably bite me in the ass later.

Last night was nothing like what I thought it would be. I can't bring myself to regret it, though. Dante and I never got to talk about what happened, not that I would have been able to. My emotions have been all over the place, ranging from embarrassment to giddiness. I may have been collared, but I gained some semblance of control. I took matters into my own hands, or rather Dante's fingers, and did something that would make me feel good. It's been so long since I've chosen me that I didn't know what to do in the aftermath.

The choice to have a conversation was ripped from me when Jenkins summoned Dante as soon as we returned. At least Dante insisted on escorting me back to the bedroom, making me promise I wouldn't open the door for anyone but him.

That was at least twenty-four hours ago. I tried to stay awake until he returned, but eventually sleep took hold. I slept on the floor since the bed was too soft, too big, too empty. My body apparently got used to the comfort since my back is aching today. Couple that with my grumbling stomach and I'm in a piss-poor mood.

I'm used to going hungry, but since Dante came, he's been ordering all sorts of foods I haven't had in years. Last week, I almost passed out when he brought me a cheeseburger. Now I'm cursing him. He's the reason my stomach is trying to eat itself.

"Where the hell are you, Dante?" I mutter at the door as if he'll pop through holding a croissant.

He's never even brought me a croissant, so I don't know why that's the food on my mind. In fact, I'm not entirely sure why I'm so focused on how hungry I am. It's not that big of a deal. I can hold out longer than a day even with Dante feeding me regularly.

As the moon hangs on the treetops, I'm no longer thinking about food. I should be in the office. If Jenkins sends Grant for me, I don't know if I can refuse. Grant would break down the door before he went against Jenkins. Hell, Grant would do it in spite of Jenkins, assuming he could get away with it. Grant would grab me just to spite Dante.

The sequins from my dress last night dig into my thighs as I sit under the window. If I crane my neck just right, I can see the stars marching their way across the summer sky. I should change into something else, but these clothes were right there. I keep putting them on after each shower, hoping Dante will come in. I'm not used to picking out my own clothes, even now. It's a silly thing and I should get up and change, but I can't bring myself to do it. The minute I do, I'll have to acknowledge that another night started and Dante is gone.

I jolt as a fist hammers on the bedroom door. Scrambling to my feet, I almost fall over when the pounding increases. Dante's command rings through my mind, and I stumble into the corner. I tuck my knees into my chest, wrapping my arms around them as nausea bubbles up my throat. I swallow it down, not wanting to end up dry heaving.

The handle jiggles violently. "Open the fucking door, bitch."

The door rattles like Grant kicked it. The thick wood should keep him out, but he might be able to get a key. I should have asked Dante about the locks. I should have asked him what to do in this situation. I should have never gotten involved in the first place.

I shake my head, digging my nails into my arms. I don't regret Dante claiming me. He woke me up after years of living in the darkness. If I die never tasting freedom I wouldn't go back and change the things I've done to help him. I swallow hard, burying my face and praying Grant will leave. If I don't respond, maybe he'll go away. I snort through the tears welling in my eyes at the thought. That's not how Grant operates.

"Get your ass out here, bit. Jenkins wants you in the office now or there'll be consequences." His muffled threat seeps under the door, tainting the air.

My limbs tremble as I push myself to my feet, causing me to sway. Closing my eyes, I use the wall to steady myself. When the dizziness passes, I pad to the bed and drop onto the edge. It takes the last of my will to strap my stilettos on. Grant pounds on the door again, cursing me and yelling more threats.

I take one last deep breath before I unlock the door, then pull it open. I'm met with Grant's face, his lips pulled up in a lewd grin.

"Got you."

***

The oppressive darkness crushes me. I wish I was back in the bedroom with Dante. I'd even take away the pillow wall I made and let him hold me all day long if only I could get out of this dead space. The walls close in on me, though I can't see them. I can tell, though. They press against me, forcing the air from my lungs. Even my closet had more room than this place.

At first, I tried to gauge how long I'd been stuck in here, but after a while, I gave up. My mind keeps wandering back to all the things Dante and I never got to. It doesn't help reel in my spiraling sanity.

It's been darkness and bruises ever since Grant tricked me. He never did have a soft hand, but I thought the threats from Dante would keep him at bay. I shouldn't have gotten comfortable. I shouldn't have thought Dante could keep me safe. I shouldn't have trusted him. This has been my world long enough to know better.

Seeing Dante, though, talking to him, getting to know him...I should have kept my heart locked up. The longer he stayed, the further I fell. Maybe I would have latched onto anyone I thought could save me. Because even though I thought I was keeping my distance, I couldn't stop myself. There was a disconnect between my brain and my heart, and now I'm paying the price.

"Ready to eat, whore?" Grant calls, and I tense, tucking myself further into the corner.

The thin door opens, barely letting a sliver of light inside, and I shield my eyes as it pierces into my skull. Slop plops on the ground as he upends the plate. It looks like he stuck spaghetti in a blender and mashed it up. And now it's splattering on my bare feet. I'm still wearing what Dante picked for me the last time we were together, so of course I'm fucking freezing. The cold mush isn't helping either.

"Well? Go ahead. Dig in," he taunts, crouching in the doorway.

I already know what will happen if I resist. The bruises on my arms and probably my face as well are testament to how far he's willing to go.

My hands tremble as I gather up the food, breathing through my mouth. The rancid smell still infiltrates my nose and I gag. I force it down, not even bothering to chew. It's going to come back up in a few minutes, anyway. At least Grant gave me a bucket to puke in. I've been peeing in it too, but that activity is getting less frequent.

"Did you think you were special? How does it feel to know he abandoned you the minute he could? Too bad he threw you away like the trash you are."

I choke, coughing as the mush slides down my throat. Grant probably assumes I'm having a reaction to his revelations. Too bad for him I don't believe a word that comes out of his mouth. He'll say anything to break me mentally. Plus, the fact he hasn't tried anything other than slapping me around a little tells me he's scared. There's only two people I've ever seen Grant cower for—Jenkins and Dante.

"Jenkins okay with you holding me hostage? Or did you fail to tell him? Again."

I flinch when he pushes to his feet. He doesn't kick me, though, like he has in the past. This time he grins, and a chill slides down my spine.

"What Jenkins doesn't know can't hurt him. Can't say the same for your owner."

He turns, slamming the door shut behind him. The lock engaging thunders through the space, and I shiver. Rolling my eyes at his tantrum, I sigh. Grant doesn't terrify me as he once did. Could he kill me? Probably. But he won't. And he gave himself away when he called Dante my owner. Not that I needed the confirmation. Grant's fatal flaw is he can't keep his fucking mouth shut.

It's been a while since he's pulled a move like this. He's right, I did think I was special. Even before Dante appeared, I was getting complacent. I'd become comfortable, strange as that seems. Jenkins has kept me in the same position for so long, never allowing anyone to claim me, I figured it would never happen. I could put up with the rest if they didn't break me completely. The insults may be new, but they're no more creative than before.

The handle jiggles and my head shoots up. Grant never comes back so soon. Nausea is already bubbling in my gut, and I swear if I puke as soon as the door opens again, I'm probably never going to stop. Which will only add to the embarrassment. Grant will probably make me eat it and then it'll never end. I gag just imagining it.

Something heavy rams against the door. It comes again and I jolt as the wood splinters. I hide my face in my arms, my knees tucked close to my chest. My heart is about to explode or pound out of my ears. Can a heart attack make your ears bleed? I bite my lip, copper flooding my mouth.

The wood cracks, the knob crashing to the floor, coming to rest at my feet. Digging my nails into my thighs, I refuse to look up. Whoever it is will probably be worse than Grant. A guard wouldn't come without a key. A member wouldn't know about the door. A councilman though...I shudder.

Rough skin brushes my arm and I jolt. I can't help it.

"Aelia. Look at me, angel." Dante's voice flows over me, soothing the jagged edges within me.

I peer up at him. He flinches, and I drop my head with a huff. I know I probably look like shit, so I can't blame him for his reaction. He coughs, and I peek out.

"Seriously?" I mutter, spotting his watering eyes.

"Sorry, angel, but we have to get you out of here. Can you walk?" He coughs again, then gags.

Maybe I just got used to the rank smell, but I feel like he's overreacting. I stumble to my feet, using the wall to steady myself. Dante reaches for me, wincing as he grips my arm.

"You don't have to touch me. I can walk on my own."

I didn't think Dante would find me. I wasn't even sure if he'd look, to be honest. Expecting him to drop everything to find me, to save me, possibly to blow his cover, would be ludicrous. A small kernel of hope kept burning deep inside, though. But I'd rather he not soil his gray suit with how dirty I am. Dried puke and nasty, rancid, mashed up food coat my skin and clothes.

His hand lands on my lower back, heat seeping into my chilled skin. I don't want to shrug him off. I want to fall into him and cry. I want to sob and tell him to get me the hell out of here. Not just this room, not just this building or city. I want out of this state, this country, this existence. I'm tired and broken.

As we step into the hall, I stop, staring at the ceiling to keep the tears at bay. I've spent so long denying that I'm broken. So many other women, girls really, come through this place who are worse off than me. They're the broken ones. I wasn't allowed to break. I wasn't allowed to complain. In my mind, I didn't have the right when they were suffering so much worse.

And yet I am broken. Probably in a way that will never be fixed. Dante, for all his grand plans to take down the Guild and save me from this world, can't find all my missing parts. I'm riddled with holes that can never be filled. I snort as the thought sends images too dirty to say out loud. Dante might not be able to save me, but I'm sure he'd be more than happy to fill any hole I present to him. I grimace as I realize I'm spiraling.

"Are you okay?" Dante asks, glancing around.

I open my mouth to blast him. Of course I'm not okay. I've been stuck in a cell for fuck knows how long, forced to eat rotten food. Not to mention Grant not caring about leaving bruises. Usually he keeps them hidden beneath my scraps of fabric, never touching my face. Not this time.

"I'm fine," I mutter.

Footsteps echo on the stairs as we round the corner and I slow, shuffling along behind Dante. He sighs, grabbing my arm and tugging me next to him. I wince, though he's not gripping me hard. Grant wasn't as careful, and Dante's thumb presses on a particularly tender spot.

"If you know what's good for you, you'll do as you're told next time," he growls, voice carrying, and the footsteps falter.

Higgins, my father's right-hand man, reaches the top of the stairs and eyes us. Dante nods and I turn away so he can't see my expression. I don't know if I'll be able to disguise my disgust from him. I'd like to kick him in the stomach and watch his body tumble all the way to the bottom. If I was lucky, he'd snap his neck. With how my life has gone, I'm pretty sure Karma hates me. Maybe I pissed her off in another life.

"Cruz, Anders would like a word with you," Higgins says, blocking our way.

"Does it look like I have time? Get the fuck out of my way. And tell Anders if he wants to chitchat to find me himself," Dante sneers.

Higgins hesitates, then steps to the side, leaving our path clear. I tense as we pass him, wondering if he'll lash out at me. He doesn't, obviously, but the fear is still there. Hurting me, physically or otherwise, isn't on his to-do list as far as I know. My father holds something over him, I'm pretty sure. I can't see any other reason he would be so loyal.

Dante's room comes into view, a guard standing in front of it. My muscles are cramping from holding myself so stiffly. I hate it, but I cower away from the burly man. I don't recognize him. Guards come and go, shuffled around from one satellite site to another. I glance at Dante, wondering if he even knows about the other cities the Guild is established in. They may be smaller, but they're fed from headquarters, so any council members would have to redo those places and reestablish themselves.

"Thanks, Jay. Any problems?" Dante asks.

"Nope. We're good."

Dante claps a hand on Jag's massive shoulder as he pulls me through the door. It shuts behind us and Dante flips the lock. Seizing me again, he marches toward the bathroom. I'm exhausted, my emotions teetering back and forth. Nothing makes sense, and I doubt that will change anytime soon.

"Take them off," Dante says gruffly.

Shuffling around the room, he grabs a few towels, then turns on the shower. I track his precise movements, wondering when he's going to finally take note of me. I may not have been expecting him to come for me, but his reactions are unsettling.

What happened to the man who handled me so gently? The one who defended me? The one who seemed ready to burn down the world for me? Either Dante locked that other man away for some reason, or it was all an act.

"Why'd you come for me?" I ask, wrapping my arms around my stomach. The spaghetti sits like lead in my stomach, but I'm sure it's about to work its way up my throat soon.

He sighs, shaking his head as he shoves his hand under the spray, not bothering to look at me. I shuffle back a step. The shower calls to me, but there's no way I'm getting in without an answer. I'll go back to my closet before I let him use me. Which is exactly what this feels like.

"I can't believe you'd actually ask me that," he finally says.

"How long?" I whisper. "How long was I in there?"

"I don't know," he murmurs. "I've been gone a week."

I nod, pulling my bottom lip between my teeth. A whole fucking week. Not that it matters. Time in this place warps until only the seasons note its passage. I couldn't say what month it was, much less what day.

The only reason I know how many years have passed is because the Auction takes place on New Year's Eve every single goddamn year. It's the only event I've consistently been to. It's vile and disgusting and Jenkins spends the entire time whispering in my ear about how one day I'll be up there, being sold to the highest bidder.

The last Auction was just a few months ago, and he complained through most of it. The woman he'd picked to abuse that night while in his private box didn't make it out alive, he was so upset. Not only was the event dampened by the Guild's ongoing war with the leaders of Synd, but Jenkins had wanted to punish one particular woman no one could seem to get their hands on. I silently prayed she'd slip through his fingers, even if it meant the rest of us felt his wrath. At least one of us would get away.

That unnamed woman gave me hope. And then there was nothing. They pulled out of Synd, set up in Rima, and Jenkins refused to entertain going back to finish the job. It was the first bright spot among the many years of darkness. If one city, one woman, could defy him, maybe fate hadn't forgotten us after all. Rachel spent weeks whispering about her to the others. Using her as a beacon of hope. As the months passed, though, and life returned to normal, that hope shriveled. As one person after another was brought in, then out of the Pit. As one after another was sold off to the Trade. We knew—no one escaped but her.

Nineteen

Dante

Hot water splashes against my hand, soaking my shirt, but I can't force myself to turn to Aelia. The last week drained me in a way I didn't think possible. Coming back to find her gone and no one knew where she was sent me into a rage. I was already riding the high of burning shit down and taking out threats, but then to find someone took what was mine to protect was too much. The small space I found her in was rank. When I finally saw her, though, nothing could have prepared me for the half-healed bruises peppering her body.

It took everything in me to not find Grant and beat him to death. I would have just for taking her in the first place, but I was in too much of a rush to find her. His beating will have to wait until I'm sure she's okay.

"Get in the shower, Aelia. The water will make you feel better," I say gently.

I can't face her. Not yet. Every time I see her bruises, the mess she is, I'm reminded of how I failed her. Telling her I wouldn't always be there to protect her doesn't excuse the fact that I wasn't there. Grant took advantage of the situation, like I knew he would. All the excuses I have are just that—excuses. They don't change the fact that she was stuck in a tiny ass concrete box for a fucking week.

"Why did you come for me?" she repeats, anger lacing her tone.

I suck in a deep breath. "Ask the question you really want to, Aelia."

"That is the question I want answered."

I spin, glaring at her. "Why didn't you come sooner? That's what you really want to know. Why did I let him take you in the first place? Why did I leave and not tell you where I was? Why—"

"Stop," she cries, covering her face. "Just stop."

She crumples to the floor, head resting against the tiles. Her shoulders heave and at first, I think she's sobbing. When I drop to my knees next to her, she pukes all over my legs.

Nausea bubbles in my stomach. When the smell hits me, bile fills my mouth and I swallow it down. I hold my breath, hoping to stop myself from throwing up on her. My father's sneering voice echoes in my head, telling me what a disgrace I am to the Raines name, as if I can stop myself from being a sympathy puker. He's been dead for five years and was an asshole, yet I'm still struggling to distance myself from his criticisms.

I gather her up, and she struggles weakly against me. I don't care about the mess. It's not her fault. It's just another mark against Grant. Slowly, I undress her, throwing her clothes straight into the trash. She shivers, pale face tipping up to me. There's no fight left in her eyes. She's a blank shell staring back at me. My chest tightens, hating that I played a part in this.

"Come on. The water will help."

She groans as I carry her to the shower. I doubt she'll be able to stand on her own. Holding her close to my chest, I let the spray wash over us both. Her shivering slowly eases as the warmth seeps into her skin, washing away the grime and tears. It only serves to make her wounds stand out in contrast, though. Soap and water won't wash away the memories.

"You can put me down," she mumbles.

"Your legs won't hold you."

"You still have clothes on. Clothes I threw up on."

I sigh, lowering her to her feet. Looping my arm around her waist, I reach for the shampoo.

"I can wash my own hair." Her voice is devoid of emotion, as soulless as her eyes.

I peel my wet shirt from my skin, throwing it in the corner of the shower. My pants follow, leaving me in just boxer briefs. I tug her around, tucking her head into my chest. A floral scent mingles with the steam as I lather shampoo into her hair. I wash it twice and still don't get all the grit out of it. Once more, I work it through her dark strands, then put the conditioner in, rinsing it each time. Her cheek rests against my chest, her breaths evening out. If she wasn't on her feet, I'd assume she fell asleep.

"I didn't think you'd come," she whispers when I grab the loofah and run it over her body.

"I got complacent. I thought no one would touch you because..."

"Because you forgot to not trust anyone?" she says bitterly.

"No. I trust you, though I probably shouldn't. I got caught up, thinking they feared me. They don't. Not yet."

She shivers, despite the hot water pelting her back. "I think it was worse this time."

I rear back, ducking to see her face. "What do you mean *this time?*"

"Grant. It doesn't happen all the time, but every once in a while he wants to teach me a lesson."

"A lesson?" Even I can hear the deadly tone in my voice. While I don't want to scare her, at least she's losing that emptiness in her eyes.

"That they're in control. They're always in control. I don't have a choice in anything, and they can take it away whenever they see fit. Dante, I know you think you're being here has done something for me, but..." She pulls in a deep breath as if bracing herself for battle.

"Aelia?"

She shakes her head. "You can't be my savior. Nothing in my life will change. Even if you succeed, nothing will change."

"You'll be free. You'll be out of this hellhole, free to live your life however you want."

"But I don't know what I want," she cries, crossing her arms over her chest, like she just noticed she's naked. She glances away, but I grip her chin lightly, pulling her gaze back to mine.

"Don't you want to find out?"

She shakes her head again, pressing her lips together. "I don't know how. Besides, this is all I've known since I was nineteen. And before that, I grew up with Anders as my father. From the mafia to fucked-up sex club. That's been the projection of my life. The shit I've seen...why are you smiling?"

She has no idea who I am, what I grew up with. An MC might be different from the mafia, but not by much. Plus, we worked with the Kings and the Byrns just enough that I'm not ignorant of how they operate. Though Anders probably is a lot more like Shane and Mason's fathers rather than mine or Helms's.

I pull her into me again, trapping her arms between us. I've tried hard to ignore the fact that she's been naked this entire time, concentrating on freeing her from whatever prison her mind has been trapped in.

"I can't tell you everything, but I can say that if you stick with me, you being raised in the mafia won't be a problem."

"It doesn't matter. Where's Grant?"

"It does matter, but now isn't the time." I reach around her and turn off the shower.

"Where's Grant, Dante?"

"Currently? Chained to a pipe in his room. I'll deal with him later."

She starts to shake, pushing away from me. "No. No, no, no. You have to let him go. You can't..."

Her breathing becomes ragged, and she stumbles into the corner. Sliding to a crouch, she runs her hands over her wet hair, then tugs at the strands. I drop in front of her, cupping her face.

"They won't hurt you anymore, Aelia. I won't let them." We both know I'm lying. They're merely words, regardless of how much we wish they were more.

"And what happens the next time you leave? He'll bide his time, and it'll be worse. He hates you and he'll take it out on me," she mutters, tears streaming down her face, though she doesn't seem to notice.

Her eyes dart around, never settling on me. It's as if she's not here, locked away in whatever hell she's imagining Grant will throw her in. I don't know how to deal with this. Her emotions skip from one to another, never settling on one for long.

What the fuck did Grant do to her to mess her up like this? It's more than the bruises or even shutting her away. She said he's done it before. So why is she so affected this time?

I tip my head back, heaving out a sigh when it hits me. This is because of me. Grant may have fucked with her before, exerted his control over her in any way he can, but this is my fault. I put her in danger, thinking I was saving her. I wanted to protect her so badly I ended up putting her straight in the path of his wrath. Every time I hit him, every time I stood up to him, I only made it worse for her.

"Then I'll kill him."

"You can't," she moans, burying her face in her hands.

"Watch me. That fucker deserves to die. And I've held back because you asked me to. Not anymore."

"And then Jenkins—"

"Fuck Jenkins. He needs me more than you realize, Aelia. You said you have access to the numbers. Tell me, when was the last influx of money besides mine? How much cash are they hemorrhaging? They can't sustain themselves without more. I'm keeping them afloat for now, but eventually, the funds will dry up and—"

"And they'll just move to another city and start again. This isn't the first time, Dante. Sure, they took a hit when they were pushed out of

Synd, but it wasn't enough to tank the organization. There's so much you don't know."

"Then tell me. Help me understand," I plead.

"I can't," she whispers.

Her dull eyes find mine and her lids droop. She's too tired to have this conversation.

"Let's get you to bed. We can talk after you sleep."

"What time is it?" she asks as I pull her to her feet.

"Just after midnight."

I set her on the bed, then go to the closet and gather some clothes for her. When I come back, I'm pretty sure she's asleep. As I slide underwear up her legs, I brush the bruises. They run all the way up her thighs as if he beat her with a pipe. Sitting her up, she sags against me, mumbling under her breath. My shirt hangs off her shoulders, practically drowning her, and I wonder how much they feed her. Probably as little as possible. Though based on the conditions in the Pit, it's probably better than they get down there.

"Why'd you come for me?" she asks as I tuck the covers under her chin.

Smoothing back the strands of hair sticking to her forehead, I wait for her eyes to open, but they stay closed. I grab the pillows, placing them down the middle of the bed. She mutters again and I lean in close. She's whispering why over and over again. I sigh, the ache in my chest pulsing.

"Because I couldn't leave you," I say.

I retreat to the closet to change, leaving my wet boxers in the corner. I should deal with my clothes, but I don't want her waking up alone again. The desire for vengeance courses through my veins, urging me to go back and finish the job. Grant can wait a few more hours. I wonder if I could convince Jenkins to let me torture him slowly. Maybe I'll put him in the same room he locked Aelia in. Recreating his treatment of her would be appropriate.

Moonlight scatters across the floor, illuminating the room. I leave the curtains open, hoping she'll wake up with the sun warming her skin. It's been too long since she's felt anything other than pain. She deserves more—more than I can give her.

Settling on my side of the pillow dam, I watch her chest rise and fall with each breath. With Jag outside, I'm not afraid of someone coming for her, but for some reason, the fear of her not making it through the night rides me hard. I expect I'll be awake long into the night, waiting for the next disaster to strike. With how things have been going, this quiet won't last long.

TWENTY

Aelia

Pulling the curtains across the windows, I cut off the rays of the setting sun. I woke up just in time to watch the edge of the glowing ball kiss the horizon. I'd love to sit in the warmth and relish its descent to the other side of the planet, but it was too bright in the room. Dante is sprawled across the bed, pillows flung everywhere. Shadows dance across his face as the fabric settles, and I sigh.

My dreams were filled with shadows stalking me through the dark. Then Dante would show up and he'd eventually chase me instead. Just as I was waking, the dream morphed to him falling to his knees, begging for something. As he dissolved, I made up my mind.

My stomach rumbles, and I press a hand against the shirt I don't remember putting on. I blush, remembering how out of it I was. Carrying on a coherent conversation with Dante was a struggle. I couldn't figure out how to feel, much less how to explain to him what I wanted to know. The only thing that stands out is that he begged me to help him. Again. It merely solidified why he's set on keeping me around.

I don't think he'd leave me to a terrible fate. He's good and decent at his core, even if his methods are sometimes on the rough side. His motives for not seeking out another woman, though, are clear. I have information no one else can give him. When he wakes up, I'll tell him.

Revealing everything I've learned over the years won't hurt. If he asks for more...I'll cross that bridge when I get to it. He doesn't understand the roadblocks in the way. Even if I wanted to risk fucking with the Guild's accounts, I doubt I can. There are so many safeguards in place for this exact reason, I'd be surprised if I could break through them. I'm no hacker or computer genius. Maybe Dante should find one of those to align with instead.

"Aelia?" Dante calls, and I meet his eyes.

I swallow hard, wrapping my arms around my waist. "Hi."

It's all I can manage. Last night was horrifying. I threw up on him, for fuck's sake. Add in all the other shit I said, and I blush again.

"What time is it?" he asks, voice still groggy from sleep.

"I don't know. The sun is setting, though." I gesture to the closed window.

"What happened to the trench?" He props himself on his elbow, swinging his head back and forth.

I try to follow his gaze, but he seems out of it. "Are you still sleeping?"

He drops back, eyes falling closed. "The pillows, Aelia. What happened to the pillow trench?"

"A trench is a channel dug down, not one built up. It's a pillow wall."

His hand waves lazily before his arm drops over his face. I didn't expect this to be what he wanted to talk about. Keeping my mouth shut is probably the best course of action. I glance at his bare chest and my breath hitches. Grant tossing me in a dark hole overshadowed what happened at the underground fight, but now I'm here. Alone. In this room with only Dante. All the memories of what we did in that supply closet come rushing back. Fuck.

I hurry to the bathroom, catching the door before it can slam. There's no lock, because of course there's not. Dante hasn't busted in when I've been in here, thankfully. I wonder where he learned actual manners.

When he talked about the mafia, especially those running Synd, I assumed that meant he was a part of that world. But mafia men do not have manners. They have guns and no boundaries. They're usually not much different when it comes to women than the ones who frequent the Guild's events. There's several who run the satellite operations in other cities.

They both run on fear, but within the mafia there's a sense of loyalty. The Guild doesn't inspire allegiance. Jenkins has had more attempts on his life than a normal person should. The council members are constantly trying to undermine each other. It's why most of the meetings are anonymous.

I start the shower, mostly because I have no idea what else to do. I need to find my apathy again. It's the only way I'll be able to survive when shit goes south. Stripping out of my clothes, I step into the spray, hot water running down my battered body. My muscles ache, though the heat helps, just like Dante said it would last night. My eyes dart to the door every few seconds. It's a nervous habit I doubt I'll ever overcome, even if I get out of here.

The others hated I have regular showers instead of using a cold bucket of water like they are forced to. At least they were afforded the privacy within their makeshift rooms. Grant leers at my body, licking his lips the entire time. Even Jenkins has come to watch me shower sometimes. I learned long ago to keep my showers as quick as possible.

Now, I stand under the hot water for an extra minute. Dante's pants and shirt are sopping wet again, a pile in the corner of the massive space. After I dry off and slip back into the clothes from last night, I gather his up and wring them out. I'm on my knees still attempting to get them as dry as possible when the door eases open.

"We need to talk," Dante says from the crack he's made.

"I'll be right out," I call, wondering how long I can put this off. Not long since he pushes the door open and strides inside.

"You can leave those. I'm going to throw them away."

"I'll get you new ones," I murmur, slipping into the bedroom.

Staring at his clothes hanging in neat rows in the closet, my mind blanks. I don't know how I got here. This room isn't meant for me. None of the other VIPs stay more than a couple nights at headquarters. They usually have wives or other places to stay, yet Dante is here all the time. Why would Jenkins allow him to house me? Why wouldn't my father push back more? I shouldn't question it, but it's suspicious. There's no rhyme or reason to Jenkins's decisions as of late.

"Are you okay?" Dante asks softly. I jump anyway, startled out of my thoughts.

"I'm fine. Just thinking. I don't know where I'm supposed to be tonight. I need to go upstairs."

I grab the outfit I wore the first day I met Dante, gripping the gray skirt tightly in my fist. It's ripped from my grasp, and I whip my head around. Dante chucks the clothes into the corner, snarling at me. Stumbling back, I track the emotions rippling across his face before he runs his hand through his hair.

"You're not going anywhere. We have shit to discuss," he snaps.

"Okay," I breathe, following him as he stalks into the bedroom.

Thankfully, he grabbed pants and a shirt on his way out. I doubt I could have this conversation with him in just underwear.

"Sit down," he says, collapsing on the edge of the bed.

I sink onto an uncomfortable wooden chair. Metal rings are attached to several spots on it, and I hop up again.

"What's wrong?"

"Who knows what the hell is on that? It's fine, I'll stand," I say.

I try to tuck my hands in my pockets before I remember I'm not wearing any pants. I end up twisting my fingers in my shirt as my thoughts jumble together.

"Then sit here next to me. I'm not going to talk to you while you awkwardly shuffle around."

He leans against the headboard, patting the space next to him. When I hesitate, he tucks a pillow next to his hip, presenting the space he's created. I wasn't worried about being next to him. This man watched me come. I could handle sitting on a bed next to him, especially one we'd been sleeping in for several weeks now.

"Do you know how I got the job? Is it still called a job if you don't get paid?" I ask, throwing the comforter over my legs.

"Probably not. How did you end up working for him?"

"Well, I told you my father sold me. I should have been sent to the Pit or the Auction. Instead, I was set up in the office. I knew how to work with computers and I was always good at math. Nothing amazing, though. I couldn't understand why Jenkins would insist I work for him. I assumed it was because he would claim me, rape me—" I swallow hard, remembering how terrified I was. "But he never did. He just wanted me to deal with the accounts. Move money around, make sure no one was shorting headquarters, things like that."

"How many accounts? What do they look like? How much money do they have?"

I slam my hand onto the pillow to get him to stop. I get he wants answers, but this isn't about him. This isn't about the Guild. This is my life. And all he's worried about is information that will assist him.

I sigh, nausea rolling in my stomach. He's not concerned with how I'm affected or what I went through. I resign myself to sticking to the facts.

"There's dozens of accounts. They come and go. I only have access to a few of them at a time. All the transactions are monitored. Actually, *I'm* monitored all the time too. I can't tell you how much money they have. As I said, I don't have access to all of them at once, so I don't know," I say robotically.

Just the facts. If I stick to the facts, then this will be over.

"Can you fuck with their accounts?" he asks, pushing from the bed to pace across the room.

"No. I'll explain how it works, how the accounts is set up, the other cities they have business in. I'll give you everything I can, but I can't mess with the money," I say, tucking my knees to my chest and wrapping my arms around them.

"Can't? Or won't?" he spits, shaking his head as he rips back the curtains and stares at the dying sun.

My heart aches and something shrivels within me. It might be the last gasp of hope Dante lit in my mind. Or something else. I don't care. Or maybe I just wish I didn't care. Either way, it doesn't change the fact that I should have kept my heart locked away behind more doors. Then it wouldn't hurt so much.

"Both." I clear my throat. "I can't because there are safeguards in place. You're better off getting a hacker to get into their systems. A good one, obviously. And I won't because while you may not care what the cost is, I do."

He swings around, confusion etched across his face. "What the hell is that supposed to mean?"

"Just that even if I could, I wouldn't do it. I'm not in a position to accomplish what you want."

"That's bullshit, Aelia, and you know it."

"You can disappear, Dante. Whenever you want." I bite my cheek to keep the accusation at bay. "I'm sorry I can't be as dedicated as you are."

"What the hell is wrong with you? Did Grant do something? Is that what this is?"

"Is he still chained up in his room?"

"Don't change the subject, Aelia. Tell me what the hell is going on." He crosses his arms, glaring at me, and I shake my head.

Burying my face in my knees, I wait for the rage. Isn't that a normal reaction? I wouldn't know, but it seems like I should be angry. Searching myself, I find nothing. No fury, no outrage, no resentment. Apparently, I found my apathy. I just wish it wasn't because of Dante.

"Nothing," I whisper. "Absolutely nothing."

Twenty-One

Dante

"What did you find, Cruz?" Jenkins asks.

Keeping my eyes off Aelia this time around isn't as easy. With her seated behind me, I hear her tapping away at the keys. Two days since I've found her, and she still won't tell me what's wrong. She won't reveal anything about what Grant did. She won't say much of anything, actually. Other than feeding me little tidbits of information she thinks will help, she won't talk to me. I don't know what I did, but I need to figure it out.

"The Night Slayers seem to have moved on. Or been taken out. I wasn't able to find which one. Most of them took off around the time I showed up. They were fighting with a rival MC, though finding which one wasn't possible. I believe it was in another city."

"And why is that?" he murmurs. I can't tell if he's paying attention. He's buried in a stack of paperwork I've been trying to read upside down for the last five minutes.

"The leader—"

"President. In an MC, they call them the president. You really aren't a blue-collar criminal, are you, Cruz?"

"Certainly not. I'd rather not get my hands dirty in that way, Jenkins. I suspect you're much the same."

Each lie burns on the way out. I feel like I'm betraying the Vipers with each syllable. None of this matters, though.

"Why do you think they're gone?"

"Headquarters burned down. Several of their shops are gone as well. Most of the remaining members scattered, probably unable to defend their territory."

"Shame," he murmurs, squinting at a piece of paper. "We could have used them more."

Unease curls in my gut, wondering what connection Jenkins had with them. He made it seem like there was a possibility to align with them.

"I believe the president's volatility would have been a detriment to the Guild."

He glances up, raising an eyebrow. "It's not as if we'd induct him. We'd continue to use them to do our dirty work, then dispose of them."

Aelia's movements behind me cease, then start up again, slower than before. I tried to tell her where I went, but she pretended not to hear me. At least she's forced to listen to it now. Maybe she'll stop blaming me for what Grant did. I don't know what lies he put in her head.

"Continue?"

He waves away my question. "Anders's idea. Thought we could use them to take out the MC in Synd. That obviously failed, like most of his ideas."

"Have you given any more thought to using Anders himself in Synd?"

"No. We've been dealing with other things." He clears his throat. "We need to discuss your continued involvement within the Guild. How high are you looking to rise within the ranks?"

I spread my hands, smirking. "As high as possible. Barring your position, of course."

He taps his finger on the desk, his eyes darting to Aelia. "We've given you quite a bit so far. We're going to require more from you."

"I assumed. What else would you like?" I cross my ankle over my leg, resting my folded hands on my stomach.

"Have you met Judge Merrick?"

"Briefly." My heart pounds, fire racing through my veins.

I haven't had much interaction with Merrick, but he's been a thorn in the Viper's side for several years. A good portion of our members have been in his courtroom, facing his draconian sentencings when they were juveniles. We were the only option they had left. Merrick could fall off the face of the planet, and I'd be perfectly content.

Merrick's stepdaughter, on the other hand, is probably the most innocent woman I've ever met. I still have no idea how my ball-busting sister fell in with Willow. One day MacKenzie showed up with a new friend, introducing Willow to a whole new world. I'd rather not have her caught up in Merrick's schemes, especially if he tries to sell her to the Guild. I don't know if I can stand by while she's sold. MacKenzie would never forgive me. I would never forgive myself.

"I'd like to see what type of assets he can bring to the table. He mentioned wanting to have more access to our amenities. Find out what he's willing to give," he says, turning to his computer.

"I'll see what I can do."

"Tonight. He's going to be at the tables tonight. Seek him out." He pins me with a look, and I push to my feet.

Buttoning my suit, I glance up. "That won't be possible. I'll get to it when I'm able."

"I fail to see what's more important..."

"You're not privy to what's important in my life. Therefore, I'll keep my current schedule. Unless you'd rather I pull my support and be on my way."

It's a risk and an ultimatum. We're still testing the waters, figuring out how far we can push one another. Sooner or later, Jenkins will break. Men like him always do. He sees everyone around him as weak. The control he wields over others is vital for his existence. But he needs my money too much. It's the reason he took it in the first place instead of insisting on what they normally do. I don't know how much power my money affords me, though.

"That won't be necessary. I'm sure you'd rather not leave behind the...benefits we have here at the Guild." His eyes skip to Aelia, but I keep my focus on him. No reason to give myself away.

"Nothing I can't find somewhere else. I'll let you know if I make any headway with Merrick."

I stride out, not bothering to close the door behind me. It's a subtle power move few think of. Closing a door conveys a respect I don't feel for Jenkins, or anyone other than Aelia in this building. The rest of the night will be spent dealing with Grant and waiting for Aelia to complete her work. I wanted to take her with me when I left, but Jenkins is already suspicious of my attachment to her. The more distance I can put between us in his mind, the better.

"Sir?" a small voice calls from the shadows of a staircase hidden away at the end of the hallway.

I stop, tucking my hands in my pockets, squinting into the darkness. A young woman peeks her face out, waving me over. She can't be more than seventeen and there's still a light in her blue eyes. Aelia told me she can always tell how long they've been here by how much of their soul is left shining from their faces. I didn't fully understand what she meant until now.

"Can I help you?"

"You know Mistress?" she asks, head constantly on a swivel, and I nod. "Can you get a message to her? Rachel said you could be trusted."

She swallows hard, face paling when I don't respond. I'd rather not be known as the person they can go to when they have issues. It'll only make shit harder for me. Having a bunch of women coming up to me to pass notes? Someone is bound to notice—namely Grant. I can't wait until I can float his ass.

"Rachel needs to see Mistress. As soon as possible."

"About what?" I ask, searching the corners of the hallway for cameras.

"They can't see us here. We're in a blind spot," she whispers. "Guards say another one is coming. Twice as big. Just tell Mistress."

She disappears into the shadows, slipping away as quickly as she appeared. I pivot, ready to go back and get Aelia. Two steps later, though, reality comes seeping back in. If someone is watching on the cameras, it would look suspicious. Not to mention Jenkins would question me.

Making my way down the stairs, I aim for casual even though my muscles are tight, unease still sitting like a lead weight in my stomach. Jag nods to me as I approach, and I motion him inside. He may not be my first choice to watch my back, but he's loyal at the very least.

"There a problem, Prez?" Jag asks, leaning against the door.

"Don't call me that here," I snarl, shucking off my jacket and throwing it on the bed.

"Thought this room wasn't bugged?"

"It's not, but that doesn't mean it's soundproof. I need you to figure out where the guards stay. I'm sure they have some sort of break room or something."

"Doubt there's a break room, but they house them a floor above the Pit. Some of them bounce from room to room. Think they've got a poker game or something."

"Or something," I mutter, collapsing on the chair. I cringe, remembering Aelia's words about what could be on it.

He drops his head, then gives me a look. "Prez, what are we doing here? You belong leading a fucking MC, not in this shithole."

"And what happens when the Guild bleeds this city dry? They'll move on to you next, Jag. You think the Phantoms will survive them coming to Harris?" I ask, digging my nails into my thighs to rein in my anger.

I'm not upset with Jag. He's doing me a huge fucking favor coming here. As Sargent-at-Arms of the Phantoms, he didn't have to drop everything and come to Rima. Ghost, the president, almost didn't even take my call, and I'm pretty sure Jag refused to help at first.

"I'm here, aren't I?"

"Fucking bikers," I grumble, pushing to my feet. "Why the hell did you pick Phantoms for a name? Sounds like a kid named you guys."

"Was named that when I joined. Didn't ask." He runs his hand through his hair. "Weird seeing you in a suit instead of leathers."

"Probably as weird as it is to wear one. Listen, I don't know what the fuck I'm doing, but I can't stand for this shit. We need to know which guards are loyal to the Guild and who we can sway. Quietly."

"Goes without sayin'. Raines, this ain't gonna be easy. No one here is loyal. And that woman you got holed up here? She can't be trusted either. You know that, right?"

I shake my head, leaning my forearm against the window. Usually, the massive lawn behind the building is dark, only the occasional animal sneaking from the forest lining the edge of Rima. Tonight, a group of mostly men spill out onto the patio, drinks in hand, partners on their arm. Several of them don't even bother to flit off into a private corner to engage in their sexual activities. I turn away when I spot a man forcing a woman to bend over the railing as she cries.

Rage swirls through me and I close my eyes. None of this should be happening. I don't know how Aelia can live surrounded by this, watching it for years, yet do nothing to help. I understand when she was alone, just trying to survive, but I'm handing her the opportunity to change things. And every time she shies away. I rear back, slamming my fist into the wall. Bracing my hands on my knees, I struggle to control my rage.

"Ghost called," Jag says, ignoring my outburst. "Wants to know when the fight is. He wants in."

I straighten, turning to face him again. "When?"

I told them both we can't have communication once Jag comes to the Guild. There's too much of a risk of being overheard. Or someone getting it into their head to play heroics or some shit. The fact that neither of them listened pisses me off. I can't keep him here if he's going to fuck with my plan.

"Calm your tits. It was before I got here. He wanted me to check shit out first, make sure this wasn't a lost cause. You know he doesn't do losing battles."

I breathe a sigh of relief. "None of us do. We're not even close to that point. But we'll need all the help we can get eventually."

"I'll figure shit out with the guards. You're better off working with the people stuck in the Pit. They got a reason to turn on the Guild." His tone is gruff, jaw ticking. I didn't realize he'd been down there.

"You ever look in their eyes?" I ask, and he shakes his head. "Aelia said you could tell how long they've been here based on how much light is in their eyes. Most of them are dead inside. They need someone to step in for them, Jag."

"Great to know we're the best we fucking got."
Rubbing my temples, I know he's right. With only the two of us, we're fucked. Thoughts of Aelia flit across my mind. Even if I don't survive, I need to get her out.

Twenty-Two

Aelia

"Where the hell were you?" Dante snaps as soon as I walk through the bedroom door.

"Working," I say, spotting shopping bags that weren't there this morning.

I ignore them, striding into the closet. It's close to four in the morning, yet I'm exhausted still. Jenkins didn't mention the bruises on my face, just smirked and went on with his night. Others weren't so subtle. The stares I could deal with, but the snarky comments wore on me. I don't have it in me to deal with Dante.

"We can't keep doing this, Aelia."

I glance over my shoulder and find him leaning on the door frame, arms crossed. I wish I could ignore him as easily as I did Jenkins. The fact I have to share a room with him makes that impossible. I've tried to keep our conversations as impersonal as possible. Dante's demands are making it harder to distinguish what is concern for me versus concern for his plan. Rummaging around a drawer, I can't figure out what the hell I'm supposed to wear.

"Where are my pajamas?" I ask, glaring at him. I don't need them right now, but they're nowhere to be found.

A vein in his forehead pulses and his hands curl into fists. "That's what you're worried about? Where your raggedy clothes are?"

The fight bleeds out of me and I turn away. I should retreat to my small closet. Was it a shithole? Yes. But it was *my* shithole. It was the first space I had that I didn't have to share. I may not have been safe there, but at least it was mine. The benefits of staying with Dante are starting to look as false as his words.

"They were mine," I whisper.

Silently, I curse the tears filling my eyes. His hand brushes my arm as I push past him, and I jerk away. I need a shower and a place where he won't bombard me with more questions and demands. The hot water can wash away my sins, absolving me from the guilt choking me. He threw in my face this morning my apparent apathy for the others like me. Thankfully, a guard came for me then or I might have pushed him out the window.

"Aelia, you can't hide forever," he calls through the door.

Peeling off my clothes, I step into the shower. I shake my head, biting my lip as I turn the handle, cold water shocking my system. I shiver my way through until steam fills the room. My motions are methodical—shampoo, rinse, conditioner, rinse, soap, rinse. Running my hand up my leg, I mourn the loss of my hair. It was one of the first things I lost when Father sold me.

The headquarters back then was housed in a mansion belonging to one of the council members. Somehow, the old man had a full-on medical office inside his damn house, with an on-call doctor. The man was terrible, obviously, but he did some type of treatment to remove the hair from my legs, arms, and other places. My cunt, as Dante so gracefully called it, is bare because I didn't have a choice. That was the point I stopped fighting. It'll never grow back, a constant reminder of when I lost control.

"Have you eaten?" he bellows, and I jolt, almost slipping on the slick tiles.

I haven't, but I have more shit to get done before the sun rises. I overheard one of the guards whispering about a disturbance in the Pit. The others down there may not appreciate my visit, but I'll hopefully get to talk to Rachel. For as much as Dante wants to tell me I'm not doing enough, at least I'm doing something.

I wrap a towel around myself and open the door slowly. Dante's tall frame leans against the wall, tracking my movements as I make my way back to the closet. I throw on new clothes, typical ones I wear to work. Always playing the part. I'm tired of wearing a mask.

"Where are you going now? We have things to discuss. You can't honestly tell me they have you going back in."

"Stop snarling at me. It's starting to piss me off," I say calmly.

"This shit is important, Aelia. And you're ignoring it."

"Just because I'm ignoring *you* doesn't mean I'm ignoring other things. Don't be butthurt about me going to the Pit."

His stunned look sends grim satisfaction through me. Serves him right. It's his penance for being an asshole since he found me. I've stopped assuming he came to save me. He never gave me a good reason to believe he didn't just stumble upon Grant leaving and accidentally find me. Until he gives me something to change my mind, I'll continue to believe it was entirely coincidental.

"First of all, I'm not butthurt."

"The air quotes are unnecessary."

"Second of all, we need to talk," he says, blocking my path when I try to walk away. "Before you go to the Pit."

"Fine. What is it then?"

He huffs, crossing his arms. "Some girl found me on my way out of Jenkins's office."

Pain rips through my chest, and I bite the inside of my cheek. I encouraged him to pick someone else, but I never thought he'd actually do it. Dante doesn't belong to me. He's free to indulge in whatever he wants. I'm assuming it was consensual, since he's not like the others around here. It still hurts, though. I wouldn't blame him for seeking pleasure from somewhere else. He certainly isn't getting it from me.

The blood drains from my face when I realize what he's trying to say. Of course, he wants to move her in here instead of me. I'll have to move back to the closet. No more showers. No more bed. No more Dante. I became complacent with him and now I'm kicking myself.

"I can understand why you'd be concerned with me going back on my word. I told you I would tell you what I know, and I'll continue to do so," I say, staring at his shoulder.

He tilts his head until our gazes meet, and I swallow hard. "What? I wasn't worried about that. She told me to tell you—"

"I'd rather not hear it. What did you do with Grant?" If I have to worry about him fucking with me again, I'd rather be prepared this time. No more having my head in the clouds, thinking Dante's presence will protect me. He won't be around anyway.

"I let him go like you told me to last night. He might have a few bruises matching yours, though."

"I wish you wouldn't have done that, but I suppose it can't be helped. Where did you put my pajamas? I'll move the rest when I get back from the Pit. Anything else?"

The old shorts and tank top are the only things I'm really concerned with. The rest of the clothes can burn for all I care. Those pajamas are the only leftover from my old life. The one where I was more than a phantom with the tiniest sliver of will to live.

His eyes narrow and his arms drop to his sides. "Move them where? Seriously, Aelia, you're all over the goddamn place lately. I need you to listen. The girl said another one is coming. Something bigger than before. Rachel wants to see you, I think."

"Wait, you didn't sleep with her?" The question pops out before I can think better of it.

I slap my hand over my mouth as if I can force the words back in. I don't even fucking care. That's the lie I'm going with at the moment. I'll examine my feelings later—or never. Never is good. Nothing good can come from deciphering some deep-seated feelings I harbor for a man who only wants me for the information in my head.

He explodes, throwing his hands up. "Why the hell would I sleep with her? For fuck's sake, Aelia. Is that what Grant told you?"

"What does Grant have to do with any of this?"

"He has everything to do with this. You're pulling away, freezing me out, and refusing to talk to me."

"I'm refusing to talk to you because you don't give a damn about anything other than what I can get you," I scream, gripping my hair and spinning around.

I can't face him. I was doing so damn well keeping shit to myself, but he just kept pushing. His arms wrap around me, body leaning over mine. I bend, whether to get away from him or something else, I don't know.

He guides us to the ground, pulling me into his lap. I sink my teeth into my arm, forcing the tears away. I've cried more in front of Dante in the last couple months than I have in years. As he rocks back and forth, fingers running through my hair, I bite harder.

"Aelia, stop." He wraps his hand around my wrist, pulling it from my mouth.

His thumb brushes over the marks I've made. Dipping his face, he presses his lips against my skin. Goosebumps erupt across my flesh, but he doesn't stop.

"What are you doing?" I whisper.

"This is called comfort. Eventually you'll have to let me in," he murmurs into my skin.

I tug my arm, but he doesn't let go. "I have to leave."

"No, you don't. Or I'll go with you. Either way, I'm not letting you go. Two weeks of fucking hell, most of it my fault." He shudders, nuzzling my neck. "I'm not letting you go yet."

"You can't come with me. They won't talk to me then. I have to go, Dante."

"I didn't throw out your pajamas. They're in the top drawer. I wouldn't get rid of them."

He nibbles my earlobe, then kisses the sensitive spot behind it. Relief floods me all while my mind slowly shuts down. I don't want to go. All the hurt and resentment flows away while he holds me. I'll give him hell for it later. Or maybe I won't. Weariness still weighs me down despite some of the things I said. There's too much built up.

"I'll be back. I promise." I crawl from his lap, expecting him to stand with me, but he stays put. "And don't have that scary guy follow me."

"Jag? He's harmless. I mean, not harmless, but he won't hurt you. I brought him for you."

I grab his hair, forcing his head back, and he grins. "Did you just say you *bought* him for me?"

He rolls his eyes. "Brought, angel. I *brought* him to guard you when I can't. Told Jenkins it was for my own protection."

"As if you need protection," I mutter. He grins again, and I shove his head away. "I'm leaving now. And I won't bitch about Jag."

I walk out, leaving him on the floor of the closet. Taking a deep breath, I inch open the door, scanning the area around the guard's massive frame. Panic floods my body, then he steps to the side and my heart calms. Every door I've opened in the last few days, I've had the same reaction. I wish I could stop my body from reacting to an unknown threat. I doubt it'll be anytime soon.

"You ready, Jug?"

His nostrils flare, black hair poking from his nose. It matches his beard and hair, giving him a dark and mysterious look. Honestly, he looks like a biker. I wouldn't put it past Dante to hire one. He seems like the kind of guy to have those connections. Every time Jenkins talks about him not being one of those types of men, Dante's shoulders tense.

"It's Jag. As in Jaguar, ma'am."

"You can't call me ma'am. You're not allowed to treat me with respect at all. You're better off just pretending I don't exist. And for the love of all that is fucking holy, do not respond to them," I whisper as I close the door softly, cutting off Dante's laughter. I didn't realize he was listening. Bastard.

"Heard. But I ain't gonna let you get hurt. So don't put yourself in danger and we'll get along swimmingly," he mutters from the corner of his mouth.

"Honey, this is hell. Danger lives in the walls, stalks through the hallways, and floats in the air. Hard to get away from it."

"Dante didn't say you were sassy."

"Well, I just screamed at someone for the first time in ten years. That might have something to do with it," I grumble, leading him down the back staircase.

The man guarding the door to the Pit widens his eyes as I approach. Whatever he's trying to convey isn't computing, but combined with what Dante said, I'm starting to worry. It's not often I'm included in the gossip. There aren't a lot of tidbits, anyway. In a place like this, it's usually reserved to which guards to stay away from and how to disassociate. Not exactly fun water cooler talk.

"Ah, Mistress. How lovely of you to come see us lowly individuals in the Pit. How is it living with a new master?" Rachel calls as soon as we descend from the stairs.

Jag snorts behind me and I consider throwing an elbow into his stomach, but think better of it. I stop in front of Rachel and tilt my head.

"It's summer."

Her lips press together in a thin line. I don't know how long it's been since she's seen the sun, but it always has been a sore spot. I hate antagonizing her, but we need a public show before the private conversation.

"How lovely. I bet all your tea parties are fraught with gnats."

I straighten, losing the smirk. Glancing around, I find most of the cages full, a mass of men crowded within. Women spill out from the makeshift rooms to my right, eyeing me. There are too many people. At five in the morning, this place should be almost empty, the others working various events on the upper levels.

"Inspection," I bark out, and my voice carries through the cavernous space.

People scramble, getting into position. A guard sidles up next to me and Jag tenses at my back. I didn't even realize he'd gotten so close, and I kick myself for not paying attention.

"Mistress, you're not allowed to call for inspection," Kirk mutters.

"Take it up with Jenkins then," I say loudly.

They won't. None of the guards go to Jenkins. If anything, they'll go to Grant, but he's been missing since Dante found me, at least from my sphere.

It hits me how much power I have, at least down here. The others will listen to me, even if they're dicks about it. The guards won't question my authority, not enough anyway. This is what Dante was talking about. Not infiltrating the servers or bankrupting the Guild. The power I hold has nothing to do with my position in Jenkins's office. It's here in the Pit.

Meeting Rachel's eyes, I try to show her what I've realized. I don't know what my face is doing, but she smirks. I nod once, then stride forward. Rachel falls into step next to me as Jag trails us.

I go to the cages first, searching for a familiar face. Most avoid my gaze, picking at their tattered clothes. I'd rather not dismiss them, but they can't help me. There must be at least fifty behind the bars, stuffed inside with barely enough room to sit, much less lie down. Not that most of them are probably sleeping these days.

Benjamin leans against his prison, arms hanging through the bars. A guard steps up, raising a small bat, but I wave him off. Some of the light has died in the man's blue eyes, leaving only a sliver behind. Usually, he has a snarky word for Rachel, but he doesn't even look at her.

"Not surprised you're still here," I sneer, tracking the guard as he moves away.

"Not for long, it seems," he says, and I raise an eyebrow. "Double or nothing."

I flinch, horror flooding me. Rachel's elbow digs into my side, and I struggle to control my face. Nodding, I wander away, the gears in my head turning.

We've never had an Auction twice in one year. The logistics alone are too hard to handle. The manpower, both to run such an event as well as getting enough cattle for the slaughter, was always something Jenkins didn't want to take on. I have to talk to Dante. He won't be able to do much, but he should be warned of what's coming.

I try to pivot, retreating to the faux safety of Dante's room, but Rachel's nails dig into my arm, keeping me on course. There's another room in the back, and she leads me straight to it. Gone are the cages, and in their place, large bars cover the open doorframes. The mass of people packed in the room ratchets up the temperature. It's sweltering despite being underground. A wail cuts through the space, rising above the quiet sobs of others.

"Trade?" I ask, expecting Rachel to confirm that these people won't be auctioned off.

There are usually only small groups in here waiting to be shipped off to other Guild-held cities. Not this time. At least a hundred people are packed into a room not meant for humans. Bile rises in my throat as I stare at them.

"Auction." She leans in close, breathing in my ear. "Something is coming."

I shake my head, not because I don't believe her, but merely because I can't imagine all these people being sold off to the highest bidder. The Auction is reserved for the prettiest or the wildest. Those both pretty and wild go for the largest sums of money. Sick bastards love breaking the ones who fight. It's part of the reason I was never considered for the Auction, at least not that I know of. I was too meek, too quiet. I didn't fight them.

"When?" I breathe.

"I don't know."

Those three words are more terrifying than anything else. I have no idea how long I have to stop this. I may have fought Dante before, told him I'd help him as much as I could, but this? I can't damn these people to the depths of hell.

Twenty-Three

Dante

"One more time," I say, laying my head on the pillow between us.

"Why?" she whines, slamming her hands on the comforter.

"Because you need it."

I scan her face in the soft light filtering through the window. It's early morning, the sun a mere hint on the horizon. She wants to sleep, but we get little time these days for this. Ever since Aelia came back from the Pit, whiter than I'd ever seen her before, we've been stealing moments to come up with a better plan than I had.

"Fine," she huffs, rolling toward me. "I'm going to move a small amount of money from an international account to a domestic account. Then wait three days to see if anyone notices. Then I'll move a slightly larger sum back. Happy?"

I grin as she glares at me. "How much is a small amount?"

She rolls her eyes. "Ten thousand."

"I still think that's too much."

"Under ten and it won't trigger anything. We've been over this a million times, Dante. You realize in order for this to work, you actually have to trust me."

Brushing hair away from her forehead, I scan the fading bruises on her face. It's enough to remind me why I'm risking my life and those of everyone else I'm connected to. Aelia made the Auction sound like an opera event wrapped in a sex trade. Rich men and women alike dress to the nines and bid on living human beings as if they're worth nothing. It turns my stomach every time I think about it.

"I do trust you," I murmur.

"You shouldn't. But I don't want to argue."

She yawns, covering her mouth with her arm. She blinks at me wearily, burrowing further under the covers. Running my hand over her hair, I rest my palm on her neck. Her pulse echoes through her skin, a slow beat reverberating through me. I should have trusted her before. My actions after I freed her from Grant's grasp didn't help. While she may have forgiven me, I'm still thinking about it a week later.

She huffs, her muscles tensing before her dark eyes find mine. "I can't sleep."

I chuckle, brushing my thumb behind her ear. "It's been two minutes, angel."

"I'm cold."

I bite my tongue before I can offer to warm her up. After our tryst in the supply closet, she hasn't given any indication that she's up for more lessons. And I won't be the one to bring it up. She's skittish enough as it is. Add in the problems we're facing, and I don't blame her.

"Sorry, but I'm not going to ask for another blanket from the front desk."

"Are you always this dense?" she asks, narrowing her eyes.

She clicks her tongue, then sits up, dismantling her pillow wall. They land on the floor with a dull thud. I rear back when one almost smacks me in the face. Before I can recover, she's wiggling into me, her ass pressed to my rapidly hardening cock. She grabs my arm, tucking it around her, and sighs.

"That's better," she murmurs, sleep lining her voice.

Her dark hair tickles my face and I burrow my nose into the strands, breathing her in. A shudder runs through me and I pull her closer. This is the longest I've gone without fucking and my fist isn't cutting it anymore. Especially with Aelia running around in my t-shirts, my scent clinging to her skin.

I've kept my hands to myself when we're alone, but being at various events for the Guild, I'm forced to keep her close. I'm not complaining, yet I'd rather have her like this. No one is playing a part, and the circumstances aren't forcing either of our hands.

I close my eyes, my fingers trailing against her stomach. Her muscles jump under my touch, and I pull my hand from under her shirt. No use torturing my cock, knowing this will only lead to sleep. When her legs tangle with mine, though, I doubt I'll fall into dreamland anytime soon. I swallow the groan crawling up my throat when she wiggles her hips.

"Stop moving," I growl as my cock twitches.

"I'm trying to get comfortable," she says, but her voice is breathless.

I slide my hand to her stomach again, this time leaving the shirt as a barrier between us. She freezes, and I wonder if I've pushed too far. I'm not doing anything, less than anything actually, but with her experience this might mean more. Hard to believe I've had my fingers deep in her cunt and I'm worried about my arm around her waist.

"Go to sleep, Aelia."

"Still can't fall asleep," she whispers not even thirty seconds later.

"Unless that's an invitation to help you relax, you'd better just close your eyes."

She hums and her hand covers mine, guiding it under her shirt again. Her soft skin is warm under my touch. Gently, I skim my fingers along her curves, hoping to lull her to sleep. Instead, she squirms against me. I try to pull my hips away so I'm not poking her with my cock through my boxer briefs.

"Consider this a formal invitation," she says, turning her head to meet my gaze.

Desire burns in her eyes, flames flickering deep within the darkness. Tipping my head back, I huff out a breath. This woman is going to be the death of me. And I'll welcome it with open arms. I kick the covers down, needing to watch the flush that's sure to wash across her skin.

Caressing her body, I memorize every dip and hollow. I catalog every gasp of breath, every twitch, filing it away for the next time. Hopefully, there will actually *be* a next time. Sliding my knee between her legs, I guide one over my hip. She moans, arching into me. The only sound she's made that's sweeter is when she comes.

I nuzzle her neck, scraping my teeth along the sensitive skin as I glide my palm along her inner thigh. When I retreat without moving between her legs, she whimpers. I cup her cunt, which has already soaked her panties.

"Don't rush me, angel," I murmur when she pushes into my palm, then nibble on her earlobe.

I want to take my time, especially since I don't know when this will end. Pushing her won't get me anywhere. Besides, savoring her will give me plenty of memories for when I'm stroking my cock in the shower later.

"What do you want me to do?" she whispers, nerves making her voice shake.

"Whatever you want." I tug the hem of her shirt higher until her tits are on full display. "You're in control here, Aelia."

"Everything," she breathes as I circle my finger around her nipple.

"Be careful what you wish for. There are plenty of things I've fantasized about doing to you."

"Oh," she says softly, mouth forming a perfect circle I could slip my cock right into.

Using my knuckle, I bump her chin. "Don't do that or you'll end up with your mouth full."

"You think I'm going to drop to my knees and suck you off?"

I chuckle, turning her head toward me. Our lips brush as I say, "I think you'll beg to have my cock in your mouth. But not tonight."

She leans in, pressing her lips to mine, and her tongue sweeps in. Gripping her chin, I angle my head to deepen the kiss. She gasps as I slide my hand down, cupping her tit and playing with her nipple. I pull back, gazing at her swollen lips as her eyes flutter open.

"Fucking intoxicating," I murmur, kissing her again softly.

She huffs as if she doesn't believe me, then reaches down. I'm about to pull away when she grabs her panties and slides them down her legs, kicking them off. Sitting up, she whips the shirt over her head, tossing it onto the floor with the pillows. I barely have time to look at her before she's pushing me onto my back and straddling me.

My hands go to her hips as I gaze up at her, raising an eyebrow. She rocks back and forth and I grit my teeth. Holding her still, I close my eyes and she whines.

"Angel, I'm going to need you to give me a minute."

"You're not even looking at me," she says, trying to move despite my hands holding her still.

"Don't need to. Your soft skin, your enchanting scent, your soaked cunt. I don't need my eyes for that."

"So you're just going to sit there with your eyes closed while I drip all over you?"

I burst out laughing, running my hands up her sides, and she shivers. Watching her through my lashes, my chest pulses as she grins. She wiggles back and forth, making my cock ache and I grind into her. Her head tips back, the column of her throat bobbing as she swallows.

I cup her tits, playing with her nipples, and she gasps, rocking faster against me. Her hands wrap around my wrists and I expect her to stop me, but instead she keeps them right where they are.

Her dark eyes meet mine, desire swimming in them. She bites her lip, drawing my gaze down, and my breath catches in my throat. She's a vision, an enchantress I never saw coming, completely enthralling me in the process. And she doesn't even know how captivating she is.

Her hands drop to my chest, nails digging into my skin. I slide my fingers to her neck, slipping them into her dark tresses and pulling her toward me. She comes willingly, our mouths colliding in a frenzy.

"Dante," she moans into my mouth. "Please."

She pulls her lips from mine, panting.

"Please what?" I run my hands down her body, settling them on her hips.

My thumbs brush against the juncture of her thighs, watching as she shivers and her eyes fall closed.

"Fuck me?" She says it as if she's requesting a side of ranch at a restaurant.

I chuckle, swiping my thumb across her clit. "Is that a question?"

She sits up, hands still planted on my chest. Her finger traces my tattoo as she tilts her head. The rearing head of a viper sits right over the grim reaper, a symbol of an important part of my life permanently inked on my body. The reaper is faded, the lines blurred, but it's no less significant to me now than it was when I got it at fifteen.

"Are you really going to make me beg you?" she hisses as I brush my thumb over her clit again.

"As much as I'd love that, no. But you need to be sure you're ready for this, Aelia," I say, pulling my hands away from her.

She huffs, dropping her head. I tip her chin up with my knuckle, raising an eyebrow.

"I want to. It's burning a hole through me how much I want this. And I hate you for making me say it out loud."

I smile, sitting up and holding her close to me. I nuzzle her neck, pressing kisses against her skin as she shivers. Her arms loop around me and she tips her head to the side as I scrape my teeth along her jaw.

"It's sexy when you ask for what you want, angel," I murmur in her ear.

"I want you to fuck me. And I want you to make it good. Make me feel good," she says breathlessly.

"No," I say, kissing her cheek, and she rears back. "Good isn't good enough. When I'm done with you, you'll never crave anyone else. You'll remember this moment for the rest of your life."

She sucks in a deep breath, eyes meeting mine. "Yes. I want that."

I capture her face in my hands, giving her a serious look. "Tell me if you want to stop. No matter what's happening or when. Got it?"

Understanding flashes in her eyes, and she nods. I lie back, taking her with me and she fits her face into my neck.

"I don't know how to start," she mutters.

"You could start by not being the only one naked."

She shoots up, wiggling down my body, and I groan as she drags herself along my length. Fitting her fingers in the waistband of my underwear, she yanks them down. I grip her wrist before she bends me the wrong way.

"Easy, angel."

Her eyes widen before she tugs them up and over my throbbing cock, and I lift my hips. She tosses them aside, then crawls back on top of me. She gives me an expectant look and I realize I'm going to have to walk her through most of this. Gripping her hips, I rub her along my length, and she coats me.

"More," she pants, eyes falling closed.

"Open your eyes, Aelia." When they're fixed on me again, I glance down to where we're almost joined. "I'm ready when you are."

She bites her lip, following my gaze. I don't know if I'm doing this right, if I'm rushing her or not. Her taking the lead will be the only way, but she's so hesitant I wonder if I should just get her off.

"Don't do that," she whispers, and my eyes fly to hers. "Don't have second thoughts just because I'm not experienced."

I lift her hips until she's on her knees, then slip my fingers between her legs. I stroke her, my cock aching with the need to be inside her when I feel how wet she is. She's already soaked my hand. Pushing a finger inside her core, I press her clit with my thumb, and she clenches around me.

I ease in and out of her, watching as lust chases its way across her face. She moans when I add another finger, stretching her. I don't want to hurt her, though she'll probably take some time to get used to my size. Her tongue darts out and she licks her bottom lip. Panting, she moves with me as I slowly build her up.

"Touch yourself, angel. Come all over my hand," I growl, increasing my pace.

Her eyes fall closed as her hand falls to her clit. She circles it, her tits bouncing with her. Just as her cunt spasms around my fingers, I sit up, capturing a pink nipple in my mouth and suck hard. She cries out, shuddering out her release. Warmth floods my hand and I groan, falling back again.

I pull my fingers from her, gripping the base of my cock. Watching her come is officially my favorite pastime. I flex my hand, hoping to relieve some of the ache, but it's no use. I breathe heavily through my nose, closing my eyes as she scrapes her nails down my chest. I grunt when her cunt envelops the tip, still pulsing from her orgasm.

"Aelia," I say in a strangled voice as she sinks down until she reaches my hand.

"More," she gasps.

I grit my teeth, wanting to savor this moment forever. Moving my fingers, she impales herself on my cock and whimpers. We both freeze as she adjusts to me.

"O-ooh," she stutters, eyes fixed where we're joined.

Sliding my hands along her flushed skin, I brush my knuckles over her nipple.

"You okay?"

She nods, then rolls her hips, and I moan. She does it again, and it takes everything in me to not flip her over and pound into her. She's playing a dangerous game and she doesn't even know it. If she keeps going, I'm going to come long before she does again. Then she rises to her knees and slowly lowers herself. Her eyes flick from my face to my cock as it disappears.

"Is this...I don't..." Her eyes roll back in her head when she rocks forward, her clit dragging against my stomach.

"Do what feels good."

Her brows pull low as she tries to find a rhythm. After a minute she huffs, flopping her body onto mine. I hug her close, kissing her head.

"Do you need some help?"

"This is embarrassing," she says, voice muffled.

I smile, rolling us so she's under me. My cock twitches deep within her and she whimpers.

"Wrap your legs around my waist," I say, then nip at her skin.

She throws them around me, locking her ankles on my lower back. I pull out slowly, then sink into her. Every time I bottom out, a sound emerges from the back of her throat.

"Faster," she demands.

I bury my cock into her, faster and harder than before. Every time I do, I grit my teeth, holding my orgasm at bay. All I want to do is empty into her, but I need this to be amazing, unforgettable. She already thinks she's broken. I'm determined to prove her wrong.

I push to my knees, and her feet drop on either side of me. Seizing her waist, I'm hypnotized by the sight of her writhing beneath me while I fuck her. She's beautiful with her flushed skin, her cunt squeezing around me with each thrust. I circle her clit with my fingers, and she gasps my name.

"Come for me, angel. Show me how much you love my cock," I growl and angle my hips until I hit just the right spot.

A desperate noise leaves her as she flies into oblivion, her soaked cunt spasming around me. I groan her name as I follow her, my cock pulsing in time with my heartbeat. Tipping my head back, I shudder as my pace slows, wringing every ounce of pleasure I can from her.

Pulling her up, she's limp, sweat dotting her forehead and her head lolls against my shoulder. We're still connected and I'm loath to leave her heat. She feels like home, and I can't help but cling to her.

"How was that?" I ask, slipping from her, and she whines. Chuckling, I lie on my side, pulling her down with me. We face each other, her eyes heavy as she smiles.

"That was not good."

I lost myself at the end, probably going too hard for her. My heart clenches, wondering if I hurt her. I've never been with someone who wasn't experienced. I open my mouth to apologize when she pushes my chin with her finger.

"It was perfect. I can honestly say that I will never forget that."

I huff out a breath, scowling at her. "That wasn't very nice, angel. I thought I'd hurt you."

She smiles lazily, then presses her lips to mine. Pulling back, she tangles our legs together.

"You wouldn't hurt me. I trust you."

As her eyes fall closed, a pulse echoes through my chest, wrapping around my heart and squeezing. I'm completely fucked when it comes to this woman. And I don't care one bit. She's mine, and I'll do whatever it takes to keep her by my side.

Twenty-Four

Aelia

Weeks. It's been fucking weeks and we still aren't anywhere closer to dealing with everything. People are still languishing in the Pit. Others are going missing. And Dante keeps dragging me to various events, telling me to wait. The only thing I've done so far is make the transfers. I conceded to Dante by lowering the deposits, but I've been slowly increasing them.

Jenkins hasn't noticed, though it may be because of all the other shit going on. He still hasn't said anything about another Auction. The extra council meetings are a dead giveaway, yet I'm not about to say anything. I may have discovered a newfound power within the Pit, but that doesn't extend beyond those concrete walls. At least he's left me alone since he's so busy.

I glare at the bathroom door as if I can burn a hole through it straight into Dante. I sigh, bracing my hands on the counter. It's not his fault. None of this is. He's not responsible for Grant cornering me every chance he gets, whispering threats in my ear. He's not to blame for me refusing to leave the Guild, even though he's told me several times he'll get me out. He's not at fault for the fact that I haven't had sex in weeks either.

I've been making excuses why I haven't jumped his bones since the last time—too much shit going on, he'll start demanding it, he wouldn't want a repeat. They're all bullshit. I'm not ready to admit that it's because

I'm too terrified of my own feelings. I don't know if I'll ever be able to give myself completely over to someone else. At least not in this place.

"Are we in a bad mood again?" Dante's voice jolts me from my thoughts.

I was so lost in my own head I didn't hear the door opening. I turn away from him as my cheeks blaze. He'll probably be able to read my mind in the curve of my cheekbone or something like that. Then again, not saying anything is eating me up inside.

"Did something happen? Was it Grant? I'm going to fucking kill him," he says, coming up behind me.

"I'm fine." I'm not. "It's not a big deal." I think it is.

"It is, so just tell me," he grumbles, which only pisses me off.

I swing around, bracing a trembling hand on the counter. Apparently, I'm not the only one in a bad mood. He's glaring at his feet, arms crossed over his chest.

"Fine. Let's get into this then."

His head pops up and he scowls, gesturing for me to continue. The words stick in my throat, threatening to choke me. I hate feeling like I don't know where I stand. The ground constantly moves underneath me and before I know it, I'll crash and burn.

"Well?" he snaps, then shakes his head. "Sorry. I just want to know what's going on. You've been avoiding me all week. I don't like it."

A week ago, Grant hauled me into my closet, pushing me onto the blankets still balled up in the corner. I thought he was going to force himself on me, but he ended up just screaming in my face. He left bruises on my arms, and while I tried to hide them from Dante, none of my clothes have long sleeves. Dante didn't even ask me about them, though.

"I'm taking all the risks." The words tumble from me without a thought. It wasn't what I was planning on saying.

"I'm not diminishing your role in this, Aelia, but you're not the only one taking risks."

"And yet I don't see any of it. You gallivant around, flaunting your money and *me*. There aren't any hazards for you. The worst that will happen is you'll flee in the middle of the night. And I'll be left here. Alone," I snarl. He opens his mouth, but I glare at him until he snaps it shut. "I'm putting my life on the line. Which honestly isn't that big of a deal. If they kill me, so be it. I don't exactly have anyone waiting for me to magically appear."

His nostrils flare, jaw ticking. "You think I would leave you here? You think I wouldn't care if you died?"

"I'm saying it doesn't matter either way," I cry, waving my hands. "That's not the worst that can happen to me. And the fact that you don't even realize that, after everything you've seen...it's fucking ridiculous, Dante."

Blood drains from his face and the scowl drops away. "I won't let that happen."

"It's already happened," I mutter, and his eyes widen. "No. I didn't mean it like that."

"Then what the hell did you mean? Is that the reason you shy away from me?" His voice softens, distress swimming in his dark eyes.

"Grant—"

He pivots, ripping open the bathroom door and stalking out. I rush after him, blocking his path as I push against his chest.

"Get out of the way, Aelia. I spared him once because you asked me to. I won't do it again."

"He didn't...he's just talking shit. I can handle it, but it's exhausting. That's all," I rush out.

"Why are you protecting him?" he growls, wrapping his arms around my upper arms.

I brace myself for him to shake me, yell at me, throw me to the ground like so many others would. Of course, he doesn't do any of that. He pulls me into his arms, pressing my face to his chest. Tension rolls off him, yet his touch is gentle. I swallow hard, rubbing my forehead on his shirt to erase the fears I harbor deep within.

"You don't understand how important he is to Jenkins. He's been a part of the Guild since Jenkins took over. The only reason he became my handler is because he asked for it. He wanted someone to torment forever, I suppose. You threaten to kill him, and you'll find out he's more important to Jenkins than you are."

His hand runs through my hair, sending a shiver down my spine. There are so many other things we need to discuss. I can't keep hiding from him. I told him he needed to trust me even though it went against everything I've learned in life.

"There's more," I whisper, my voice muffled by his body.

"I'm still going to kill him. Or maybe I'll teach you how to do it and stand back while you beat him with his own spine," he chuckles.

I huff, shivering at the image that pops in my head. "They set the date for the Auction."

He tenses, hand freezing, then resumes its path along my strands. "When? Soon?"

"One month. They're shooting for Halloween. They put my father in charge of it."

He sighs, hugging me close. "We don't have enough time to stop it. Not unless something drastic happens."

"Father went off the rails, asking where Judge Merrick went."

"Don't call him a judge. He's more of an executioner," he spits out. He nuzzles my neck, then presses a kiss to my temple.

"Whatever you call him, apparently he wanted Merrick to help him set things up. Jenkins told him to fuck off when Father wanted to do the Auction in Synd. He's still obsessed with bringing them down."

"Merrick disappeared two weeks ago."

I rear back, and he drops his arms from me. "Where'd he go?"

He shakes his head, grabbing my wrist and tugging me to the bed. He settles against the headboard, then pats the space next to him. I hesitate, not because I'm upset with him anymore, but if I sit down, I might fall asleep.

His eyes fall closed and he tips his head back. "Unless you'd rather sit on my face. Both would be perfectly acceptable to me."

Rolling my eyes, I crawl next to him and he pulls me close. "We both know men don't like doing that shit. They do it for brownie points. Seeing as how we're in the weirdest fucking relationship ever, I don't think that'll be necessary."

His fingers seize my chin, forcing me to meet his gaze. "First of all, relationship? Second, I can wholeheartedly say that I would die a happy man if you suffocated me with your pretty little thighs while you came all over my face."

I squeeze my knees together as heat builds between my legs. "We'll just pretend you didn't say any of that."

He murmurs in my ear, "Because your wet cunt is begging for my cock?"

I shudder, digging my nails into my thigh. "Where'd Merrick go?"

He sighs, pulling back. "I believe he went to Synd, but I'm not entirely sure."

"What the hell is it with Synd? Seriously, I don't remember much from when I lived there, but it's not some gem."

"I grew up in Synd. I regret leaving every day," he murmurs.

Commenting on the little tidbits he's been dropping seems like a gamble. I'm afraid he'll stop if I ask any questions. I crave anything from the outside world, though I often don't fully understand what he's talking about.

"What's the next step?"

"Convincing you to sit on my face."

Shaking my head, I lean against him, his warmth seeping into me. "Tell me how you really feel."

"I'm starving for you, angel. But I'll shut my mouth," he says, pulling his arm from behind my back.

"What? Why?"

He pushes from the bed, then stares down at me. "I tried to give you space. Then I kept it subtle. Now I'm telling you point blank and you're brushing me off. Contrary to your belief, I can take a hint, Aelia."

Studying his face, I bite my lip. I didn't realize he would think it was him and not me. We stare at each other, both waiting for someone to break the silence pressing down on us. He nods once sharply, tucking his hands in his pockets and turning away.

"I'm scared," I whisper, panic flooding me. I roll to my knees, folding my hands together and squeezing.

He freezes, not bothering to face me. I wonder if he thinks he'll scare me off if he does. Honestly, he might.

I take a deep breath, forging onward. "You make me feel things I shouldn't."

"Shouldn't?"

"I just don't know how to do this."

He turns, watching me with a blank face. It doesn't help. How do I tell him that even though I'm well into my twenties, I don't know what it means to be in a relationship? How do I tell him I'm terrified all the time? How do I convince him I'm too broken?

So I don't.

I stare at my hands, waiting for him to walk away. Because that's what I would do in his position. I'd wash my hands of that hot mess. He's clearly more skilled, more worldly, more stable than I am.

"Rachel asked about you. Wanted to know where my bruises came from," I say.

"What did you tell her?" It's the curiosity in his voice that punches me in the chest.

"I told her you weren't like the others. She'd be able to take care of you." I gather the strength to meet his eyes, hopefully showing him I don't care, even if it'll break my heart. "You should do that instead."

He crosses his arms and widens his stance. "Instead of you."

It's a statement, but I nod anyway. "Then I can focus on the money trails. You'll be taken care of while I'm in the office."

I know he'll never let me move back to the closet. I've stopped throwing that option out there, mostly to avoid his scowls.

"What about everything I've said makes you think I would fuck another woman?"

"Because it's logical."

"Sex isn't logical, Aelia. Not to me. And I don't want anyone else. So, if that's what you're worried about, let me put your mind at ease." He leans down, bracing his hands on either side of me. "You're mine. I want you and I will continue to want you."

"But what if—"

"Only you," he says, then covers my mouth with his.

Twisting my hands into his shirt, I pull him closer. His tongue tangles with mine as if he's trying to devour me. I shudder when his fingers grip my waist, guiding me down until his body covers mine. With my knees tucked under me, I'm in an awkward position. I wiggle, trying to straighten them out without breaking our kiss.

He rips his mouth from mine, gazing down at my body. "What the hell are you doing?"

"My legs are stuck," I whimper as they start to tingle.

He lifts off me and I squirm, unfolding my legs. Blood rushes back, leaving pins and needles behind. He kneels between my legs, running his hands up my sides, taking my shirt with him. Leaning down, he kisses me gently.

"I'm going to strip you down and take my time devouring you," he murmurs against my lips. "I'm going to show you exactly how much I love the way you taste."

"Promise—" My gasp cuts off my words as he sucks on my nipple through my shirt.

He chuckles as he cups my breasts, kneading them as he wraps his lips around my other nipple. My back arches, fingers spearing into his hair. This is what I was missing—what I was afraid of missing. I thought if I pretended I wasn't horny, then it would just go away. I got too much into my head, and I fucking hated it.

"I promise you'll love it. And so will I."

His fingers slide under the hem of my shorts, pulling them and my panties off. I press my legs together, blushing. Before the lights were off, only the moonlight filtering through the window. Now the lamps around the room are a spotlight seemingly pointed straight at my vagina.

Dante drops to his knees next to the bed, then slips his warm hands between my legs and pries them open. I'm not trying to resist him, but nerves skitter up my body. Grinding on him in the dark is one thing. Having his face shoved between my legs is something completely else.

"Do you want to stop?" His breath coasts across the sensitive skin on my inner thigh.

"Uh, no?" I keep my gaze on the ceiling.

"That sounded like a question, angel. Look at me."

I glance down, preparing myself for the wave of embarrassment that's sure to come. His dark eyes bore into mine, demanding I spill my secrets. I can't pull my gaze from his as he kisses his way up my thigh, then nips at my flesh and I shiver.

"Do you want me to stop?" he repeats, raising an eyebrow.

"No," I gasp, my pussy clenching around nothing.

He grins, his nose nudging my clit as he switches to my other leg. He starts again, running his mouth from my knee to the juncture of my thighs. When his eyes flick to mine again, I bite my lip, legs already shaking. His hands grip my knees and he yanks me to the edge of the bed, my ass almost hanging off, and I yelp.

"Relax, angel," he whispers.

I take a deep breath, letting it out slowly, and my muscles unclench one by one. He guides both my legs over his shoulders and glances at my face one last time, smirking. He buries his nose in my pussy, licking me from core to clit.

"Holy shit."

He groans, then does it again, and my body jerks. I don't know if I'm trying to get away or force him closer. Either way, I've never felt like this before. His arms trap my thighs, keeping me still as he devours me. His tongue circles my core, then spears into me, and I cry out again.

I squirm, heat building in my gut as he swirls around my clit. He hums as he laps up the wetness. I moan and my fingers grip his hair. Something comes over me and I grind my pussy into his face. I'm pretty sure he's chuckling, but his tongue never slows. Then his finger thrusts into my core, stroking several times before he adds another one.

Rocking against him, my eyes fall closed as my orgasm builds. He mumbles something, but I can't hear him over the roaring in my ears. When he sucks my clit in his mouth, I fall over the edge, shuddering out my release. He licks me as I come down, fingers still curling inside of me.

I huff, my hands falling from his hair as I stare aimlessly at the ceiling. He licks me one more time and my pussy spasms before he pulls his hand away. His arms fold over my stomach and he rests his chin on them. I can feel his eyes on me, but I'm still floating above my body, a weightlessness infiltrating my bones.

"Well?" he asks, laughter tinging his tone.

"Well indeed."

His chuckle rings through me, filling some void I didn't even know existed inside me. I can only hope it stays that way.

Twenty-Five

Dante

"What the hell you mean, he's missing?" Jenkins bellows from behind his desk.

His office isn't large enough for the dozen council members, plus me and Aelia, who's stuffed in the corner. She vacated her chair ten minutes ago when a fistfight erupted between two men. Being stuck across the room, standing behind Jenkins like a personal bodyguard, I couldn't get to her. Thankfully, she slipped away seconds before it started.

"I'm sorry, sir, but he left in the middle of the night without a word to anyone," a nervous-looking man says. I'm pretty sure his name is Timothy, but I haven't been cataloging their names.

"Then how do you know he's missing?" Jenkins growls, an edge of violence lacing his tone.

Timothy's watery blue eyes dart to me, then back to Jenkins. The leader spins around, nostrils flaring as a vein pulses in his forehead. I wait, though I shouldn't antagonize him. I'll make him ask the question. He'll either take it as insubordination or respect. Either way, I don't care.

"Cruz, what do you know?"

"Anders Drake left the premises at roughly midnight. He didn't take any transportation until he was several blocks away from headquarters. I followed him to the train station, where he bought a ticket to Synd. It was one-way."

His eyes narrow as if he expected me to stop the older man. Even if I could have, I wouldn't have bothered. The best thing for Aelia will be if he dies while in Synd. I doubt he will, though. He'll probably come crawling back to the Guild like the cockroach he is.

"Everyone out," Jenkins bellows, waving them away.

As the men file out, I wonder if any of them will be tapped to take care of the Auction. From what Aelia has told me, usually it's one of the council members who organizes it, though Jenkins is heavily involved. He doesn't seem to be in the right state of mind to pull off this event without losing it completely.

Jenkins glares at me when I round his desk, intent on following the others. He points to the chair in front of him, and I sink into it. I wasn't expecting this.

"Where's Merrick?" Jenkins asks when the door clicks shut behind the men.

"He's disappeared. No one has seen him. His office put out a press release—"

He waves away my explanation, grimacing. "I saw that bullshit they're pushing. I want to know where he is and what he said before he left."

I cross my legs, buying time. Giving Jenkins information is a delicate dance. Too little and he'll dismiss me. Too much and he'll use it against innocent people, and I'll only have myself to blame.

Aelia's chair squeaks, drawing his attention, and his eyes narrow on her.

"He said he would be using his stepdaughter for his entry fee into the Guild. He seemed hesitant, combative about it," I say, attempting to draw his eyes back to me. Thankfully, it works.

"Why is that?"

"Not sure. He was meeting with the son of another high-level official within Rima. Perhaps he had a deal with him regarding her. Either way, all three of them seem to have fled the city."

"Media said they're looking for her," he grumbles.

"Grasping at straws to link her to Merrick's disappearance. I believe he's dead, though I have no proof."

"The Auction needs to move forward," Jenkins grumbles, shuffling through his papers.

"Who do you think is capable of taking over?" I ask, holding my breath.

This was the first time I've seen most of the members in one place before. Trying to find more information on them was a bust. I'm still not convinced I've met them all. Asking Jenkins which of those men he plans on assigning Anders's role is a risk. Even after all these weeks weaseling my way into his good graces, my position isn't secure. Not that I want it to be, but it would make this whole thing easier.

"None of them. They're all idiots, incapable of doing anything for the Guild. I'd kill them all and start over, but—" He cuts himself off abruptly, shaking his head. "We may need to postpone."

I nod, nerves building in my stomach. "It certainly is a massive undertaking. And to have one so close to the usual one at New Year's…"

"What do you know about the Auction?" Jenkins asks cautiously.

"The others talk. Tragic I missed this past year's," I murmur.

"Not happy with your choice?"

"Hardly. Though the thought of training another one has crossed my mind." My skin crawls as the words come out.

He smirks, eyes darting to Aelia, then back to me. Leaning back in his chair, he tracks her movements, the clicking of her keys stuttering into the sudden silence.

"You. Come here," he barks at Aelia.

Her soft footfalls against the ornate rug are the only indication that she's behind me.

"You look more or less intact," Jenkins says, eyes tracking down her body.

I force my muscles to relax. If Jenkins tries to take her, there's little I can do unless I want to jeopardize my identity.

"I prefer to keep them submissive as long as possible, Jenkins. Breaking them in is tedious and exhausting for me," I say, cutting off whatever he was about to say next.

I finally glance at her, running my finger along the strip of skin exposed at her waist. Compared to her other outfits, this one is downright modest. If she bent over, most of her ass would be on display.

"You're a strange man, Cruz."

I nod, then press my hand to the back of her knee. Aelia sinks down, dropping her head and folding her hands in her lap.

"This would be impressive had I not laid the groundwork for you years ago," Jenkins sneers. Aelia's breath hitches, but I don't think Jenkins notices.

"A feat, I'm sure."

"Go back to your desk." Jenkins's hungry eyes follow her, and I curl my fingers into fists.

"While I don't want to question your decisions..." I start, and his sharp gaze whips to mine.

"Tread carefully, Cruz. You haven't been in the Guild long enough to cross the line you're dancing around."

"Which is exactly my point, Jenkins. Anders has been here for years. Some of your council members as well, and yet you chose me to confide in." I raise my eyebrow, daring him to lie.

"You've met Anders. That man has vengeance at the forefront of his mind. I saw in you the same thing that I was twenty years ago. You can't buy that, son."

I nod, even as confusion runs through me. He waves me away and I push from the chair. It takes everything in me to keep my emotions from my face. Snapping my fingers, I don't slow, and Aelia rushes to my side.

"Cruz," Jenkins calls, and I pivot to face him. "Don't fuck me over. You won't like the consequences."

"Don't threaten me, Jenkins. You'll be sorely disappointed at how I react."

"As long as we understand each other."

"I believe we do."

Aelia shuffles after me, closing the door softly behind us. Her chin is practically resting on her chest, and I grab her wrist. I'd rather she not run into something because she's not watching where she's going. Her arm brushes mine as she hovers close to my back.

"Do you think he'll die?" she whispers.

I glance around at the empty hallway we're walking down before answering.

"I wouldn't be surprised if Merrick is already dead. Your father? Not likely. I imagine he'll pop back up in a few weeks," I mutter.

A guard turns the corner ahead, nodding to me and sneering at Aelia. I don't understand why they're so openly hostile toward her. Most of the members ignore her presence because she's claimed. The guards are a whole other story.

I push her through the door, tipping my chin at Jag as we pass. He's been disappearing at random intervals, refusing to tell me where he went. He blushed when Aelia asked, then took off again. Whatever he's getting himself into, he's not fucking us over. I wouldn't be surprised if he found a woman, much the way I did.

"Do you think I could ever kill someone?" Aelia murmurs, sinking onto the edge of the bed.

I sigh, sliding out of my suit. "I know you want me to say yes, but honestly, it's not as easy as you'd think."

"How many people have you...sorry. That's probably not a good question, is it?"

I chuckle, sitting next to her. "I didn't keep count. Not that it's so many I can't, but I grew up hard, Aelia. Dying is a way of life."

She shakes her head, leaning away from me. "You're in the mafia, aren't you?"

"Would it bother you if I was?" A lead weight drops in my stomach at the look on her face.

"I don't know. Roman, my brother, always told me I wasn't built for that life—the one of a mafia wife." She turns to me in horror. "Not that I'm saying I'd be...I just meant when I was younger. Dammit."

She stares off, not focusing on anything as I try to keep my laughter in. I grab her hand, intertwining our fingers, and she jolts. I should put her out of her misery, but it's hilarious.

"You're laughing at me. I wasn't proposing to you," she grumbles, tugging to get away from me, but I hold on to her.

"I'm not in the mafia. But even if I was, I'm sure you'd make a perfectly fine mafia wife," I say, grinning.

She rolls her eyes. "He wasn't saying I wouldn't make a good wife. Just that I was meant for other things. I don't think this is what he had in mind, though."

She scans the room, sadness creeping into her brown eyes. I can't imagine what it's like to lose a sibling. If MacKenzie died...my stomach rolls just thinking about it. The fact I don't even know where she is right now, if she's okay, eats me up inside. She's strong enough to take care of herself, but she won't go to Maddox for help if she needs it. Honestly, I don't know who she'd run to. The thought sends a pulse through my chest.

She clears her throat. "Didn't mean to bring down the mood."

"I'm in an MC," I blurt out.

I really hope she knows what an MC is, because saying motorcycle club doesn't encompass what the Vipers are.

I didn't plan on telling her until we were on the outside. If shit goes sideways, I don't want the information to be tortured out of her. They probably wouldn't believe her if she said she didn't know anything. It's a catch-22 I never fully understood how to navigate. Thankfully, since my father died, we haven't had to deal with anything extreme enough to hurt someone. A few nights locked away in the dark are enough for most people to break.

She turns, gazing at me as she studies my face. Her lips purse, drawing my eyes to them. When her tongue darts out, my cock swells. I subtly try to adjust myself, but she glances down, a small smile playing on her face.

"Does thinking about being in an MC make you horny?" She giggles, the sound dancing around the room.

I smirk, squeezing her hand. "*You* make me hard, Aelia. Honestly, it's becoming a problem."

Her eyebrows crawl up her forehead. "A problem? I'd better start wearing baggy sweatshirts and stop showering then, huh?"

Dropping her hand, I cup her cheeks, brushing my nose along hers. "You could wear a potato sack and I'd still be hard around you."

"Cliché," she mutters, eyes falling closed.

I chuckle, pressing a kiss to her lips. "It's not what you wear. It's how you move, how you smell, everything about you."

She pulls away, sighing. "I hate to tell you this, but I don't think it's any of those things."

Sliding from the bed, she walks to the window, peeking out the curtains as if someone might be listening in.

"What exactly do you think it is, then?"

She turns to me, leaning against the window. "You're stuck in here with me. You've got this idea in your head that I need to be saved even though I never asked for that. I'm not saying I'd be able to get out of here by myself. Clearly, if that were the case, I'd already be gone. But you thinking you're infatuated with me?"

"I'm not infatuated with you, Aelia," I growl, stalking toward her. She doesn't move. Her face doesn't change—just a resigned look in her eyes.

"Dante, this isn't some love story where you're the hero and we're going to live happily ever after. You don't deserve to have to deal with me after all this." She gestures to the room as if it embodies the whole Guild. "I'm grateful just to be here with you, in this moment. But I won't put you in a position to keep me around just because you feel like you should. Trauma bonding and all that."

She snorts, shaking her head, then gazes out the window again. I don't know where shit went wrong—what I said to make her think I chose her as if she was the first woman I came across. Thinking back to all our other conversations, it hits me.

"That's not what trauma bonding is. You think I picked you because you were in Jenkins's office the first time we met, don't you?"

"I think that was a large part of it, yes. I'm not mad. It was a smart choice, though other people might be able to do more for you. Or at the very least, they can help you when I can't. It's why I thought you should move on to someone else. Gathering more people to your side—"

"Stop," I grunt, holding my hand up.

I just need her to get out of her head. She's spent long enough watching, waiting, deciphering ulterior motives. It's time she realized that not everyone is like that. I don't know how I'll get her to realize I want her for who she is, not what she can do for me, but I'll figure it out.

"I'll say this as many times as it takes, Aelia. I don't want anyone else. And while you may not believe that now, eventually you'll see that this wasn't a coincidence or a clever ploy on my part. You're who I want and that's not going to change...whether we're stuck here or out there. You're it for me. Get used to it."

Twenty-Six

Aelia

"Can't we just shoot him and get it over with?" I whisper in Dante's ear.

His hand at my hip squeezes, though I don't know if that's to get me to shut up or because he agrees. Perching on his lap while he gambles isn't exactly the way I wanted to spend my night, and I was already exhausted when my father showed up.

"He's hurt," I breathe and Dante shudders.

I'm not trying to turn him on, but his cock hardens even more, poking my ass. His hand slides in my hair, forcing my head back. His teeth scrape up my throat, then he tilts my head away and I catch my father's eyes. I force my face into an emotionless mask. If he gets wind that I'm actually enjoying this, he'll do something to Dante. Jenkins won't interfere, not when I'm pretty sure Dante's money is keeping the Guild afloat at the moment, but my father is unpredictable. He always has been.

"Where?" he grunts softly.

He tucks my face back into his neck, skimming his fingers down my side. When he reaches my thigh, he digs his nails in, probably leaving marks on my skin. It's a common move he's used recently to readjust my skirt, covering my body from other's prying eyes. I wiggle back to help, draping my arm around his shoulder as I do.

"Shoulder, maybe. Right arm stiff."

Dante throws some chips into the pot, not bothering to respond. He doesn't need to. He'll observe Anders and we'll talk about it later. It's become routine at this point. I don't know what else Dante is waiting for, what he's searching for coming to all these events, but I stopped asking. Honestly, I don't think he knows himself.

"When you going to get rid of your bit and upgrade, Cruz?" Byron calls from the other side of the table.

Dante taps my wrist, and I slide from his lap. Peeking from under my lashes, I watch Byron's eyebrows climb up his forehead as I sink to my knees between Dante's legs.

"Why would I upgrade when she's obedient to a fault?" Dante says coldly.

He taps my shoulder, and I crawl back into his lap, tucking my head under his chin. I hated the lessons, as I called them, at first. Every time Dante would teach me another command—a pinch of his fingers, a tap of his hand, a nod of his head—his face would morph into one I didn't recognize.

When I finally mentioned it, he admitted to having to distance himself from everything, even me. After, he'd tuck me into the bed, holding me long past when he assumed I fell asleep. I don't mind doing this, but he doesn't believe me. I wish we were anywhere else, learning how to navigate the things we like together.

Out of everything I've endured, this feels like I'm in control. It's silly, since he's the one directing my movements, but not having to think, to worry, about anything because he'll take care of it is liberating. I'm used to constantly being on high alert, waiting for the next person to ambush me. I can't do anything about their treatment of me, but I sure as hell can anticipate it.

Byron's booming laugh washes over me, making me tense. I wouldn't put it past the man to try to steal me away, expecting me to go with him willingly. Men like him convince themselves that the women in this place secretly crave their touch. We're just playing hard to get. He's almost worse than the ones who take without thought. At least I can see them coming. I know what to expect, but with Byron it's all a game.

Byron moves closer when a woman curses violently as she loses and vacates the seat next to Dante. There aren't many women who are members in the Guild, but the ones who come to these events are callous and cold. Men have made the mistake of trying to take them and usually end up dead.

As the woman stomps away, she glances over her shoulder, glaring at me as if I'm the one who took all her money. She can't blame Dante, so she'll take it out on me.

"Cruz, when are you going to get me a higher status? I've been languishing, trying to get a seat on the council for six months now, and I can't even get a meeting with the man upstairs," Byron says, leaning close to us. His hot breath hits the back of my neck, and I sink my teeth into Dante's neck.

Dante shuffles me around until I'm straddling him, his free hand gripping my ass. At least I can rest my chin on his other shoulder instead of being subjected to Byron's nastiness.

"You know the price, Michaels."

"But I don't have anyone," he whines, throwing his hand down. He sounds like a toddler, stomping his foot because he can't have ice cream before dinner.

"I doubt Jenkins will allow you, then."

"Word on the street is you didn't need to turn someone over."

"I'm not at liberty to discuss my induction into the upper levels of the Guild." It's a line Dante has used before, but I doubt it'll work this time.

"I'm the one who brought you in, Cruz. You owe me," Byron spits out. "If you won't help me advance, then you'll pay your debt with her."

Byron's sweaty hand grips my arm, yanking me toward him. Dante's tightens his grip on me, his cards scattering across the floor. I cling to him, clamping my lips tight to keep my cry of pain from escaping. Dante's foot lashes out, kicking Byron in the kneecap, and the man releases his hold on me. Dante stands, tucking me behind him as he faces off against Byron.

Byron stumbles to his feet, grinning as he holds his hands out as if to fend off Dante.

"Settle down, Cruz. I'm just playing." He hobbles a step back. Obviously, Dante didn't kick him hard enough.

I press my forehead against Dante's back, not wanting to see what else is coming. He steps toward Byron, leaving me fumbling with whether to follow or let him deal with the asshole.

A yelp leaves me when someone grabs my hair, dragging me back, then throwing me to the sticky floor. My father's face glares down at me, his lip curling. I try to scramble away from him, but his shoe lands on my stomach. He lifts his foot, then slams it into me. I cry out, curling in on myself.

He kicks my shoulder, rolling me to my back again, then kneels on my chest, forcing the air from my lungs. I cough, fingers curling into fists as I fight for my next breath. His sharp blue eyes, the exact shade of Roman's, spew hatred, dripping onto me like acid burning its way through my body. Each drop is another memory of his abuse—the things Roman could never shield me from.

In all the years we've been here, he's never addressed me, never talked to me, never done anything to save me from the fate he shoved me into. Why he's attacking me now, especially when Dante is here, doesn't make sense. Unless that's exactly what he's going for.

"You're going to pay for his sins," he hisses, spittle hitting my face, and I cringe away from the vitriol.

Squeezing my eyes shut as the edges of my vision darken, my hands flutter at my sides as I fight for consciousness. Suddenly, the weight is gone, a roar ringing in my ears. I'm not sure if it's my heart fighting for the right to live or someone fighting for me. Dante's face floats behind my lids and my mind resets.

My eyes fly open as I gasp for breath. Byron's wide gaze is the first thing I notice, but he's not watching me. Everyone seems to have forgotten I'm here. I crane my neck to take in the rest of the room. Half the tables are still playing, music still pounding, women still dancing on the stage.

Dante's fist plows into Anders's shoulder, the one I suspected he hurt. My father crumples to the ground, his limbs twisting in ways that aren't natural. I blink, rolling my head around, and my vision blurs.

Dante leans down, grabbing my limp body, and slings me over his shoulder. My stomach rolls and I shudder. If I puke on him, he'll be forced to toss me aside. The public display would be too much to explain away.

"Don't pass out on me," he says when we reach the hallway.

I moan as I bounce on his shoulder. It doesn't help and neither does the fact that blood rushes to my head the longer I'm hanging here. I don't know what damage Anders did to me, but I doubt I'll be able to follow Dante's command to stay awake. He moves faster, then swings me into his arms as the hall lights vanish.

Darkness descends upon us, and I worry that I've done exactly what he told me not to. His heavy breathing says otherwise and I curl into his warm body, soaking up the safety. My head pulses, pain radiating down my neck. I don't remember anything other than my father kicking me, but maybe I hit my temple.

"What happened?" Jag's voice floats through my head. Then a door slams shut and Dante's warmth is gone.

The soft mattress envelops me, and I roll to my side, groaning. My stomach clenches and I swallow reflexively. Gentle hands grab my shoulder and turn me to my other side.

"Garbage can right next to ya," Jag says in his deep voice.

"Dante," I gasp as light pierces my vision, and I slam my eyes closed.

"He's getting shit from the bathroom. Your temple is bleeding."

"Run," I breathe. "Make him run."

His radiating presence disappears, and I can only hope he's warning Dante. Going up against my father, especially over me, will only put him in danger. Dante needs to leave, to disappear as quickly as he appeared in my life. There's no way he'll make it out with me.

The alley was our escape plan, but one of the guards mentioned how they put a bouncer on the doors along with cameras. Every other exit is blocked, mostly to keep us in, but also so the members can't steal us away from the Guild. We're their property and they protect their assets.

"Aelia, stay awake. I'm going to clean your cut," Dante says next to my ear.

"Go," I moan.

"I'm not leaving. They won't touch me. Anders is on thin ice with Jenkins as it is. I'm more important to him right now."

"Jenkins wants Synd." I swallow hard. "He'll start the Auction again. They'll kill you."

"I'm not running, Aelia. This might sting."

I barely feel the pain as he swipes a bandage across a wound I didn't even know I had. When did it happen? Did I pass out? Why isn't he running? Each question stabs at my temple, demanding an answer I don't have.

Pounding on the door has Dante's hand jerking away. I groan when Jag picks me up. He smells like gunpowder, and I wonder what the hell he was doing while I was getting the shit beat out of me.

"Sorry, but you're not going to like this," Jag says. "Gotta make it look real."

He lowers me onto the tiles in the shower, then turns on the water. The cold spray blasts me and I whimper. I was cold before, but this has my body convulsing. I tuck myself into the corner of the space. Pressing my cheek against the glass, tears stream down my face. Not that I notice as it mixes with the water.

"I'm dealing with her," Dante growls. "Get the fuck out of my face, Grant, or I'll rip off your dick and shove it up your ass."

The door slams and I jolt. The water warms slowly as Jag turns the knob and I shiver my way through it all. At one point I dry heave, but nothing comes up.

Another knock has the burly man sighing and flipping the handle again. Gradually, the spray chills. If my father didn't do irreparable damage to my body, this certainly will. I turn my head to listen to Dante's voice, but get a face full of water instead.

Sputtering and coughing, I tuck my face into my arms, making myself as small as possible.

"Why the fuck do you think I did it? That asshole fucked off to Synd leaving me to pick up his goddamn mess. And then he had the audacity to touch what was mine. I don't fucking care if he's her father or not. He sold her and therefore has no rights to her," Dante bellows.

"Who?" I stutter, my chin trembling uncontrollably.

"Big boss," Jag mutters. "Pretend you're afraid."

"No pretending," I whisper, but he doesn't hear me. His eyes are firmly fixed on the open door.

I can't see or hear Jenkins, but that's probably for the best. I don't know if I'd be able to school my face. The dizziness has passed, and my stomach has settled at least. Exhaustion weighs on me and my eyes feel heavy. It's more than my lids drooping. It feels like rocks are sitting in my sockets, burrowing into my skull.

"See that you do," Dante sneers and Jenkins rumbles out a response I can't hear.

The door slams shut again, and Jag adjusts the water once more. Apathy spreads through my body, invading my pores and dousing my spirit. This isn't worth it. I could handle it if it was just me. I'm used to the abuse.

Dante putting himself in the line of fire for me, though...it's too much. It's too risky. Believing in his plan before was hard, but the further we come, the more I think he really might accomplish taking down the Guild. I won't be the reason he fails.

"I seen that look before. Don't do it," Jag says gruffly, and I turn to him.

He pushes the shower head down until the water rushes over my body. At least I'm not being waterboarded anymore.

"I'm serious, Aelia." He stares down at me, and I have to crane my neck to see him.

"You should have told him to run," I croak, burying my head in my arms when a coughing fit takes over.

"No point. He wouldn't have and you know it. That man is—"

"Jag," Dante says, a warning in his tone.

I roll my head toward him, taking in the blood dripping from a cut below his eye. With his knuckles stained red and a menacing look on his face, he's every inch the deadly man he warned me about. The one who doesn't keep track of how many people he's killed.

His face falls as he scans my body, mouth parting as he takes in whatever injuries I have. My head aches and I'm pretty sure my ribs will be covered in bruises. Every time I breathe, my right side pulls, as if my skin is too tight for my bones. That's not normal. I've broken ribs before, but never this badly. When I first got here, maybe, but that was a long time ago.

"We need to get her into warm clothes," Dante says, his face closing off again.

I swallow hard, glancing at Jag as Dante stomps from the room. Ignoring the hand Jag holds out to me, I push to my feet, biting my cheek to keep in my yelp of pain. I shuffle half bent from the room, shivering all the while. Jag drapes a towel over my shoulders but doesn't touch me. How he knows that I'll break into a million pieces if he does, I don't know.

"Lie down. No use piling on more," he mumbles, hands hovering over me as if he'll catch me if I fall.

I turn toward the closet. Having the bed be soaking wet because of me isn't going to help anything. Between the adrenaline wearing off and the cold water, I can't stop shaking. I don't know whether they'll go away if I get dry clothes on, but I won't be sleeping naked, especially if Jag doesn't get out of the room.

"I can get them for you. Just go lie down."

"Leave me alone," I mumble.

With Dante walking away, vacillating between being sweet and acting like I've fucked up everything, I can't take it. I'm done. Everything I've accomplish thus far has been washed away with the water, the will pounded out of me with each lash of my father's foot. I'm too exhausted to fight anymore, and I realize why I didn't do this before.

Dante asked why I didn't help the others, and this is why. Because no matter what I do, it'll never be enough. My father was just the latest sign why it'll never work. Why I'll never be enough to save them.

I'm too weak to fight.

TWENTY-SEVEN

Dante

I shouldn't have walked away, but every time I spotted a new bruise marring her skin, I was reminded of before. Grant coming to the door, offering to take her to perform some form of justice only he could deliver, didn't help. Then Jenkins showed up when all I wanted to do was take care of her. It was just too much.

No matter how much information I gather, how high I climb in the ranks, it's never enough. For months now I've been playing the system, searching for a way to bring them down, and I feel like I'm no closer to my goal than I was when I first got here. This shit is too difficult, and I'm not even the one suffering. All my choices leave Aelia the one with bruises, with scars on her soul that will never fade.

I slam my fist into the wall, accomplishing nothing other than damaging my knuckles more. They'll turn black and blue for sure now. When I knocked Anders clean off his feet, I probably would have gotten away with mere redness. Maybe it'll lend credence to disciplining Aelia. Jenkins's only concern was whether she'd be able to work tomorrow. Apparently, with Anders back, Jenkins plans on going forward with the Auction, though he'll be pushing it back.

"Great to see you're still an asshole," Jag grumbles as he grabs a blanket off the bed.

"I'm not in the mood, Jag." I sigh, resting my forehead on the window. The cold seeps into me, chilling my flushed skin. It'll snow soon probably.

"Oh yeah? I'm sure all this shit is really fucking hard on you," he snarls.

I swing toward him and he squares up, pushing his chest into mine. He narrows his eyes, daring me to make a move. We may not be in the same MC, but I'm the Vipers' president. Jag is a Sargent-at-Arms, below me in the hierarchy. Someone like him stepping up, trying to put me in my place, isn't done. It's grounds for me to beat the shit out of him. He doesn't look like he's going to back down, though.

"Go ahead. Hit me. I'll even give you a free shot. And then I'm goin' back in that closet and gettin' that woman the fuck out of here."

"The hell you are," I growl, balling my hands into fists.

"Maybe you were too busy feelin' fucking sorry for yourself, but that woman is drowning. If you won't save her, I will."

He stomps away, and the rage that filled me so suddenly extinguishes in the blink of an eye. He's doing what I should be—taking care of Aelia. I can't make my feet move. I'm frozen, wondering if Jag smuggling her out would be better. At least she'd be safe then. I don't know how he'd get her out of here. Aelia is adamant we'd get caught.

I drop my chin to my chest, my chaotic thoughts bombarding me. No matter what choices I make, she'll suffer. And I'm no closer to bringing Jenkins to his knees than I was months ago. The bedroom door clicks shut and I whip my head up, ready to rush after them.

"Dante?" Aelia calls from the closet, and I deflate.

"I'm here," I say, rubbing the back of my neck.

"Can I wear your sweatpants?" she asks in a small voice.

I force my feet forward in measured steps. With every stride, a little more of my resolve bleeds away, streaming behind me to float away into nothingness.

I stop in the doorway, scanning the marred skin not covered by her towel. "I'm going to have Jag get you out."

She's shaking her head before I've even finished. "It won't change anything. We'll just get caught."

I nod, not really listening to her excuses. There has to be a way, and even if it doesn't work, I have to try.

"I'm getting you out, Aelia. This isn't up for discussion."

Her head snaps up, eyes narrowing. "Is that so? You're just going to take over and make all my decisions for me? And what happens when it all falls apart?"

"It won't," I growl. "The bruises on your body show just how well I've been able to take care of you. I'm eliminating the suffering now. I'll try to stay on the inside and bring them down. The worst that will happen is death."

She scoffs, pushing to her feet. When she turns away, dropping the towel, I avert my eyes. She may not have an issue with the small scars scattered across her body anymore, but it still sends a bolt of rage through me each time I see them.

Glancing back, she's pulled on a shirt and is rolling up the waistband of a pair of my sweatpants. They hang off her hips even though I've been feeding her more. What little weight she gained was lost when Grant locked her up and she can't seem to put any more back on. The stress doesn't help.

"You don't get it. After all the time you've spent here, you still don't fucking get it," she mumbles as she presses a hand to her side.

"Enlighten me. Because all I see is me failing and you paying the price."

She turns slowly, anger lining her dark eyes. "Let's say I run, with or without you. The worst for you is if I died. You're willing to take that risk, but you have no fucking clue."

My heart clenches at the thought of her dead at my feet. I don't know what she sees on my face, in my eyes, but hers softens, pity etched within them.

"They won't kill me. In fact, I'd welcome a bullet. I'd *beg* for one. A quick death would be preferable to what they'll do to me—what I've seen them do to others. You sit up here, wondering why those below don't overthrow the guards and the leaders. It'd be simple during the day, wouldn't it? All you'd need is a few people willing to sacrifice their lives."

"You can't tell me they never tried," I murmur.

She lets out a sharp laugh, shaking her head. "Course they did. Which is exactly why I know it wouldn't work. The ones who are caught aren't killed. That's too easy. No, if I was caught, they'd keep me alive. They'd torture me, taking bits and pieces of me until there was nothing left. I've watched them do it, and death would be a blessing."

I open my mouth, but she snarls, cutting me off. "Don't throw platitudes at me. Don't sit there and tell me it's worth the risk. You have no idea the shit I've been through."

"You're right," I whisper, then clear my throat.

"What?" Her chest heaves with each breath and her eyes dart around the space as if seeking answers swirling through the air.

"You're right. I have no idea what you've been through. I have no idea what it's like and I'll never know. But I can't keep putting you in danger, hoping the next time I'll be able to protect you."

"You don't have to protect me." Her lips purse as I advance on her.

Her hands flutter by her side and her bottom lip slides between her teeth. I reach up, freeing the flesh from her mouth, and brush my thumb across her skin. She shudders, finally meeting my eyes. I slip one arm around her waist, then kiss her softly. She sighs into my mouth, all the tension leaving her at once.

"I'm sorry," I whisper against her lips. "I can't help but try to protect you."

"Why?" She jerks back as if she didn't mean for the word to slip out.

Her cheeks flush, and she grimaces as her body curls into mine. I hold her gently, mindful of the injuries her father gave her.

"Let's go to bed," I murmur, pressing a kiss to her hair.

She shakes her head, fingers curling into my shirt. "You should run."

"I'm not going anywhere, Aelia. I belong here—with you."

My heart breaks when a sob escapes her. I've fucked up so much here, not only with her, but with this whole thing. I shouldn't have come, thinking I could bring down the Guild by myself. To be fair, I didn't think I could do it alone. I'm not qualified for this type of mission.

I run guns and drugs, keep my family together, and give men the chance to be a part of something. I'm meant to lead an MC, not bring down a corrupt organization. Eventually, I'll have to call someone.

"Why?" she breathes again when her tears subside.

I tip her face up, scanning her eyes. She's too exhausted for this conversation. Resting my forehead against hers, I breathe her in, letting her scent fill my senses and seep into my pores. I'll have to admit my feelings soon enough, but not tonight. She's too fragile, like spun glass. One false move and she'll shatter into a million pieces with no hope of gluing her back together.

"I'll tell you tomorrow. Right now, I'm putting you to bed."

"I'm not a toddler. You don't have to tuck me in," she says, but there's no heat behind her words.

"Let me take care of you. It's what I should have done before."

I tug her along after me, but she's obviously still in pain. I lift her into my arms and bring her to the bed as she nuzzles my neck. My stomach rolls when she yelps, and I push her shirt up. The smattering of bruises along her ribs stands out starkly against her pale skin.

"It's fine. I think I just bruised a rib." She tries to pull the fabric from my fingers to cover herself, but I grip it tightly.

"It's not fine. He broke one, didn't he?"

I drop her shirt, pivoting as my focus goes to the door. I'll fucking kill him. I should have before, instead of worrying about how Jenkins would react if I painted the room with Drake's blood. It would have been an improvement to the decor.

Aelia's fingers circle my wrist, stopping me, and I glance back at her. "Don't go."

I drop to my knees next to the bed, brushing her hair back. "He deserves to die."

"I know. But I want to be the one to kill him. You owe me that for being a bastard." She attempts a smile, but it turns into a grimace.

"If you want to be the one to end him, then you'll have to learn how to do it, angel."

Her eyes fall closed and a grin spreads across her lips. "You think I didn't learn how to kill a man? Oh, Dante. You sweet delusional man. My brother made sure I could take care of myself. I just need a refresher course."

"I can definitely help with that," I murmur.

"This fucking sucks," she says, her breathing shallow.

I climb in behind her, nestling her back to my chest. My arm loops around her waist and she sighs, the last of the tension leaving her. That one sound settles into my soul and I close my eyes. I may not believe I'm capable of bringing down the Guild, but she's more important right now.

As her breathing evens out, I slip from the bed. The hallway beyond our door is bright, empty save for Jag. He swings around, raising his eyebrow.

"This isn't working. We need to make a move before shit goes sideways."

"The Auction is shit going sideways," he mutters.

"It's too close to the annual one now. He'll postpone, probably push it beyond New Year's. We need to get our shit together before then."

A minute passes, both of us lost in our own thoughts. I don't know what else to do beyond starting to blow shit up randomly. If I could get some help, have them hit some of the other sites in the city the Guild has taken over, it might be enough to tip Jenkins over the edge.

It won't be enough, though. I need Aelia to fuck with their money or get further into their system at the very least. She's no hacker and asking only puts her in more danger.

"We need backup," he says, breaking the silence.

"When you figure out who, let me know."

"Call your guys. Hell, call Helms. He called you when they came to Synd. Time for him to repay the favor."

"I'll think about it. Right now, I'm focusing on how to keep Aelia safe."

"About fucking time," he grumbles, turning away and settling into a chair set up against the wall.

I close the door, not bothering to say good night. Pulling off my clothes, I drop them next to the bed before climbing in next to her. She rolls, cuddling her face into my chest. I flip the light switch, plunging the room into darkness.

Twenty-Eight

Aelia

Three weeks of healing has taken its toll on me. Sitting in this chair every night hasn't helped. Jenkins watches me the entire time, refusing to let me leave. Holding my bladder that long is probably going to give me an infection. Dante hasn't bothered to come to the office, lying low. My father has been even more absent, never leaving his room.

"Get back to work, whore. I'm not keeping you around to stare blankly into space," Jenkins says. He doesn't raise his voice. He doesn't have to.

I focus on the screen again, inputting more numbers from the last quarter. It's mind-numbing work, double checking every entry to make sure it's all correct. Jenkins made me go back through every quarter for the last three years, redoing every spreadsheet.

Busy work. That's all this is. I don't know if he noticed the transfers I've been making, but I doubt it. If that were the case, I'd probably be locked away in some forgotten space while Grant played out whatever sick and twisted fantasies he's had over the years.

"Get Cruz in here. Now," he growls.

I glance up, then realize we're the only ones here. I jump up, smoothing my skirt down as the sequins cut into my palms. It's one of the monstrosities Grant dropped off, smirking as Dante accepted the outfit without a word.

When the next day rolled around, it was the same thing. I took them and wore them even when Dante raged about the control they were exerting over me. It's nothing new, so I don't care. Maybe I should.

"Hurry the fuck up." He jabs at his keyboard.

He rarely uses the computer, and I'm pretty sure he barely knows how to turn it on. He asked me a few years ago to show him how to search for something, but I think it was an excuse to harass me. His eyes never left my ass and his hands...well those will be the first to go if I ever get the chance.

I've taken to whispering to Dante in the early morning hours about how I'd take him apart. I've gotten pretty creative on how to disassemble a body with his help. Apparently using his bowels to create a noose isn't possible, but I told Dante to let a girl dream.

As soon as I step from the office, Grant appears at my elbow, shadowing me as I walk down the hallway. He's become bolder since Dante has been keeping a low profile. I hate it, but at least Grant has kept his hands to himself for the most part.

My side cramps as I pull in a deep breath. I'm still not entirely healed and it's almost as frustrating as Dante telling me to back off our plans.

Jag is nowhere to be found when we reach Dante's bedroom. It's still hard to think of it as mine instead of just another stopover, not a destination. Grant crowds into my back as I knock on the door. Usually I'd just walk right in, but with Grant here, I'd rather he not follow me inside. If Dante isn't here, I don't know what he'll do.

"Open the door, slut," Grant whispers, his fingers pinching my bruised side.

I swallow the yelp, but I can't suppress a flinch. Stepping to the side, I gesture for him to try the door. It's a subtle sarcastic move I can get away with. Anything else will result in a punishment I just don't have the energy to combat. Grant's lip curls, indecision swirling in his eyes—open the door or retaliate against me.

Just as his eyes turn hard, I'm saved by the door popping open. Dante frames the doorway, glaring at Grant. He turns to me, silently asking me a question.

"Jenkins requests your presence," I murmur, bowing my head.

Grant grabs my elbow as if he'll direct my movements. Dante's arm comes down on his, breaking his hold on me, then slides between us.

"Honestly, Grant, I would have thought you'd learned your lesson by now," Dante says, pushing me ahead of him.

I tip my chin up, marching past a guard turning the corner. Worry worms its way through my chest at leaving the room unprotected. Jag is probably sleeping, dreaming of whatever ridiculously massive men who never talk about themselves dream of.

"Jenkins is done with you, Cruz. I'm going to have so much fun breaking her while you watch."

I press my lips together, keeping in the snort. If he wasn't worried, he wouldn't have said his threat so quietly. Dante doesn't bother to respond.

"What exactly does Jenkins want?" Dante grumbles.

"He didn't say," I murmur, opening the office door and stepping to the side.

Grant hovers by my shoulder as Dante sweeps inside, then slides in front of me, blocking my way. His grin turns manic as his eyes rake down my body, stripping me bare. He leans forward, then suddenly he's sprawled on the floor at my feet. Ten seconds have passed. I didn't even have a chance to move, much less react. Dante grabs my waist, swinging me through the door.

"What the fuck is going on out there?" Jenkins grunts, still squinting at his computer and jabbing at his keyboard.

"Nothing. However, you'll need a new handler for her," Dante says, shoving me into my chair.

He's not rough, but he's perfected the art of seeming like he's throwing me around when in reality it's mostly me fish flopping for dramatics. As he drops into the seat across from Jenkins, I note the tension in his shoulders. Focusing on my computer, I input more numbers.

"Anders is refusing to continue until he's allowed to kill you. He's convinced you had something to do with Merrick disappearing. And he's back on his push to take over Synd," Jenkins says, jumping straight in as if he hasn't been waiting for Dante to break first and come crawling back to him.

"I doubt he'll be able to focus appropriately on the Auction with his attention diverted to Synd. Why did he go there this time?"

"Merrick. Apparently, they were a lot closer than I assumed. Merrick has dropped off the face of the planet. His stepdaughter as well. Anders wants us to track her down. I'm loath to get involved."

Dante spreads his hands in supplication. "Then don't. Cut him loose or use him to your advantage."

Jenkins nods, eyes focused on the opposite wall. "We need access to someone who's good with computers. Someone discrete and without traditional morals."

"A hacker?" Dante's sharp voice pulls my eyes to them. I glance away quickly when Jenkins leans back in his chair.

"We had one who set up our systems many years ago, but they dropped off the face of the planet, just like Merrick."

Dante snorts, shaking his head. "Not surprising, since they pride themselves on being able to become ghosts."

"No one else has been able to breach our programs. I'm sure that will be expensive," Jenkins mutters. His implications aren't very subtle.

"I'll see what I can do. Anything else?" Dante says, pushing from his chair.

"Council meeting in two weeks with the satellite sites. I expect you to be there."

Dante nods, then makes his way to the door. I save the document and close out of the program. Since Jenkins has blocked most of my access, I have nothing else to work on. I don't know how the bills are actually getting paid, since I'm not doing it.

"I'm taking her," Dante growls, flipping his hand toward me as he stalks through the door.

I pop up and my chair rolls back, smacking into the wall. I freeze, eyes darting to Jenkins, but he doesn't pay me any mind. Scrambling after Dante, I don't dare glance behind. Jenkins will pull me back in and give me more mindless work.

Grant pushes off the wall when he sees me, scowling when he spots Dante, and takes off down the hallway in the opposite direction. I follow Dante, just wanting to slide into bed and fall asleep. Nothing else is as important as that to me. When he passes the turn off to the room, I let out a heavy sigh.

"This won't take long," he murmurs.

He leads us down to the Pit, nodding to the guard who scrambles to step aside. I don't know what changed since the last time we were down here, but they're submitting to him as if he's in charge. Whatever he's been doing over the past three weeks, he's clearly made some type of headway. My palms itch with the need to question him, but not here.

"Rachel," Dante calls, voice bouncing off the stone walls.

Rachel's head pops around the corner of the nearest makeshift room, then disappears again. She appears once more, a young woman shuffling after her. I don't recognize her, but her eyes narrow when she spots me. Her hair might be blonde, but with the layer of grime covering the strands, it's darker.

"This her?" Dante sneers.

He walks around her, eyes raking up and down her body. My chest seizes, but I tamp down on the panic. Dante has made himself perfectly clear that he won't be taking another bit or replacing me. I need to trust that he knows what the hell he's doing.

"Yes, sir. She's new, just brought in. We left her as is, like you requested," Rachel says as she slides next to me.

Her arm brushes mine, then she slips a piece of paper in my hand. I curl my fingers over the note and tuck it into my waistband. I wrinkle my nose against the smell of too many bodies in too small a space. There may be more than last time, though it's hard to tell with how they're shoved together.

"I'll take her. Mistress?"

My head whips around, butterflies fluttering in my stomach. Dante tilts his head at the woman, who silently starts to cry. I don't know what he's expecting me to do. Getting the women Jenkins requests involves a whole process. Dante can't be asking me to prepare her for him, nor do I think he wants me to tell her what we're up to. New assets will use whatever they can to garner special privileges. Oftentimes, they think the guards will let them go. They learn quickly none of their words matter. Giving this woman any leverage will only end up with Dante dead and me in a crimson chamber.

"Yes, sir?" I ask, keeping my tone even.

"Deal with her...privately." His dark eyes meet mine and I nod.

Pivoting, I march away, my heels clicking against the hard stone. I glance behind, but she's not following me. Rachel nudges the woman, and she stumbles after me. When she reaches me, I link our fingers together and tug her along. I tense when we reach the top of the stairs.

The guard grunts at us, knocking his shoulder into mine. I drop her hand, then turn on him, snarling. He steps in front of me, backing me against the wall. He usually isn't like this, though I don't even know his name. As he towers over me, I wonder if I'm going to have to slip off my heel and stab him or something. Dante told me it was possible if I aim for soft parts. I doubt I can reach his balls from this angle, but his eye socket would be perfect.

"Watch yourself, Mistress," he sneers, slipping another piece of paper into my waistband.

"Get your fucking hands off me," I snarl, shoving him away.

He goes willingly, and my mind scrambles to put together all the pieces. The guard lets out a snide laugh, stepping back into position. I tip my chin up and grab the woman's hand again. The further we get, the more my muscles relax, though I'm still tense when we reach the next staircase.

"What's your name?" I murmur.

"Avery," she answers, her voice barely above a whisper.

"I'm Aelia."

"Ellie?"

I shake my head, immediately being transported back to when we moved to Westmont from Synd. None of my teachers could figure out how to pronounce my name, insisting I was spelling it wrong. I was only eight and very shy, but Roman stepped in when one of the teachers kept telling me I was being a brat.

"El-ee-ah. It's Norwegian."

I tug her along, not wanting to have this discussion out in the open. When we reach the top of the stairs, I glance down the hallway. Grant saunters away from Jag, who's posted in front of Dante's door. The woman ducks behind me, muttering under her breath.

"He's not going to hurt you." My reassurance doesn't seem to register as she grabs onto my tank top, practically ripping it. The sheer fabric isn't meant to be yanked on.

I turn my wide gaze to Jag as we pass, and his eyes narrow, zeroing in on the woman. She shuffles along, tripping over my feet in her haste to get into the room. I swear she kicks the door closed with her bare, dirty feet, cutting off his silent inquisition.

Avery drops to her knees, covering her face with her hands. She's completely still, not even a twitch of her muscles. I don't know what to do. Do I comfort her? Demand she get up? Wait her out? I've never been in this position before, but Dante trusted that I could deal with this.

"Avery? Are you alright?"

"Why is he here?" she asks harshly.

"Dante?"

"No, Jag. How did he get here?"

I shake my head, though she's not looking at me. I don't have answers for her. If she knows Jag, it would make sense why Dante chose her.

"He just showed up. He knows Dante. Do you know him?"

She lifts her face, misery etched in every groove and drowning in her light blue eyes.

"My brother is the president of his MC. He's the third in line. He's going to fucking kill me."

Well, shit.

TWENTY-NINE

Dante

"Get in the room, Jag," I say, striding toward him.

His pensive face turns stormy. "What did you do?"

"I found her. Get in the damn room."

He bursts through the door, scanning the room as soon as he makes it over the threshold. I push the wood closed, stopping him from storming into the bathroom where the shower is going.

"No use scaring her more. You can wait."

"How the hell did she get here?" he growls, pacing back and forth as his fingers dive through his dark hair.

"I told Rachel to keep an eye out for anyone from Synd or Harris. She told me about this one today, so I think she just got in. Maybe we'll be able to keep her in here, away from the rest of the shit going on." I lean against the door, tracking his movements.

He's already shaking his head before I've finished. "We have to get her out. She can't be here."

"Jag," Aelia calls, closing the bathroom door quietly behind her. "She'd like you to contact her brother and tell him she's safe."

His explosion is slow, building gradually and marked by the curling of his fingers, then a flush overtaking his face. His eyes are the last to blow, darkening in a way I thought only happened in books.

"Safe?" His voice is deadly, echoing through the silence, and I step in front of Aelia, directly in the line of fire. "She's the furthest fucking thing from *safe*."

Like a curse, the last word drops in front of him as if he's throwing down the gauntlet, begging me to deny it. I'm not stupid enough to poke the bear. I thought I'd seen him go off the deep end before, but this is a whole new level.

I wonder if he's in love with her, watching from the sidelines while her brother controls where she goes and who she sees. I shake my head, unwilling to go down that rabbit hole. I have enough issues dealing with my own relationship without inserting myself into his.

Aelia steps next to me, placing a hand on my arm. "Avery is much better off than many other women who come through here. She just arrived and while she's dirty, she isn't hurt. Dante found her before anyone else could and claimed her, thereby placing her under his protection."

His lip curls as he advances on her. "Is that supposed to make me feel better? I've seen what his protection gets you, Aelia."

She straightens her spine, tipping her chin up. "Our situations are vastly different. You can't judge mine against anyone else's. We'll keep her in here until we're able to find a way out for her."

"I'm taking her now," he growls, and I step in front of the door, pushing Aelia toward the closet.

"Knock it off, Dante," she hisses, batting my hand away. "Jag, either you're going to listen to me or you're going to get the fuck out. She's terrified, and your presence doesn't help."

He rears back as if he's been slapped. "What does that mean?"

She sighs, glancing at the door, then back to Jag. "She thinks you're going to be upset with her. I believe her words were, 'he's going to kill me.' No matter what I said, she is convinced you're going to be pissed."

The water shuts off and his body sways, his feet at war with his mind. I've never seen him this gutted, as if his entire world has tilted on its axis.

I knew Avery, being Ghost's sister, was important to the Phantoms, but I didn't realize how close Jag was to her. Then again, maybe it's a situation like Helms and MacKenzie.

I always suspected those two would get together given the right circumstances. Then all of us were thrown a curve ball and most of the leaders died, including Helms's dad, leaving him to take over. When our dad moved us to Rima, Mac left part of herself with the Reapers, and I don't know if she'll ever get it back. I thought when we went to Synd to help them deal with the Guild they would reconnect, but Helms had to be his usual asshole self.

"Jag, I'm not going to tell you what to do, but just know if you start bossing her around, she's only going to fight you harder. I've seen it before. Be the one she runs to, not away from," I say, regret swirling in my gut.

I think I fucked up with my younger sister. Mac stopped coming to me, and I took that as a sign she was coming into her own. Maybe she just didn't bother anymore. Her relationship with our half-brother is strained, but I always thought they'd get back to who they were when they were kids.

"Dante? Are you okay?" Aelia asks, stepping in front of me.

I swallow hard, anxiety spiking inside me. Shaking my head, I don't know how to answer her. Something is wrong, or maybe I just realize how much I let everyone in my life down.

I was a shit president, trying to change the fundamentals of our club. I was a shit brother, ignoring my sister's concerns and my brother's outbursts. I even was shit at being a friend, dropping off the radar when it came to Helms. I thought it would be easier, but maybe it was just easier for me.

"I'm fine." My throat is tight and I'm barely able to get the words out.

Glancing at Aelia, I wonder how I'll let her down. Will she end up paying the ultimate price for my own shitty behavior? I won't survive that. My life would crumble around me, breaking me into a million pieces and scattering me to the furthest corners of the earth. I'll never recover if I fail her.

"Dante?"

I run my finger down the deep grove between her brows, smoothing her skin until the lines soften. Concern still swirls in her chocolate eyes, but I can't do anything about it. Nothing I say will assuage her fears. If anything, I'll only add to them.

The door behind me opens, and the spell between us is broken. I step to the side, pulling Aelia with me. The woman, Avery, yelps when she lifts her head, light eyes fixed on Jag. I almost don't recognize her with the dirt washed from her blonde hair.

"Stop staring," Aelia hisses, and I turn my head away.

"Avery, what the hell are you doing here?" Jag growls, glaring at her.

My eyes dart to Avery and she transforms. Her spine straightens and she clutches the towel to her body. Her eyes narrow, becoming shards of ice ready to cut him down to size.

"Fuck you, Jag. The last week has been a shitshow and your first words to me aren't asking if I'm okay? Not making sure I'm not losing my mind or was hurt? No, you go straight to blaming me for being in this hellhole. Well, fuck you."

He smirks, but it holds an edge of something else to it. "You said fuck you twice. Can't come up with a better comeback?"

"You insufferable, arrogant, selfish asshole." Each insult is punctuated with a slap of her bare feet on the hardwoods as she invades his space. "Get the fuck out."

She flings her hand out, pointing at the door. They stare at each other, in a war all their own, oblivious to spectators. Aelia tucks her body into mine and I loop an arm around her waist. Neither of us says a word, too entranced by the situation unfolding in front of us. It's not often I have a front-row seat to something like this.

Jag leans down, getting right in her face and bares his teeth. He might be trying to grin, but it only comes across as predatory.

"This isn't your room, sunshine."

"It's not yours either, kitty cat." She spins, stomps back to the bathroom, and slams the door behind her.

Aelia buries her face in my neck, then sinks her teeth into my shoulder as her shoulders shake. Her laughter is such a rare thing, and I wish she would let it out, if only so I could experience her joy given life. Then again, by the stormy expression on Jag's face as he glares where Avery disappeared, maybe now isn't the right time.

"Uh, Jag. You're more than welcome to take her to your room. Might be more..."

I snap my mouth shut as he slowly faces me, a warning clear on his face. I nod, clenching my teeth to keep the grin from my lips. He strides out the door, hopefully to calm his ass down. Avery's appearance is the last thing we need right now, especially if it pulls Jag's attention away from dealing with the Guild.

"Do you think they had a thing?" Aelia whispers, tipping her face up.

I drop a kiss on her soft lips, relishing her response. She opens for me, tilting her head and I slant my mouth over hers. There are a million other things we need to deal with, but I'll take any stolen moments I can with her. I grip her waist, sliding my thumbs under the fabric of her skirt. Brushing against something, I pull away and glance down.

"What the hell is this?" I ask, pulling out a piece of folded paper.

She yelps, snatching it from my fingers, then her hand dives into her waistband. Her cry of triumph echoes around us as she produces a second note, neatly folded.

"I forgot."

"Who gave you them?"

She unfolds one and reads it, mumbling as she scans the paper. Her eyes narrow, then she smooths the other one out and her eyes dart back and forth as her teeth pull her lip in her mouth.

"Aelia," I say sharply and she jolts, meeting my gaze.

"Sorry, yeah. Rachel gave me this one. The Pit guard gave me the other one." She waves them around as if I'll be able to decipher the words through osmosis.

"What exactly do they say?"

"It's just a list of names. But I'm pretty sure they're who would be with us if there was a coup." She's practically mouthing the words by the time she's done.

"Burn them," I say, then grab them out of her hand.

Nothing good will come from having these around. If someone finds them, the names on these lists will die. And that would be merciful, which the Guild is not known for. Crinkling the notes in my fist, I rush to the bathroom door, intent on flushing them down the toilet.

"Dante," Aelia sputters, grabbing my shirt and yanking me back.

"We can't keep them, Aelia," I snarl, tugging the fabric from her fingers.

"Stop. Avery is in there, you asshole," she hisses.

I stop trying to get away and sigh, torn between banging on the door and just waiting her out. I don't have to do anything, though, as the door pops open. Avery jerks back, eyes bouncing between us. She's wearing the same dress as before and it's filthy. At one point it was probably a bright yellow, but it's streaked in dirt and ripped in places.

I turn to Aelia. "Get her some proper clothes."

"What, am I too dressed for you?" Avery spits out, nostrils flaring.

Aelia steps in front of me. "Listen, I know you're upset and probably confused, but Dante isn't the enemy."

"He certainly *looks* like the enemy. And what is Jag doing here?"

I mumble under my breath, retreating to the hallway while Aelia tries to calm her down. I close the door behind me, leaning against the wood next to Jag.

"She still spitting venom in there?" he asks gruffly, crossing his arms.

I slide my hands in my pockets. "She's not exactly happy. Think she's more scared than anything, but she hides it well. You two got history?"

"Ave isn't scared. That woman doesn't have an ounce of self-preservation in her body. Constantly running headlong into whatever trouble she can find without a care for anyone who's sent to pull her ass out of the mess she's made."

Scanning the hallway, I really hope no one is watching from the cameras tucked in the corners. I wouldn't put it past Grant to be hiding in the shadows, eavesdropping.

"So a lot of history then." I grin as he curses under his breath. "Why is she so pissed at you in particular?"

He huffs, crossing his arms over his massive chest. "The last time I saw Avery, she was flitting around Harris with some redhead. They got into it with a rival MC up there, burned down some buildings and pissed off a lot of people. Then her friend disappeared off the face of the planet. I had to swoop in and clean up their mess. May have had a few words with Ave about it."

I hide my grin behind my hand, then rub my jaw. "Can't imagine why she'd be upset at you scolding her like a child."

"I didn't scold her. Just told her she should pick better friends," he grumbles. "And now she's here in this shithole, which is a thousand times worse than a little arson on a Friday night."

I sigh, fear slicing through me. We're getting closer every day to bringing down the Guild which only puts Aelia, and now Avery, in more danger.

"We'll get her out, Jag."

"Can't promise that, Dante. No more than you can promise we'll survive this. Or that your woman will."

"You saying Avery is your woman?"

He scowls, tucking his chin to his chest. "I'll be dead either way. If I come home without her Ghost will kill me. Let's call her my insurance."

"Sure, Jag. Whatever you say," I murmur, clapping him on the shoulder. "Whatever you say."

THIRTY

Aelia

"Think he'll stay gone?" Dante asks.

I swallow the snort I want to let out. Instead, I chance a glance at Jenkins seated at his usual place behind the desk. He shakes his head, scowling.

"If he knows what's good for him. I'm tempted to send you after him just to finish the job," Jenkins grumbles.

"I offered to kill him two weeks ago," Dante says, glancing out the window as if he's not ridiculously invested in what Jenkins has to say.

"And I refused for good reason. He's still an asset to the Guild, though his usefulness is dwindling with every asinine decision he makes."

"And where exactly did he slip off to this time?" Dante brushes his hand along his leg, ever the picture of indifference.

"Synd. At least this time, he told me he was going. Convinced he'll be able to topple the mafia families there and pave the way for us." Jenkins shakes his head. "The council meeting is tonight."

"Well aware."

"This is a private meeting, Cruz. Not a time to flaunt your whores around."

Dante tilts his head, and I imagine he's smirking, though I can't see his face. "I'll bring whomever I like to the meeting. However, I'll reserve the favor for my most submissive bit."

A shiver rolls through me, knowing that will be me. I've never attended a council meeting, though I've seen the aftermath. Jenkins is always in a bad mood when the members meet. I don't particularly want to go, but Dante doesn't trust Grant not to take advantage of his absence, even with Jag still guarding his room.

Jenkins looks like he might insist Dante leave me behind, but then thinks better of it. The change in Jenkins only puts me more on edge. He's still the worst human being I've come across. The way he's conducting business now, though, speaks volumes. He hasn't had me pick someone for him in weeks. He hasn't harassed me either. I'm not complaining, but the switch in his demeanor, coupled with the way he's allowing Dante to control things, is concerning.

Dante doesn't care why Jenkins does the things he does. As long as Dante has access to the top tier of the Guild to set whatever traps, he won't bother to figure shit out. He should. Jenkins will eventually double-cross Dante, and we'll both be fucked. We need to make a move before Jenkins catches on. And before the Auction goes through.

"Have we chosen a reset date for the Auction?" Dante asks.

"One of the things we'll speak on tonight. This is the first year we've had to postpone."

Not to mention it's the first time you bit off more than you could chew by trying to do two Auctions in one fucking year and then had to abandon the plan, asshole.

"Is this the first year it will be in the same city as headquarters?" Dante already knows the answer since I told him last week.

Jenkins isn't even hiding shit anymore. He used to have the perfect poker face. Maybe Dante really has worn the man down and made himself indispensable. The lines of exhaustion on Jenkins's face are pronounced as he nods at Dante, giving away every secret the Guild has kept for as long as I've been here.

Hopefully Dante will be able to use it to get me more access to the system. If we can bankrupt their cash flow, it'll shut down the satellite posts. That'll be the first step, but with Jenkins punishing me for being injured for almost a month, I don't know how I'll be able to do that.

"Perhaps you should allow someone else to take over certain aspects. I realize Anders was your first choice to organize the event, but this is too much for him."

"Are you volunteering, Cruz?" Jenkins asks, raising an eyebrow, but the look doesn't hit the same as it did a few weeks ago.

"I'm ill-equipped to organize an event of that magnitude. However, since I'm bankrolling the majority of it, dealing with the money might be more plausible."

Jenkins taps his fingers on his chin, contemplating Dante's suggestion. I hold my breath, my body perfectly still. I click on an icon on my screen I don't recognize.

It's not unusual to have programs come and go as my access to certain ones is often revoked. It's the Guild's fucked-up way of keeping me on a need-to-know basis. Though it makes my job harder, it also protects them from someone like me coming in and stealing their money.

"Do you know why I put her in this office?" Jenkins gestures to me. I keep my eyes fixed on my computer as the program boots up, subtly starting to breathe again.

Dante glances over his shoulder, murmuring, "No. I did find it strange you would put someone who can't be trusted in such a position."

Jenkins lets out a sharp laugh. "I trust no one, Cruz, much like yourself. Embezzlement comes in many forms, I've found."

"Embezzlement is only funds, Jenkins. Are you saying she's embezzling from you?"

"Certainly not. She wouldn't dare. Which is exactly why she's in that chair. I've had men dealing with our money, with the assets, with the Auction. Yet every time, they fucked me over. Eight years ago, Anders waltzed into my office—we were in some shithole city, needing to move on. And who did he drag with him, but her."

Jenkins pushes from his chair, rounds his desk, and steps next to me. He doesn't touch me, probably because he saw my father's face after Dante got done with him. His hand lands on the back of my chair, fingers brushing my back. I lean forward to get away from him, but it's not enough.

"The others before her stole more than money from me. They took assets, business, and more. But the money, well, that I couldn't forgive. When it happened for the third time, I decided I needed to approach things differently. Drake's daughter, his price for entry, was young, moldable, and had experience with computers. She may not be an expert, but at least I know fear will always hold her back from fucking me over like so many men did before her."

His hand latches onto the back of my neck, forcing my head down. I gasp as pain ripples through me at the odd angle.

He leans down, whispering harshly in my ear. "Isn't that right?"

I whimper, not able to answer. Dante can't save me, and there's no way I can fight back. A wave of rage rolls through me, but it's quickly doused with the fear that he'll snap my neck.

"Jenkins, try not to break my sub. It's so hard to find good ones these days," Dante calls nonchalantly.

I notice the bite behind his words, though I doubt Jenkins does. He squeezes, pinching a nerve in my neck, and I flinch. He lets go, chuckling.

"My apologies, Cruz. I'm sure she's no worse for wear. Making sure she remembers her place is important, don't you agree?"

"I'm sure you put safeguards in place regardless of how well you're able to control her."

"Of course, so why would I give you access that I wouldn't even allow her?" Jenkins asks, settling in his chair again.

Dante glances at me and I avert my gaze. Ever since he showed up, I haven't been able to handle this place as well as I did before. He may have woken me up from my apathetic state, but he made me weaker in the process. I still don't know how to deal with it. Toeing the line gets progressively harder with each interaction. Everything is building within me and eventually I'll blow. I can only hope I take down Jenkins when I finally erupt.

"Actually, I believe you should have her do it. You've obviously trained her well, allowing me to come in and mold her to what I expect. Between the two of us, we should be able to avoid any issues you had before."

Jenkins leans back in his chair, contemplating Dante. When his eyes flick to me, I focus on the banking program that's popped up. It's blurry from the tears, but it doesn't matter. I still don't know what this is. There's no log-in, no indication why I'd have access to this. Blinking rapidly, I try to clear my vision.

A communication box pops up, then disappears into a black coding box. I only know basic code, though I've probably forgotten everything since I haven't used it since I was a kid. Ember pushed me into the class, claiming we could be secret hackers who traveled the world and made our own money. It was a five-month fad for her, but I found out I actually liked it. Unfortunately, it was short-lived since I ran off after my ex a mere two months later. Words appear in the box instead of the usual string of numbers, letters, and symbols.

Let me in fuck this shit

I frantically click out of the box, making sure Jenkins isn't watching me. It pops up again and I panic, my breath stalling in my lungs. This time a string of actual code appears as if someone is hacking into the system. Nothing happens and it devolves into more curse words being strung together in an incoherent rant.

I click out of the entire program, then send it to the recycling bin. I empty it, but it's not gone forever. I don't have access to the hard drive to erase it permanently. Hopefully Jenkins doesn't look too deep. He's got enough to deal with that I might not get caught.

"I'll consider it." Jenkins's voice breaks into my chaotic thoughts, and I scramble to remember what Dante asked him.

"I'm going to enjoy a show before the meeting." Dante stands, flicking his wrist at me.

I shut down the computer, even though I'd usually leave it. Falling into step behind him, I fold my hands in front of me, ducking my head. When the door snaps shut behind me, I let out a sigh of relief.

"What the hell was going on back there?" Dante mumbles from the corner of his mouth.

"Not here."

The walk back to the room is brutal. I'm bursting to just blurt out everything. I prod his back when we reach the door, and Jag steps in behind us. Avery shoots off the bed, squaring up as if she's being attacked.

"Your thumb shouldn't be in your fist, sunshine," Jag grumbles. She glares at him, but drops her hands to her sides.

Dante pivots, planting his hands on his hips. "Are you okay?"

His question takes me off guard and my lips part. "Uh, I'm fine. But someone's fucking with the system."

He doesn't take the bait, instead brushing my hair over my shoulder and inspecting my neck. His fingertips skim over my skin, searching for bruises, probably. It doesn't hurt anymore, though my muscles might be sore tomorrow.

"Dante, someone was trying to hack into the Guild."

He rears back, hand cupping my face. "How do you know that?"

"Because a coding box popped up with someone trying to gain access. I don't think they could see anything, since it seemed like they were still trying to get in, but they're out there. If Jenkins finds out, he'll trash the whole thing and probably blame me." I wrap my arms around my waist, some of the old anxiety seeping back in.

"Wait, it just popped up?" Avery asks.

"There was a new program and I clicked on it. Then a command box came up and someone was writing code into it. I freaked out and got rid of it."

Avery's mouth drops open, and Jag starts yelling. Dante drops his hand and steps back, studying me. None of them understands the position I'm in.

They haven't spent countless hours walking the fine line between life and death. They haven't spent years in the depths of hell, without even a glimpse of freedom.

I spin around and walk away. I can't handle their bullshit when they're screaming and have no idea what the hell they're talking about. There aren't many places to run to in this room and I'm afraid one of them will follow me into the closet, so I escape into the bathroom. It doesn't stop Dante, though, which I should have assumed.

"Don't even fucking start," I snarl, pacing the space.

He steps in front of me, hands landing on my shoulders. I glare at the door, not bothering to meet his eyes. He cups my face, guiding my gaze to him.

"They don't understand." He gives me a look when I open my mouth. "And that's not their fault. But I need to know what the code said."

"Do you know anything about code?" I raise an eyebrow, crossing my arms.

"Not really, but you do."

My annoyance bleeds away, leaving exhaustion to settle in my bones. Part of me wishes I could go back in time and protect my heart more. If I had kept it under lock and key, behind all the walls I built up, I wouldn't be sitting here waiting for something to happen. I wouldn't be terrified all the time.

I should have been scared back then, but I didn't care what happened to me. I didn't have anyone else who cared either, so what did it change if I was gone? Nothing. Now, I have everything to lose and I know it.

"I have a teenager's knowledge of code." I shake my head and his hands drop to my waist. "That doesn't make sense. I just mean, I don't know very much either. But it looked like they were trying to get in. I don't know how else to explain it. Oh, and they dropped a bunch of f-bombs."

"Do you think you could have helped them?"

"And get myself killed? Absolutely not," I growl, trying to pull away.

"I didn't ask if you *would*. We need to know who it is. Then maybe we can get ahold of them. Call them when the time is right."

Rolling my eyes, I drop my chin to my chest. "And when is that, exactly? Because all it feels like we're doing is pretending we have a plan. The only one taking any risks is me."

He tips my chin up, then brushes his lips against mine. Resting his forehead on mine, he sighs.

"You're right. I'm making this up as I go along. I wish I could give you more, Aelia, but I can't. Bringing down an organization like this isn't something I have experience in," he says.

"You're used to running an MC," I murmur, watching his face for the lie.

He sends me a lopsided grin, skimming his thumb across my cheeks. "Clever girl. Not that it's easy to keep shit from you."

"It's not. So you should stop trying."

"I'll work on it, angel."

THIRTY-ONE

Dante

I should have left Aelia behind. Bringing her to the council meeting was a mistake I didn't realize until we walked into the room. A dozen men swivel toward us the moment the door opens, scanning her body with lust-filled gazes. I want to scoop every single one of their eyes out for daring to look at her.

Instead, I tug on the leash, guiding her forward. I didn't want to use the collar again, but Aelia insisted. I'm starting to wonder if she enjoys being submissive. Being in her position for so long, she might enjoy giving over the control freely. It's something we'll have to discuss later once we're free of this place.

I drop into the only open chair at the conference table, pushing it away slightly so Aelia settles on her knees in front of me. I'd rather have her in my lap, but this way she'll be hidden from most of the others. Jenkins' face across from me is unreadable, and he turns away before I can decipher anything.

"There a reason he's here again?" a middle-aged man with a shock of white hair calls from the end of the table.

"Cruz is here at my request. Anyone have a problem with that?" Jenkins asks, scanning the members.

No one speaks up and he nods to the man at the front of the room. He flips a switch, and a large screen lowers, then flashes as he sets up the computer. Two dozen boxes pop up and I realize they're setting up a conference call. Panic floods through me, realizing there are twenty-four cities the Guild is set up in. Shadowed faces fill each one with no indication of who they are or where they're specifically from.

I slide my hand to Aelia's shoulder, tapping my finger on her collarbone twice. She tilts her head slightly, eyes flicking to the screen before staring at her folded hands again. How the hell are we going to tear down that many outposts? Setting headquarters on fire, burning their entire fucking world to the ground, wouldn't be enough. Because it's not their entire world. They have all these other places to run to and start anew. I wonder how many times they've had to do this.

"We're here to discuss the Auction," Jenkins says, addressing everyone. "I understand we're running behind our normal schedule, but with the issues we've run into lately, that's to be expected."

Jenkins drones on, talking about logistics and who will handle what. At least he took my advice to split the duties up. Hopefully, that will allow more issues to arise and push the timeline out even more. I don't know what damage we can do in two months, but I'll push it as far as I can.

"Why are our dues being raised again, Jenkins? We just had an increase six months ago," a woman asks, her voice crackling from the speakers.

I flinch, not expecting a woman to be a member. They're few and far between at the events I've been to, and Aelia is the only one in this room. Aelia wasn't fazed by it when I brought it up to her. She merely said evil comes no matter what's going on between your legs. With so many other women locked up beneath our feet, though, I can't wrap my mind around it. Then again, there are men in the Pit as well. And no one seems to care that they're being abused, too.

"Because we supply you with product. If you have a problem with it, then I'll find someone else to run your city," Jenkins sneers.

"And how exactly will you pay for that if I don't pay my dues?" the woman says, and Jenkins's face reddens.

I clear my throat, waiting for him to turn to me. He waves his hand dismissively, collapsing in his chair.

"Our revenue streams within Rima are still being established. Once we've set a firmer foothold within the city, new assets will be pushed to your cities. This will allow you to expand your current reach and justify the increase in dues," I say, tapping my finger on my knee.

Aelia leans into my leg, silently giving me strength. I won't let my guard down in this room, or anywhere within these walls, but having her with me keeps me sane.

The woman falls silent, appeased hopefully, and Jenkins starts up again. I don't understand a lot of what he's discussing as most of it is past issues they're rehashing. I file it all away, regardless. Something might help us later. Plus, being here keeps Jenkins from becoming suspicious. As the meeting wraps up, though, I wonder why I needed to attend. I could have been meeting with Rachel or planning with Jag.

"Cruz, a moment," Jenkins says as the others file out.

I sink back into my chair, pushing Aelia back to her knees. Jenkins can't see her over the table, thankfully.

"I gave your suggestion some thought." He brushes his hand across the table, not meeting my gaze. "If I agreed to allow her more access, you would be entirely responsible for her actions."

He finally looks up, piercing me with a look. I tighten my grip on the chain linking Aelia to me, waiting for more threats. When they don't come, I glance away.

"While I trust she won't disobey, I would need more oversight in what she's doing."

"You shouldn't trust her."

I smirk even as an ache in my chest pulses. "I don't. I trust in my ability to control her."

Jenkins nods, an evil grin forming on his lips. "Noted. She'll be monitored still, but I'll allow her to get into more programs at once. I'll also send the records for the last Auction to your room. I trust that it's still to your liking?"

"The room is fine." I push to my feet, tugging Aelia to her feet.

"Perhaps you'd prefer another one? Certainly with two bits now, you might prefer more space."

My stomach turns even as I smirk. "The chair is enough to tame the other one."

Jenkins licks his lips, probably imagining Avery shackled to the chair in my room. "I notice you have a man stationed outside your door."

I slide one hand into my pocket. "You noticed? Or Grant informed you?"

"Does it matter?" Jenkins asks, leaning back in his chair.

"Certainly. You see, I've had my man there for several months and yet he's only informing you of this now. Perhaps he doesn't have the Guild's best interests in mind after all."

I pivot, heading for the door. Jenkins doesn't stop me, thank fuck. After the mind-numbing meeting, all I want to do is strangle him with the chain hanging from my fist. Several council members glance our way, one even lifting his hand as if we're buddies. I've never seen him, and I have no intentions of forging any new faux-friendships.

Aelia's words from last night bounce around my mind, catching on all the excuses I've made for not making a move against the Guild. The risks she's taking far outweigh what I've done so far, yet I've acted as if we're on an even playing field. And now I've set her up to take on more. Putting her in more danger isn't the way to dismantle the Guild. We need help.

I tip my chin to Jag when we reach the bedroom, and he follows us in. Aelia sighs, tearing at the lock on the collar. I push her fingers away, unhooking the leather, and it drops to the floor. Her neck is irritated, red marks scored into her skin. Rubbing my thumb along them, I rein in the outrage coursing through me. I hate that I can't prevent her flesh from becoming marred.

"I'm done waiting," I say, breaking the silence.

"Maybe you could be done with leading her around like a fucking dog," Avery mumbles, just loud enough for me to hear.

I sigh, but Aelia's face morphs, nostrils flaring and indignation flashing in her eyes. I shake my head, silently telling her it's not worth it. Of course, she doesn't listen. Aelia pushes me aside, rounding on Avery.

"You have a lot of fucking opinions for someone who was rescued the minute you stepped foot in this building."

"Apparently you don't have enough after being here for, what? A couple months?" Avery sneers.

Jag's arm lands on my arm, stopping me. I didn't even realize I'd moved. Shrugging him off, I retreat to the window, leaning against it. Jag settles next to me, crossing his arms.

"Seven years," Aelia says, crossing her arms and popping her hip out.

Avery flinches, eyes darting to us, then back to Aelia. Her mouth flops open, then snaps shut again as she searches the floor for her next argument. Aelia taps her foot, then looks at her wrist as if checking an invisible watch.

"I thought you said *he* wasn't like the others?" Avery throws her thumb at me.

"And? Doesn't mean I'm allowed to act differently. Plus, wearing that shit?" Aelia gestures to the collar still sitting at her feet. "That allows me more freedom than I've ever had within the Guild. I wouldn't expect you to understand."

Avery's lip curls and she narrows her eyes. "You have no idea what I've been through."

"I may not, but that doesn't mean that you can go judging situations you don't understand. I get it—this sucks. But get your shit together and stop blaming the rest of us for the shitshow you're in. Jag has offered to get you out and you refused. So get on board or shut the fuck up."

Aelia pivots, snatching up the collar, then marching to the closet. She'll strip out of her ridiculous outfit and slide into my clothes even though I bought her sweatpants of her own. I won't stop her since it's adorable watching her trip over the hem. She covers her feet with the ends and shuffles around. When we get out, I'm buying her a dozen of them.

If we get out, I remind myself.

"You could have fucking said something," Avery hisses at Jag, smacking him on the arm.

"Think again, Ave. Nice to see someone else verbally handing your ass to ya." Jag grins, then busts into laughter as she huffs and stomps away.

She reaches the corner of the room and slides down, wrapping her arms around her knees. There's nowhere to run in this place and now that we're cramped in here together, it doesn't help. Jag has been taking Avery to his room to sleep, but he refuses to leave her alone with other guards right next door while he's guarding my space. It's not ideal, yet it's the best we can do.

"You mentioned something about not waiting?" Jag asks, eyes fixed on Avery.

"We need to start blowing shit up. Fucking with their cash flow while Aelia lays the groundwork for cutting off their funds. It's going to be a process, but I'm sick of doing this shit," I grumble.

"You think burning down a gambling hall or two is going to do much?"

"Probably not by itself, but Jenkins is already worried. As soon as I stop contributing, he'll be in a tight spot." I watch Aelia stumble out of the closet, hiding my grin behind my hand.

Jag runs his hand through his dark hair. "Which puts you at risk of being exposed and fucks us all. What else?"

I shrug, completely at a loss. "If we had contacts in the other cities. Or hell, knew where they were located, then we could try to cut them off as well."

Aelia approaches Avery like she's taming a wild animal. She crouches in front of the other woman, tilting her head as they talk quietly. An image flashes through my mind of Mac meeting Aelia, completely taking my woman under her wing. I jolt back at the thought of her being mine—at planning for the future. I don't even know what's going on outside these walls, which makes my palms itch.

"You good?" Jag asks, breaking through my thoughts.

"You worried about anyone out there?" I gaze out the window as if I can see all the way to Viper territory.

"Ghost can take care of himself. I don't have anyone else to worry about," he murmurs, eyes fixed on Avery.

"Sure you don't."

He scowls, pulling his gaze away from them. "Don't start. Shit is convoluted enough without adding more complications."

"You really shouldn't call your woman a complication." Quashing the grin isn't easy, but I manage it—barely.

He grits his teeth, fingers curling into a fist, and I step back. "Knock it off. She might get it in her head and use it to torture me. All I want to do is get her the fuck out of here and deliver her to Ghost. He'll deal with her."

"Deal with her?" I raise an eyebrow.

He waves away the warning in my voice. "She's always been a wild one. Does whatever the hell she wants. He's the only one she listens to and even that is only half the time."

"You think she landed herself in here because she was reckless?"

He scowls, poking my chest. "Don't fucking blame her for being here. These people shouldn't exist. The world would be better off without them in it. No matter how she got here, it's not her fault."

I hold up my hands. "Wasn't saying that. But we need to know if they're in Harris. If she followed you here, thinking she could help..."

He deflates, eyes skipping to the women huddled in the corner still whispering to each other.

"I don't know. I'll ask her, but we gotta stop this before more people like her get caught by the Guild."

"Reinforcements. We need backup."

He nods, but he's not paying attention anymore. He's too wrapped up in whatever horrific scenarios that are running in his head. I walk away, all the ways this could go wrong—Aelia's death playing over and over in various ways in my mind.

Thirty-Two

Aelia

"What do you mean we can't afford it?" Jenkins growls, and I shrink down in my chair.

Dante slides in front of me, pointing at the screen. "There's not enough liquidated assets to pay for the luxury the Auction normally has. Couple that with the recent influx of more bodies and the funds just aren't there."

"What about the raise in dues? That's why I upped them." A flush travels up his neck the more agitated he gets.

"Unfortunately, many of the council members are dragging their feet," Dante says, shaking his head as if this is a terrible turn of events.

It's not. And it's totally because of Dante. He's been stringing them along ever since Jenkins put him in charge of communication between headquarters and the satellite cities. One month isn't enough to do any real damage, but it's pushed the Auction date out at least. New Year's is right around the corner and most of the members are grumbling about the delay.

"I thought you were dealing with that. Why did I allow you into the Guild if you aren't going to deal with these things?"

"Because I infused your business with hundreds of thousands of dollars," Dante growls, facing Jenkins and crossing his arms.

A chill runs through me. All the escape plans we have include us just running for the nearest exit. That won't work here. And since Jenkins has a strict no weapons rule, we don't even have the added protection.

I close my eyes, planning the route to the closest exit. The problem will come if Jenkins overpowers Dante or he hits the alarm. He had it fixed last week, along with the addition of steel sheets capable of blocking the windows. Dante said something about total lockdown, which I don't fully understand, but I know it's not good.

"I bent all the rules for you. Fix this. Now." Jenkins storms from the room, leaving us alone.

I push back from the desk, standing abruptly. The chair knocks into the wall, and I stutter to the side, eyes darting to the door. My hands tremble as I shuffle into the corner, praying to whatever god will listen that he won't come back to investigate the noise.

I've never been left alone in here. Someone is always watching. Even when I go into the Pit, Jenkins has said he follows me through the cameras. Grant usually isn't too far behind.

Dante steps toward me, but I throw my hand out, making a point of glancing at the camera in the corner of the room. His face changes, brows pulling low, and I remind myself it's all an act on his part.

"Get back here, now," he grunts, pointing at the chair.

The command in his voice overrides the panic, and I woodenly walk back to him. Sinking slowly into the chair, I roll it back toward the desk as I pull in deep breaths to calm my racing heart. My eyes flick to the door again and again, unable to fully smother the anxiety rushing through me.

He leans over me, pointing at the screen as he murmurs in my ear. "Are you okay?"

"He's never walked out while I'm here," I breathe, fingers shaking as I pull up another program.

It takes me four times to enter the right information to access the files. Dante wants me to siphon more money into an offshore account, but after Jenkins's outburst, I'm not sure it's such a good idea.

A phone rings and I jump until Dante fishes it out of his pocket. I rarely see him use it, but over the last month he's been taking more calls. He's also been disappearing during the day, refusing to tell anyone where he's been. Then Jag snuck off, coming back smelling like gunpowder and smoke. No matter how much Avery badgered him, he refused to say what he'd been doing.

"While I understand your position, dues are a part of life. Unless you'd like us to pay you a visit." Dante paces away, then leans against the front of Jenkins's desk.

I focus on the screen, biting my lip as I pull up a file I've never seen before. The last time I did this, someone tried to hack in, but I doubt it'll happen again. My chest still seizes until the screen fills with numbers and descriptions of people.

I gasp when I realize it's a list of every person they have locked in the Pit. At first, I think the numbers are to keep them straight, but then I see that they're age-ranges. There are hundreds of them, separated into different documents, but at the top—the city's name.

Remembering twenty-four cities shouldn't be hard, but as soon as I move from one, I forget the previous one. My eyes flick to Dante, silently trying to get him back here. He's too busy arguing with the person on the other end. The red light on the camera lasers through me, and I glance around.

I jerk my arm and knock over the pencil cup. Pens scatter across the floor and Dante's head shoots up. He hangs up mid-sentence and stalks over. As I scramble to pick up my mess, he leans over the desk. He tenses, nudging me with his knee. Sitting back down, I scroll through the data, allowing him to memorize the various cities. When I reach the last one, he raps his knuckles on the desk, and I close out of all the programs.

We need to get somewhere we can talk. I don't know where any of those cities are, but Harris wasn't on them, at least. Dante stalks from the room and I trail after him, peering down the hallway as we go.

Jenkins might be pissed we just left, but I'm not in a position to say anything. I'm never in a position to have a voice, unless it's with Dante, but lately even he dismisses me. He comes to me for information and that's about it these days.

"Are you ever going to fuck me again?" I ask, tripping down the stairs. He throws out his arm, catching me before I crack open my skull.

"What the fuck, Aelia? Not exactly the time to discuss that."

I follow after him, horror and embarrassment swamping me. I didn't mean for that to tumble out. Clearly, we have more shit to deal with other than sex. And it's not like we're in an actual relationship. We weren't fucking like rabbits and suddenly there was nothing. Most of the time we fall into bed each morning after Jag and Dante stay up putting a strike plan into place. Avery and I fall asleep long before they're done.

Dante slams the door behind us, startling Avery and Jag. I stop, head swiveling between them. They're posted on opposite ends of the room, studiously ignoring each other. I drop onto the bed next to Avery, tracking Dante's movements as he approaches Jag. Rolling my head to the other woman, I peek over at the book she's reading.

"Where'd you get that?" I ask, leaning forward to see the cover. A half-naked man chest stares back at me.

"Jag brought it. He's not exactly happy I found his stash," she murmurs, turning the page.

"A stash of romance books?" The only romance books I've read were historical and had a man with wavy blond hair on the front. My father burned them when he found my small collection.

"Smut mostly."

"What's that?" I lean over, trying to read over her shoulder, but she sighs, closing the book with her finger keeping her place.

"You don't know what smut is?" she asks, finally looking at me, and I shake my head. "It's explicit."

She raises her eyebrows as if that's an actual answer.

"I read some historical stuff when I was a teenager," I mumble, realizing how much I've missed being locked away.

She busts out laughing, and I turn to slide off the bed. She grabs my arm, gasping for breath.

"Sorry, it's not your fault, obviously. I just forget how sheltered you are while at the same time being surrounded by sex." She sobers as I plop down again.

"I wouldn't call what happens within these walls sex. More like violations."

"Well, I read books with explicit consent and nary a mention of manhood."

My eyes widen, and she bursts out in laughter again. I scrub my hands on my cheeks, trying to erase the blush I'm sure I have. Avery leans over, grabbing another book from the nightstand.

"Here. Read this one and then we'll talk about it. By the time you're done, I'll have finished book two."

"You just had this lying around?" I ask, raising an eyebrow as butterflies erupt in my stomach.

"I finished it an hour ago." She goes back to her book, and I realize she's already halfway done with it.

Tears fill my eyes as I stare at the cover. I haven't done anything as simple as reading a book since I was sixteen. Avery doesn't understand the gift she's given me, though I doubt I'll be able to finish it by the time she's done with hers. What would we even talk about? The sex scenes? I feel like I would spend the entire time being embarrassed.

"It's just a book, Aelia," Avery whispers.

"Yeah. Just a book. I'm going to go take a shower. Oh, and we found where the other sites were. Don't know how much it'll help." I slip from the bed, clutching the paperback to my chest.

I pivot back to her. "Oh, and Jenkins is on a rant. You might want to reconsider Jag getting you out of here."

"And what happens then?" she asks, eyes fixed on the pages.

"What do you mean?"

She sighs, laying down her book again. "Let's say he actually gets me out. Which is a big *if,* mind you. But then what? Do I just go home and pretend none of this is here? Does Jag come back to help? And I'd be leaving you alone to deal with everything. You obviously don't have anyone in your corner, because as much as Dante seems to feel some sort of way about you, he's got too much on his plate to really protect you."

I don't know how to respond. She's right—no one is truly in my corner. Dante doesn't have the capacity to fully protect me. Hell, he can't even do it now. Which is why Grant had such an easy time throwing me in that room. I don't blame him, but no one has cared since Roman and Ember. Not like that.

"Some sort of way?" Dante grumbles from behind me, and I tense. "I don't feel 'some sort of way' about Aelia."

I can practically feel the air quotes he uses, though I don't understand why he's making fucking statements. If he doesn't want to have feelings for me, fine. I knew going into this it was a weird situation. There isn't even a future for us, since I probably won't make it out of here. He's wily, so I'm sure he'll go back to his normal life, whatever normal means for him. I don't actually know a lot about MCs, and he won't talk about it. To talk about what we are to each other in front of Jag and Avery is just disrespectful.

My cheeks burn and I clamp my lips together. I'm not going to stand here and listen to him stutter his way through an explanation. Except he wasn't even stammering. His voice was as bold and smooth as usual.

Bastard. How he can be so calm and collected tells me all I need to know. Now I'm really pissed I blurted out my question earlier about us fucking. I should have stuck to getting myself off in the shower.

Pivoting, I march to the bathroom. Jag huffs as he leans against the wall, but I ignore him. No use dragging him into this either. He probably wants to be here even less than I do. I barely make it before the tears fall, dropping onto my shirt and disappearing into the fabric under the garish sequins. At least no one will know I've been crying after I get under the water.

I kick the door closed behind me, but it doesn't shut. Spinning around, I glare at it, but then jolt back as Dante calmly closes it. He leans against the wood, crossing his arms as he studies my face.

My mind and body war with one another. I want to be upset, though I should have suspected something was coming. But my body can't decide whether to light up for him, or cry because I lost something I never actually had.

"You want to talk about what just happened back there?" Dante asks, his face unreadable.

I tip my chin up. "Well, Avery gave me a book I'll probably never get around to reading. I freaked the fuck out being left without a handler. And you and Jag came up with a way to destroy all the Guild sites in other cities."

"And what Avery said?"

"You're going to have to be more specific."

I bite my tongue, hoping to stop my tears. I don't know why because it never works. It only makes my eyes water more, and it looks like I'm a blubbering fool.

He tips his head back, then meets my eyes again. Something burns deep within the darkness, sending a shiver down my spine.

"What about your question earlier?" he asks.

My gaze skips away, and I wrap my hands around my waist. Can I have secondhand embarrassment from myself? Or is that just regular embarrassment? He doesn't owe me anything. I'm acting like a teenager in my first relationship, which isn't surprising since I have no experience, anyway.

"Can we just forget I said anything?" I mumble. Spinning around, I put the book on the counter.

Heat from his body sinks into me as he presses his chest against my back. I glance up, breath hitching, and our gazes collide in our reflection. Shit, he looks pissed. Apparently, my answer wasn't enough. His hands land on the counter, boxing me in.

"You can't keep running from conversations, Aelia."

"I'm not running. It slipped out, I thought about it, then realized it was not a question I should have asked in the first place." I try to hold my voice steady, but his nearness is messing with my head.

"We're a little busy with other things and there's usually two other people hanging around. There haven't been many chances to fuck you, angel."

I sigh, closing my eyes. "Which is exactly why I don't want to talk about it. It's fine."

"It's not, but I doubt I'll be able to convince you of that. What about Avery's assessment?"

"What about it?" I attempt to step away, but he doesn't move. I huff, glaring at him in the mirror, and he smirks.

He brushes his lips along my shoulder and up my neck. I tense, locking down the urge to give him more access, to melt into him, to force him to reassure me. Even with my limited experience, I know I don't want someone who makes an effort merely because I told them to. He shouldn't have to force himself to seduce me just because we had sex before. I don't even know if that's a fucked-up view or not.

He rests his chin on my shoulder. That can't be comfortable, but he doesn't seem to mind. Whatever he's searching for in my eyes, I doubt he'll find it. I have nothing to give him.

"You have no idea how I feel about you, do you?" he murmurs.

"Avery brought it up. We don't have to talk about it." My words are rushed, tumbling out of my mouth in an effort for him to just stop.

I don't want to hear his explanations or excuses. My hand lands on the book and I stare at the cover instead of him. The man holds a woman, one hand around her throat as she throws her head back, ecstasy stamped in every line of her body. His face is harsh, commanding. But there's something in his blue eyes, a softness around the edges and a promise within their depths meant only for her. How the artist was able to capture the sentiment in colors and lines is beyond me. No one has ever looked at me like that. I've never seen my future in someone's eyes. I don't know if I'd recognize it even if I did.

"Aelia, look at me," he whispers in my ear, and I meet his eyes. "I love you."

The world drops away and I'm in a free fall. Every doubt that's been running through my mind pierces through my heart. I shake my head slowly, not knowing how to respond. He straightens, hands landing on my hips, and I curl my fingers into fists.

"You may not believe me, but I do," he says gruffly.

"I know," I say, then clear my throat. "I know you think you do."

"I'm not expecting you to say it back. I can wait." He presses a kiss to my hair, then steps away.

I turn, leaning against the counter, keeping my gaze on my feet. "It's not that simple, Dante. I don't know how to love. Everything I've ever touched falls apart and tumbles away into nothingness. I'm broken. I can't give you what you need. I can't love you because I don't know how." I swallow hard, tears filling my eyes again. It's one of the truest things I've ever told him, certainly the most vulnerable.

And he chuckles. My heart clenches in my chest, the urge to lash out smothering the sharp pain. My hand swings toward him, my palm connecting with his face.

He jerks back, startled. I didn't hit him that hard, but his pink cheek shows exactly where I struck him. Covering my mouth, I hold my breath, waiting for his retaliation.

He rubs his fingers over the redness and stretches his jaw. "Solid hit. Maybe I should call you wildcat instead of angel. Next time, don't hold back."

My hands drop along with my mouth. "What?"

He grins, shaking his head. "I deserved that. But I wasn't laughing at you, which is what you thought, right?"

I nod, not trusting myself to say anything else. In fact, both of us should walk away. I just want this to end, to go back to dealing with the things that actually matter.

"Can you go now? I'm going to take a shower."

He steps toward me, pressing his body into mine. Butterflies erupt in my stomach, threatening to send me into a frenzy. Having him so close always makes me lose rational thought. And I know he's about to say something I won't be able to process. If he tells me he loves me again...I might throw up on him.

"Aelia, I love you for who you are right now. I love your imperfections, because it makes you perfect for me. Your brokenness calls to my own. Your broken pieces fit into my own—they make me whole. You'll change. You'll grow. And I'll love who you are then, too. I'll fall in love with each version of you over and over until you're ready to love me. I told you I'll wait, and I will. For as long as it takes."

I suck in a deep breath, staring into his intense eyes. There it is. That piece I thought was missing that I'd never find. My future plays out within his dark eyes. And it terrifies me.

Thirty-Three

Dante

I should be sleeping. The sun is still high in the sky, though the curtains block most of the light. Instead, I'm counting Aelia's breaths, watching her chest rise and fall with each one. The last three nights she's jolted upright, terror in her eyes. She never admits what her nightmares are about, but I'm pretty sure they feature Grant. Or maybe Jenkins. The horrors she's seen have probably plagued her for years. She didn't have them until Jenkins walked out of the office two weeks ago, though.

I sigh, sliding my palm along her arm, up and down. We're no closer to enacting our plan than I was when I first stepped foot in this building. I kept thinking I was making progress, setting shit up to topple them, but everything is in a holding pattern.

Delaying the Auction is my number one priority, which seems to be working, but it's getting harder the more time passes. Jenkins has been on my ass about giving more money, but the accounts Nemesis set up for me are dwindling. Contacting her would be terrible, mostly because I have no idea how to get ahold of her.

"Dante?" Aelia's sleepy voice pulls me out of my thoughts.

I brush my lips over her cheek. "Go back to sleep."

"Why are you awake? What happened?"

"Nothing," I whisper. "Everything is fine. Sleep."

Her droopy eyes meet mine, filled with confusion. I kiss her softly and she sighs. Tucking my arm around her waist, I pull her closer. She turns toward me, burrowing into my chest.

"What are you thinking about?" she mumbles, still half asleep, I'm sure.

"You," I breathe, burying my nose in her dark hair.

She snorts, lifting her head, and I swoop down, capturing her mouth with my own. I kiss her slowly, sweeping my tongue against hers. My cock hardens, but I ignore it.

After I confessed my feelings, I didn't bring it up again, but I also didn't follow her into the shower. She has enough to process without me badgering her about how I feel. The minute I told her, though, it was as if life had meaning. As if I was finally where I belonged. Aelia may not believe she's meant for me, but I'll wait until she does.

Her small hand glides down my chest, then my stomach. My muscles jump, and I skim my hand under her shirt. She shivers, a soft gasp leaving her, and she pulls her mouth from mine.

"You keep that up, angel, and I'm going to end up devouring you," I mumble, rubbing my nose along hers.

"Fucking finally," she breathes.

She hooks her fingers into the waistband of my boxers, attempting to shove them down, and I chuckle.

"Need some help?" I ask, my voice tinged with amusement.

"Nope," she says, popping the P as she grins up at me.

Her hand dives into my underwear, wrapping around the base of my cock, and I groan, eyes falling closed. She strokes me once, then twists, squeezing me. Her thumb brushes over the tip, and I dig my fingers into her hip. Already my balls are tightening, and I haven't even gotten her naked.

I shove the covers down, my body jerking with each swipe of her hand. She bites her lip and I collapse on my back. When she lets go, I reach for her, but she bats me away, attacking my boxer briefs. I lift my hips as she shimmies them down, and I kick them off.

She whips her shirt over her head and tosses it to the floor. Her underwear follows, and I rake my eyes down her body. Swallowing hard, I fix my eyes on her as she crawls up my body and grabs me again.

A flash of her teeth is all I see before my cock disappears into her wet mouth. I kick my hips up without thinking, and she coughs. Sliding my hand into her hair, I brush my thumb along her jaw in apology. Her tongue swirls around my tip and I moan, flexing my fingers in her silky strands.

When she hums, I force her mouth from me as I pant. "Angel, I'm going to come down your throat if you keep that up."

"You say that like it's a bad thing." She grins, licking her lips.

I growl, reaching down to grab her waist to haul her on top of me. My cock slides across her wetness, coating me, and I swear my brain short circuits. She yelps as I roll us, trapping her underneath me. Her legs wrap around my thighs as she tries to pull me closer. I tease her, slipping my tip inside and rocking my hips. She whines, fingers digging into my biceps, and I inch forward until I bottom out.

She gasps, back arching as she adjusts to me. I slide my hands up her body, then duck, capturing a nipple between my teeth. She wiggles underneath me, trying to force me to move. I pull out slowly, then sink back into her heat. Groaning into her flesh, I repeat the move, relishing the feel of her cunt wrapped around me.

"Faster," she pants, and I release her nipple, lapping at the hard bud.

Moving to the other one, I keep my steady pace, building her body up slowly. If I go any faster, I'll come too soon. I kiss my way up her neck, nuzzling her as she squirms and whimpers.

"Don't rush me, Aelia. It's been too long since I've been in your sweet cunt, and I want to savor you."

She shudders, grabbing the back of my neck and pulling my face to hers. I devour her as everything rights itself in the world. It's ridiculous and before I would have chalked it up to not fucking her for so long. Now I see it for what it is—she's meant for me. I gentle the kiss, pecking at her lips as she meets my thrusts.

Her eyes flutter open, desire dripping from them. She glances down to where we're joined. I follow her gaze, watching my cock vanish inside her cunt until I can't tell where I end and she begins. No other experience has been half as mesmerizing as this is every time I'm with her.

"Dante," she whines. "Please."

"Since you asked so nicely."

I smirk, nipping at her bottom lip before sitting up on my knees. Seizing her hips, I retreat, eyes fixed on where we're joined. She moans as I bury my cock into her and she arches her back again. I speed up, thrusting into her harder as her cunt spasms around my length. I can't pull my gaze away from her.

When her hand drops to her clit, I grit my teeth, forcing my eyes from the sight. This isn't like the last time, where she struggled to find a rhythm. No, she knows exactly what she's doing. She thrashes, meeting my thrusts each time, and then unravels. Her face goes slack, bliss flashing across it. I stop, buried deep in her as her cunt pulses around me.

She sighs, a flush splashed across her skin. "You didn't go."

"I'm not done with you," I growl, rolling my hips, and she squeezes the fucking life out of me.

I slip out of her and she whimpers, knees falling open. Her wet cunt is like a beacon I can't resist, luring me in. Sliding down, I wrap my hands around her thighs and lick her. She jolts in my grasp. Her fingers grip my hair as I consume her. I suck her clit into my mouth, flicking my tongue against the sensitive bud as I push two fingers into her, and she comes again.

"Good girl," I hum against her flesh, stroking her through her orgasm.

"What the fuck," she breathes, hands falling away.

I glance up, her eyes meet mine, and I grin. She doesn't even have the energy to roll her eyes. Sitting back again, I curl my fingers and she moans. I love the way she responds, not holding back. My cock twitches as she clamps around my knuckles. Pulling my fingers from her, I cover her body with mine.

"Do you trust me?" I murmur, nuzzling her neck, and she nods. "Do you want to come again?"

"I don't think I can."

"You will. Tell me to stop if it's too much." The last thing I want is for her to get in over her head.

I push off of her, kneeling between her legs. "On your stomach, Aelia."

She scrambles to obey, trying to tuck her legs between mine. I grab her ankles and guide her to her knees. Gliding my palms along the back of her thighs, I admire her ass presented to me like my own personal gift. She wiggles back, and I slip my hand between her legs, stroking her soaked cunt. My cock aches, and I grab the base with my other hand to relieve some of the pressure.

Lining myself up, I pull my fingers from her and replace them with my tip. I ease into her slowly, fascinated as she stretches around my cock. I groan as I slip into her further, giving her time to adjust. She grunts, pushing back, and I grab her hips to stop her from impaling herself on my cock.

"Did you just growl at me?" I ask as she clenches around me.

She snarls, glancing at me under her arm. "Stop teasing me."

I loosen my grip and she slams back, her moan mingling with mine as I bottom out. I'm so much deeper in this position and I know I won't last long.

"Rub your clit, angel," I say through gritted teeth.

Her hand slips between her legs, and I thrust into her hard and fast. Leaning over her body, I intertwine our fingers as I bring us both closer to the edge.

"Dante," she moans, shuddering as she erupts.

Her cunt clings to me as I fuck her through her climax. She turns her head, sinking her teeth into my arm, and I crash into oblivion. My vision blurs as I groan her name. My hips roll as her cunt quivers around me, squeezing out every last drop.

When I try to ease from her, she whimpers. I shush her, caressing her skin. I wrap my arm around her stomach, tipping us to the side. Her ass nestles into me and my cock hardens inside her. There's no way I'll come again, but I'll give her whatever she wants.

Skimming my hand across her skin, I circle her nipple, then pinch the bud, and she jolts. I nibble on her earlobe, walking my fingers down her flesh until I reach her clit. Her sharp intake of breath is quickly followed by another moan.

"You want me to stop?"

"Fuck no. Make me come again," she demands, throwing her leg over my hip, giving me full access.

I chuckle, rubbing her clit as she rocks her hips. Sliding my other arm under her head, I play with her nipple while my fingers work her into a frenzy. Her movements are erratic as needy sounds fall from her lips. I could drink her in for hours if she let me.

"You're intoxicating with your wet cunt wrapped around my cock," I murmur and she spasms. "Do you have any idea how beautiful you are when you come? Your pussy can't get enough of me. She's a greedy little thing, begging for more."

She shudders, then cries out while she implodes, curling her body. Her leg slides off mine and she clamps her knees together, trapping my hand. I press my fingers against her clit, and she jerks away, moaning.

"No more. I can't," she gasps.

I kiss her neck, slipping away from her. She rolls toward me, throwing her leg between mine and cuddling up to me. She sighs, her hand landing on my heart. It's still racing, both from the fire burning through my veins and the emotions pulsing through me.

"Dante?" she murmurs, eyes already closed.

I brush her hair away from her forehead, kissing her softly. "Hmm?"

"Don't leave."

Even half asleep, I can hear the vulnerability in her voice. I hug her close, covering her hand with mine and intertwining our fingers.

"Never."

Thirty-Four

Aelia

There's something in the air.

A heaviness that blankets my senses, muffling everything around me. My stomach turns with the taste of it on my tongue. The hair on my arms stands on end, sending a bolt of anxiety through me.

Something is coming and I don't think I can stop it.

It's more than the looming Auction. More than the thinly veiled threats from Grant. More than the side glances from Jenkins. And I'm not the only one who feels it. Avery kept shooting me looks as I got dressed, eyes bouncing between me and the bedroom door. Jag shuffled around, muttering under his breath as Dante and I left.

Now I'm perched on Dante's lap as he pretends to watch the women on stage dancing. He's so tense, I swear he'll fracture with one wrong move. Trying to pinpoint the source of my unease isn't easy. I scan the crowd over his shoulder, searching—always searching.

I know this feeling well. It's the same one I had when I stepped out of Dante's bedroom and Grant snatched me. The lead weight that dropped in my stomach when Jenkins almost raped me five years ago. The panic that flooded me when my father sold me to the Guild. It was even present when I was driving to Synd ten years ago. Sure, I was excited, riding the thrill of doing something I knew I shouldn't. Underneath it all was that soft warning bell ringing in the back of my mind that something wasn't right.

My father has been gone for almost two months—the longest he's ever been away recently. That's who I'm looking for now. He has to be the reason I'm so off. Jenkins refuses to tell Dante whether or not he's reached out. I doubt he has, but with the coldness Jenkins addresses Dante, we wouldn't know either way. Maybe Jenkins sent my father to some of the other cities to collect the dues. We've never had a problem with people paying before, so I have no idea what action the Guild would take against them.

"Stop fidgeting," Dante mumbles in my ear.

He taps my arm and I slide from his lap and onto my knees. Byron's booming laugh precedes him and I shiver, pressing closer to Dante. His hand lands on my neck, massaging the tense muscles.

"Cruz, heard you got another bit. Double dipping."

I peek at the man as he plops into the chair next to Dante, grinning manically. There's an edge to his smile now. His eyes dart to me and I avert my gaze, hoping he didn't notice me watching him. In that split second, though, I saw a razor sharp clarity that was missing before. I concentrate on my breathing. The last thing I need is him thinking he has an effect on me. When I peek back, he's making a show of glancing around.

"Where is the new one?" he asks, shouting over the music.

"She's not ready for outings yet," Dante says, fingers flexing against my neck.

It's the line he's used whenever someone asks. When Jenkins questioned him, he talked about it being a process to subdue some of them. I don't know how Dante knows about all this stuff, but he plays the part well. Unless it's not an act at all. He's never acted like this when we're alone, though, so probably not.

"I don't understand you, man," he chortles. "I see you cowed your other one."

"Watch yourself, Michaels."

He holds up his hands, still grinning. I don't understand how someone can hold the same expression for so long. Don't his cheeks start to hurt? It has to be an act but keeping it up for hours seems exhausting.

"Heard some talk about a certain special event. Any chance I can get in on that?"

I sigh, grateful that he's finally getting to the point. Whatever is waiting on the horizon for us has nothing to do with this man. He's just a blip on the radar, an annoying gnat I wish I could swat away.

"Unfortunately, Michaels, I doubt you'd be able to afford this one."

The other man bristles, nostrils flaring. "I think you forget who paved the way for your entrance, Cruz."

Dante sighs, straightening his cuffs. "The starting bids are twenty-five thousand. But none of them go for that. This is an elite event, with exclusive invitations sent out. If you haven't received one, I doubt there's much I can do about it."

He's lying, since the invitations are still sitting on my computer waiting for a date. We were able to secure another delay by setting fire to the space Jenkins has people fixing up for the Auction. I wish I could have been there to watch the fallout when he realized he'd have to push it back yet again. Dante assured me no one died from the electrical fire one of the workers engineered. I almost wish it would have spread, taking out the entire building.

"I'm starting to regret introducing you," Byron grumbles, crossing his arms like a petulant child throwing a temper tantrum.

"If it wasn't you, it would have been someone else. Be careful, Michaels. You don't want to be on my bad side."

I swallow a snort. Dante sounds like he's in a mobster movie. Apparently, Byron doesn't have the same reservations as he makes a show of huffing and puffing. He throws out his chest as if he can intimidate Dante into his way of thinking. He sputters when Dante doesn't react, essentially ignoring the blustering man.

Dante lifts his hand and I lean to the side, peering around his body. Security stops several paces away, glancing between the two men. Byron spots them, sobering as his eyes spear into Dante.

"Can't even fight your own battles, Cruz?" he hisses.

"I could, but what would be the point when I can pay someone else to take out the trash for me?" Dante's hand slides through my hair, tugging when he reaches the ends.

Byron explodes, screaming obscenities as he throws himself at Dante. I scramble back, cowering under the table as Dante slams his fist into Byron's Adam's apple. The burly man drops to the floor, clutching his throat as he wheezes. With one move, Dante has incapacitated him.

I've seen him give Grant a beating, but never something like this. He's calm, his face never losing that passive look. I shiver, wetness gathering between my legs, and I squeeze my thighs together. Now is not the time to get horny.

Dante snaps his fingers and I crawl to his side. When he hauls me to my feet, I stumble, my heels getting caught on the thin, aging carpet. Jenkins should have replaced it by now. I glance up once I've steadied myself and lock eyes with the reason this entire night has been off.

My father narrows his gaze on me, then dips to Dante's hold on my arm. He bares his teeth, and I realize how unhinged he looks. Burn marks scar the side of his face and he leans, favoring his left leg.

I knock my foot against Dante's, trying to get his attention. He's too busy watching Byron being hauled away. I step on his toe, digging in and he flexes his fingers. When he glances around, though, my father is gone—disappeared into the crowd.

"He was right there," I mumble, ice sliding through my veins.

Dante doesn't respond, yanking me toward the exit. Byron's shouts precede us, filling the foyer with his objections at being unceremoniously tossed out. This will be another test for Jenkins regarding Dante. If he lets Dante's decision stand, then maybe we're not in as much of a shitshow as we thought.

"Who was it?" Dante asks from the corner of his mouth, still dragging me along. I can barely keep up, still stunned by the appearance of Anders.

"My father," I breathe.

I swivel my head around, searching for the familiar blue eyes, so like my brother's, yet not. Roman always looked at me with love, whereas my father only had indifference for me. I never was told why he despised my existence so much. It hardly matters now, but the little girl inside me, the one who craved his approval, cries out for answers. I wish we could go back to him ignoring me, but since Dante came, he's been around so much more, openly berating me, all while he obsesses over Synd's leaders.

"Get in the room. Don't leave. Wait until I get back."

He pushes me toward Jag, his face a mask of detachment as if he didn't even register what I said. Jag's hand lands on my elbow, ushering me through the door, cutting off Dante as he strides away. I thought the off feeling would dissipate since seeing my father, but it's only amplified.

A fog floats through my mind, muffling my thoughts as I stand in the middle of the room, not registering anything around me. Jag's voice is a rolling thunder through the room as he talks to someone—probably Avery—but I close my eyes, trying to block them out.

My father's image floats behind my lids, the deranged glint in his eye is nothing new, but the fact that it was directed at me is. As my chest tightens, I dig my nails into my arm to distract myself. Something was off with him. Something doesn't fit right. The scene wavers as a scuffle to my left breaks out and I plug my ears, squeezing my eyes tight.

There. A voice whispers.

"Blood," I whisper.

"Aelia?" Avery calls and I shake my head.

He was shot. Or stabbed. Something injured him to the point where there was blood seeping through his light gray slacks, staining the fabric. I may not have seen him actually limping, but I'd put cash money he's hurt more than he'd like others to know..

My eyes fly open, searching for Jag. "Something happened in Synd. You have to find out what."

"Aelia, why don't you sit down," Jag says, his wide eyes searching mine.

"Don't fucking dismiss her. Are you going to tell her to calm down next? For fuck's sake." Avery shoves him, but he's like a brick wall, not moving an inch. I'd probably laugh if my stomach wasn't rolling.

Avery grabs my hand, tugging me gently toward the bed. I sink onto the comforter as a vise clamps around my lungs. Avery shoves my head between my legs, then rubs my back as I struggle to pull in a full breath. Thoughts ping around my brain, never settling long enough for me to think them through.

"What happened?" Avery asks when I sit up, my head still swimming.

"My father is back. He's injured, but I think he's going to target me." I wave my hand when she opens her mouth to interrupt. "That's not the problem. He's hated me my entire life. The issue is, he was in Synd. He's determined to bring down the people running the city for some ridiculous vendetta. Keeps pushing Jenkins to send the Guild there again."

Avery glances at Jag. "Again?"

"The Guild tried to take over Synd last year. It didn't go like it usually does. They got pushed out, but then Jenkins settled here. They'll probably try to go back if they have the chance, but my father is obsessed. He'll never stop trying to burn Synd to the ground."

"Do you think Drake will be able to convince Jenkins to pivot? If we could shift the pressure from Rima to Synd, we might be able to stop the

Auction and bring them down." Jag pulls out his phone, swiping at the screen frantically.

"Jenkins won't. He's already pissed about the fact he wasn't able to have two Auctions this year. Then having to postpone the one they have every year...add in the money issues and he'll focus on one thing at a time. My father doesn't give two shits what the Guild wants unless he can exploit them, which is exactly what he's going to do."

"Exploit the Guild? How?" Avery's hand drops from my back as she jumps up to peek at Jag's phone.

"I don't know. He doesn't exactly share his plans with me. But if he found out who Dante is..."

Jag whips his head up, eyes meeting mine. I press my lips together, swallowing the words I want to scream at him. I want to tell him to run—get Dante and run. I don't even know what the implications of Dante's identity are. All I know is he's from Rima and the president of an MC. Frustration hammers at me, and I wish I wasn't so isolated. The only motorcycle club I've heard Jenkins talk about...

Horror floods my body, locking my muscles. Slowly, I push from the bed and shuffle to the side. The closer I am to the door, the better.

"Jag?" I murmur. "What do you know about the Night Slayers?"

Jenkins was giddy when he learned about the MC in Rima sowing havoc and chaos throughout the city. He kept saying they'd be a great ally for the Guild. The leader, who he never met, wanted to do whatever they could to align themselves with Jenkins. Dante has never indicated he'd be a part of them, but it doesn't make sense why Jenkins wouldn't know about another MC.

"Going somewhere?" Dante's voice from behind me has my breath stalling in my chest.

I turn, knowing I won't be able to run even if I wanted to. And I really don't want to. I may have told Dante I don't know how to love, but I thought I could learn with him. It's hard to wrap my mind around the fact he might have been playing me this whole time.

"What MC are you in?" I whisper, begging for him to tell me I'm wrong. That no matter what the signs point to he's not one of them.

"It's better if you don't know. We talked about this, Aelia."

"He's in the Vipers," Jag cuts in.

Dante glares at him, annoyance clear on his face. "Thanks a lot, fucker. What happens if they separate us?"

"Better than her thinking you're a Night Slayer?" Avery retorts. "I don't even know who they are and I can tell they're bad news."

"Avery, stay the fuck out of it," Jag hisses, and she rolls her eyes.

"Like you just did?" she sneers.

Dante grabs my hand and leads me to the closet. I glance back at Avery and Jag bickering in the middle of the room. Sighing, I let him tug me inside. No matter what he says, I have a feeling everything is going to change. I'm not sure if I'm ready for any of it.

He drops his hold on me as soon as the door clicks shut. There's not enough room to pace in here, but he tries anyway. Three steps away from me, pivot, three steps back. Running a hand through his hair, he finally stops, staring at the dark wood lining the back of the closet.

"Did you honestly think I was a part of the Night Slayers?" he asks harshly, and I flinch.

He spins around, eyeing me, and I shrug as I twist my hands together, refusing to meet his gaze.

"That's fucked up, Aelia. I thought we knew each other better than that."

I sniff, biting my lip. "We do, but I don't know."

"You don't know."

I throw my hands up, spinning around to escape his harsh gaze, then I fling my body around again to face him. I jut my chin out as all my insecurities fall away. How fucking dare he make me feel bad about this?

"You know what? I do know. I've spent my entire life second-guessing everyone around me. I've lived in a world where no one can be trusted. Then you waltz in, and I'm just supposed to, what? Turn that off? Because not only would that be a surefire way to get me killed, but it's not possible. I won't apologize for worrying that maybe I was too naïve."

He drops his chin to his chest and crosses his arms, fingers flexing against his biceps. I don't fucking care what excuses he has for his behavior. I won't allow him to jump down my throat every time I question something.

I've lived so long without knowing someone's true intentions, I don't know how to fully trust. It's one of the reasons I don't think I can ever fully love Dante. If I could pick anyone to trust, though, I'd choose him every time. I want so badly to force my mind to stop second-guessing him, but I can't.

"You're right," he murmurs, glancing at me from under his lashes.

I jump, taken aback by his sudden agreement. "What?"

"I said you're right. I don't know what it's like to question everyone around you, even someone you think you should trust. Doesn't make it any easier that the woman I love thinks I'm aligned with the Guild and actively working to keep her enslaved, but we'll figure that out later."

Startled, I stare at him with wide eyes. I'm always caught off guard when he mentions his feelings. He's not overt about it, which just means I'm blindsided by it when he does. He covers his mouth, hiding his grin, but I scowl.

"What happened with the Night Slayers?" I ask, tipping my chin up in an attempt to get us back on track.

He reaches for me, pulling my body into his. "You're cute when you're trying to hold your ground."

I push against his chest, grumbling under my breath. He tips my head up, then kisses me hard. I sputter, curling my fingers into his chest. I'm torn between pushing him away and pulling him closer.

"You can't just kiss this away, Dante. Tell me what happened."

He leans against the wall, pulling me with him. "I burned their shit to the ground. The Vipers keep to our territory up north. I went to Synd when the Guild came through and knew they would hit us next, which is why I'm here. I've been avoiding Viper territory for months now."

"You were in Synd?"

He nods, resting his head against the wall. "My sister and I went to help the Reapers."

I wince, realizing how little I know about him. "Sister?"

"There's a lot we can't talk about. I want to, Aelia. I do, but the more I tell you, the greater danger you and my family are in. I won't do that to you."

"No, I get it. I just don't understand how..." I suck in a deep breath. "Never mind. We have other things to deal with. My father—"

"I know. Jag texted me. But I can't find out what he did in Synd. I tried to find him. He's sequestered with Jenkins, and I wasn't about to push my luck by interrupting them. I'm already walking a thin line here." He sighs, sliding his hands up my sides.

I shiver, some of the tension leaving me as his warmth sinks into me further. Nothing will fully ease my nerves, though. Not until we're out of here. The lack of a guarantee that we'll ever escape eats away at my soul a little more every day.

"Should we run?" I whisper, resting my forehead on his chest.

He drops a kiss on my head, murmuring into my hair. "Not yet. We have a little more time. I'll find out what's happening with your father. And what went down in Synd. We still need to deal with the Auction. If we can drain their resources some more, that would help."

I feel like we're just delaying the inevitable. The longer we wait, the more likely one of us will be killed. I'm sick of waiting. Eventually our luck will run out. I'd rather not come out at the end with nothing at all.

"Dante, something is coming. My father coming back injured. Jenkins's attitude. Grant's boldness with his threats..." I shudder. "I'm scared."

I've never admitted how terrified I am. Once I decided to help him, I plodded forward. Even when I was yelling at him, calling him out on his shit, or dealing with whatever terrible circumstances popped up, I've never given into my fears. He holds me closer, but it doesn't help.

"Me too, angel. Me too."

THIRTY-FIVE
Dante

I should have listened to Aelia when she wanted to run a week ago. Since then, it's been nothing but one damn thing after another. Drake has disappeared, floating like a wraith through the halls. No one can tell me where he is or what he's doing. Or they've been told not to. Either way, I know he's still hanging around.

Jenkins vanished two days ago, leaving Aelia to fend for herself at night. The first day she walked into the office, saw Jenkins wasn't there, and walked straight back out. Yesterday, Grant showed up, insisting she do her fucking job. She came back looking like she'd seen a ghost, but no new bruises at least. She wouldn't talk about it, but said he was his usual shitty self. I don't know what to make of that.

"Hurry the fuck up," Jag hisses from the shadows. "I don't like leaving Avery alone."

I slip into the alley, pulling the mask from my mouth. "You think I'm just lollygagging around for funsies?"

"You sure we should do this tonight? Seems like we're pushing the limit."

"If not now, when? Shit is falling apart. Sooner or later, they're going to catch on that I'm not who I said I am and then we'll be fucked," I say, pulling out my phone and checking the time.

"We're already fucked," he mumbles, leg jiggling as he scans the mouth of the alley. "You sure we can trust this guy?"

"Probably." My phone lights up, giving us the go-head.

"Seriously? We're doing this on a probably?"

I shrug, walking toward the door hidden in the darkness at the back of the alley. The smell of rotten food taints the air and I pull the mask over my nose again. Knocking on the metal, I wait until the small slit opens, then flash the text on my phone. No one says anything as it slams shut before the door swings open, admitting us. As we step through, I shut off all my emotions. It's the only way I'll get through this.

The roar of a crowd mingles with the barking of dozens of dogs. I can almost hear Jag gritting his teeth. I didn't want to bring him to a dogfight, but hitting the smaller operations first makes more sense. Plus, we might actually help some of the animals. My phone buzzes again, but I don't pull it out. I already know what it says.

The dank hallway opens up to a large open space with a dirt ring in the middle. The crowd, mostly men, shakes their fists with wads of cash clutched in them at the two dogs tearing each other apart.

Jag steps past me, but I hold him back. He never told me why he's so triggered by these types of fights, but it's obvious how much he cares. Rage flows across his face, lining his muscles as he tries to shrug me off.

"Wait, Jag. Not yet." I shout over the yelping and cheers as one dog pins the other.

Two men jump into the ring, separating them. I'm surprised they stopped it. The ones I've been to before the fight was to the death, much like the underground ring I took Aelia to. I didn't tell her several of the fighters were probably dead, but it was clear by the amount of blood left behind.

I yank Jag away from the scene and direct him toward the makeshift bar. It's just a slab of wood slapped on two barrels in the corner. A greasy kid probably not more than sixteen pours beer after beer as one of his buddies takes the money.

I assumed most of the people here would be either underage or in their fifties. Instead, it's a mix, but they're all obviously hard up for cash. No one wears a suit or looks like they've seen a shower in weeks, adding to the general stench hanging in the air. I'm glad I wore clothes I don't care about, since I'm pretty sure I just stepped in someone else's piss.

I hold up two fingers as Jag hands over the money along with a generous tip. The kid grabs it, shoving it into a bag, then snatches his hand out again, staring at the thick wad. His wide eyes find mine and I nod. He taps the bartender on the shoulder, then takes off, upending the wood in the process. I barely step back, avoiding the spillage. Others aren't so fortunate, and they yell in outrage.

Next, we approach someone near the cages lined at the back of the room. A boy even younger than the other two doesn't notice our arrival. He's too busy being hit with what looks like a cricket bat. Where the hell the man even got one is beyond me, but Jag grabs the wood as the man tries to hit the boy again. He rips it from the man's grasp and tosses it away. Jag pushes into him, baring his teeth. The man stumbles back and lands on his ass.

The boy scrambles to his feet, and I snag the back of his shirt. He digs his heels in, but all he accomplishes is to choke himself. Another fight breaks out, dogs snarling viciously. Grabbing the kid's arm, I shake him a little to get him to stop trying to flee, but he kicks my shin.

"Would you knock it off? Little shit," I hiss, hopping back so he can't land another blow while still keeping hold of him.

"Let me go," he says through gritted teeth.

I yank him toward me, bending so I'm right in his face. "You want the pups to go free?"

The boy sobers, staring at me with the solemness of a kid who's seen more death than a ten-year-old should. He glances at the dozen cages, then back at me, and nods.

"Then listen up."

I mutter in his ear what to do and to wait for the signal, checking to make sure he understands. He nods again, then scampers behind a box in a crouch. His dark eyes pop up from over the top, widening when I don't move.

Jag has dealt with the abusive asshole, now crawling to get away from the larger man's fists. Anyone watching will assume we just lost a bet, and no one is going to interfere with a man like Jag, especially with the evil glint flashing in his eyes.

Pulling my phone out, I stab at the screen, my fingers trembling. It's been a while since I've done anything other than live out a stranger's life that's filled with money and wealth. Adrenaline courses through my veins, amplifying my surroundings.

"Get it together," Jag says, glaring at me.

I slip my phone back in my pocket, then glance around. A few men are watching us, and I meet Jag's gaze. Striding over, I kick one of the cages and the dog cowers in the corner. I set my jaw, then swing around. A man who looks like a guard stomps toward us and I cross my arms, waiting for him to reach me.

"You got a problem?" he asks.

"Nope. We dealt with it." I gesture to the man Jag beat, still crawling away, leaving a bloody trail behind him.

He nods, narrowing his eyes. "These are your problem now. Get them ready."

When he walks away, I smirk. I didn't expect that to be so easy, but apparently, they don't give a shit who deals with the dogs. My phone buzzes one last time, and I lift my hand to Jag. He glances around, making sure all the workers who were kids are out before hustling to the back door next to the child still cowering behind a box.

Following him, I barely make it through the door before Jag pulls the fire alarm. We had a different plan, counting on the system to not be working anymore, but my contact assured me it was. There's no shrill ringing and only one strobe light next to the door we just exited.

"You sure they got to the rest of the lights?" Jag asks, glancing back at me as we hurry down the hallway.

"Since no one is rushing from the building, I'd say so. I need you to hang out and make sure the kid makes it out."

"You think I'd leave him inside? I'm an asshole, but I ain't a child killer," he growls. "We should have stayed to help him."

"The others have it."

He swings around to face me, stopping me in my tracks. "Others?"

"You think they don't take care of their own? Those bartenders didn't take off. They're hiding to get the kid and the dogs out."

"Who the fuck is your contact?"

I grin, pushing him toward the exit. When we burst outside, the cold winter wind whips through the empty alley. Sending off one more text to confirm our part is done, we rush away from the building. We make it to the rendezvous point, and I breathe a sigh of relief when a woman steps from the shadows.

"Raines. Or is it Cruz now?"

"Raven, good to see you. Everything in place?" I ask, glancing at the five other women, all dressed in black, gathered around her.

"You realize this is a big ask, right? We don't do anything for free." She smirks, crossing her arms and tapping her booted foot against the concrete.

"You owe me," I grunt, glancing behind me.

She snorts and I turn back. "Fair enough. Better get the fuck out of here before the fireworks start. Wouldn't want to tarnish your image."

Shaking my head, I sigh. "If you don't hear from me, get ahold of Ryker Helms in Synd. Tell him what's going on."

Concern flashes across her face. "You thinking of getting yourself killed?"

I shrug, feigning nonchalance all while my body itches to get back to Aelia. I hate that I had to leave her behind. The sooner I get back, the better I'll feel.

"With these people? You never know what they'll do. Don't underestimate them, Raven."

The ride back to Guild headquarters is tense as scenario after scenario runs through my head of what I'll come back to. I miss my bike. I'd already be there if I was riding instead of stuck in traffic. Horns blare around us and I'm about ready to sprint back. Convincing myself that Aelia is fine doesn't work. Only seeing her in person will settle my nerves.

An hour later, we finally pull up in front of headquarters, and I rush up the stairs. The guards barely get the doors open before I'm barreling through. Once inside, I slow my pace, trying to project a calm I don't feel. The night is in full swing, members spilling from various rooms into the hallway. I'm able to slip through them without catching anyone's attention. It's the only saving grace right now.

When I reach the hallway of our bedroom, it's blissfully silent and I breathe a sigh of relief. If someone got to them, I'm sure it'd be chaos, or Grant would be waiting around to gloat.

My feet slow as I approach the door, my brain not processing what my eyes are seeing. The knob hangs at an odd angle, scuff marks surrounding it. I push the wood with my fingers, barely putting any pressure on it, and it swings open. Deep gouges line the door frame and my heart stalls in my chest.

Empty. The room is completely devoid of any life. Aelia's scent still lingers in the air, but nothing else remains of her. I don't even need to check the rest of the space, but I do anyway. The closet is a mess, clothes strewn about as if someone were searching for something. I blink and I'm suddenly in the bathroom with no recollection of moving. Blood splatters the tiles, the red a stark contrast against the white.

I blink again and I'm on my knees, hands braced against the floor as her blood—it has to be hers—smears across my palms. My vision darkens, a roaring taking over the silence that presses down on me.

Get up.

I groan, slamming my eyes closed against the voice. She's gone and it's my fault. I should have run when she asked. I should have gotten her out. I told her I loved her, then I abandoned her.

Get up.

Sitting up, I tip my head back, yelling at the ceiling, hoping I can drown out the voice. I'll stay here, waiting for them to find me. I don't give a shit about the Guild. None of it matters anymore with her gone. I don't know how long I stay there, attempting to turn my brain off, but eventually I open my eyes.

There's not enough blood for her to be dead. Now get up.

The voice that sounds suspiciously like Mac's rings in my ears, dampening the roar of my heartbeat. I swallow hard, then scrub my hands on my jeans. Stumbling, I haul myself to my feet, and stagger back to the bedroom.

A lead stone in my stomach weighs me down, making my movements slow and clumsy. Other than the damage to the door and the blood in the bathroom, there's no evidence of a struggle. The bed is mussed as if she was asleep when they came for her.

The thought pulls me up short. Aelia wouldn't sleep in the middle of the night. She's spent the last decade living in the dark. In my despair, I forgot about Avery. How the hell am I supposed to tell Jag, who didn't even want to come tonight, that she's gone? Ghost will go ballistic and retaliate against me. I have to find them.

I turn to rush out the door when my eyes snag on Aelia's pajamas. It's not one of my shirts, which she's taken to sleeping in every night. No, this is her ratty tank top she freaked out over when she thought I'd tossed them. The one thing that was truly hers. It's been stuffed in the back of a dresser drawer for months now. There's no reason she would have randomly taken them out.

Running out the door, I dash to the stairwell that was probably once for staff to remain unseen. I'm panting by the time I reach the right floor. I wait by the door, listening for anyone on the other side. Easing the wood open, I peek out before I slip back into the muted light of the stairs. I shoot off a text to Jag, warning him away and giving him a location to meet at. He sends a barrage of messages almost immediately, but I ignore them. I'll deal with the fallout if I can't get Avery out.

There's no use acting normal. If someone is watching the cameras, they already know I'm here. They're probably banking on me to go to Jenkins to get Aelia back. I'd do it too—if I thought it would work. With the way shit has been around here lately, I'm fucked.

I sprint for the closet I found Aelia in all those months ago and rip open the door. Quiet sobbing meets me, and I tear the blankets from the makeshift bed, reveling a cowering Avery. Tears stream down her blotchy face, terror radiating from every line in her body. Grabbing her arm, I yank her upright and she yelps.

"We don't have time. Where's Aelia?" I snarl.

She shakes her head, her entire body shaking with the force of her sobs. "She brought me here and took off. She said she'd be back."

Slamming my eyes closed, I count to ten. It's the most I can give myself right now.

"We need to get out. Now."

I drag her into the hall, then toward the stairs around the corner. We'll have to enter the main hallways eventually, but I'll delay that as long as possible. Several times, she stumbles into me as I rush us down the stairs. When we reach the end, I swing open the door and stalk into the crowd.

Music and the chatter of dozens of men fill the space, spilling from the gambling room. Avery stops, her arm slipping from my grasp. Turning around, I brace myself to fend off whoever interfered, but no one grabbed her and she's not running.

She's frozen, eyes fixed across the room. I spin back and spy Anders Drake. He limps down the hall, grinning at the man he's talking to. A woman literally hangs off his arm. I'm pretty sure the only reason she's still standing is because of the grip he has on her waist.

When he turns, limping toward us, I grab Avery and pull us into the gambling room. Most of the tables are filled and a mass of men are clustered by the stage where women dance. I've never seen this many people just standing around, though. We squeeze through a cluster of them as I try to lose us in the crowd.

We reach the corner by the bar with a clear shot to the main doors. I'm hesitant to pass any of the guards. I pull Avery close, wrapping my arm around her waist and putting my mouth to her ear.

"We'll stay here until he passes, then make a break for the front doors."

She nods, and I keep my head buried near her neck as I scan the crowd. Drake wanders in, laughing as if he doesn't have a care in the world.

"Dante." Avery's voice is carried away, lost within the mass of people, and I lean closer. "She said to make the call."

Ice floods my veins and I rear back, searching her face. My discussions with Aelia revolved around how to escape, never with something like this. The only person I talked to about calling in others was Jag.

"Jag told you our plan. And you told Aelia."

Guilt flashes in her eyes, but it doesn't matter. Calling the Vipers, the Reapers, hell, even the mafia families in Synd was always a last resort. They dealt with enough when it came to the Guild. They lost more people than they should have. We can't do this alone, though. Especially since I no longer have the advantage of being on the inside. With Aelia missing, my focus is on finding her now, not bringing down the Guild.

I slide my phone from my pocket, dialing my brother's number. Maddox might not be my first choice, but I left him in charge of the Vipers. He should at least be able to get ahold of the rest. It doesn't even ring, an automated message about the line no longer being in service picking up instead. I curse, hanging up. My thumb hovers over the screen. I don't want to drag Mac into this, but I might not have a choice.

A guard approaches and I'm about to take off when I realize I recognize him. He casually posts up next to us, then slides closer.

"Go," he grunts, then melts into the crowd again.

I dial Mac, then push my way through toward the double doors. Avery yelps when she gets elbowed in the head, and I drop my arm as the line rings over and over. I seize her hand, pulling her behind me. There's a click and I let out a whoosh of air.

"Mac?" I yell.

The line crackles and I glance at the screen to make sure it's connected. The timer clicks on, counting the seconds.

"Mac!" Still nothing, but I don't have time to make sure she's there.

"MacKenzie, I'm sorry. I don't have time, and I hate to ask, but I need you. Call everyone. I'm in with the Guild in Rima. I think I can—"

Avery cries out as a man trips into her, then his body crashes onto a table, scattering chips. Men jump up, bellowing and adding to the general chaos. Another man grabs Avery and she shrieks, trying to free herself. I shove him, clutching my phone tight.

"Back the fuck off. She's mine."

"You can share, pretty boy," he slurs, bloodshot eyes finding mine.

My lip curls in disgust as Avery slips behind me. "Touch her and I'll cut your fucking dick off and shove it down your throat and make you thank me for the service."

I remember I'm still on the phone and bring it to my ear again, grunting when Avery's elbow slams into my stomach in her haste to get away from another man leering at her.

"Mac?" My heart clenches when I still hear nothing. "Just get here. I can't bring them down alone."

I hang up, then drop the phone in an abandoned drink. No use keeping it. Who knows what type of tech Jenkins has to track me. I've spent enough time in here I'm sure he's got eyes on me. No use giving him another way to find me.

Spinning Avery in my arms, I mouth, "I'm sorry," then throw her over my shoulder. She doesn't react, just digs her nails into my back as she clutches my shirt. We finally make it out the doors and into the hallway. I turn to the left when a shout from behind rises over the din of voices. I don't bother glancing back as adrenaline courses through my body.

We make it to the front and another guard, one whose name was on the list Rachel slipped Aelia, spots me. He hurries to open the heavy wood and I slip through, narrowly clearing Avery's head. The driver I used all those months ago waits at the end of the drive, and I sprint toward the black SUV.

More shouts ring through the night and I push myself harder. The back door pops open just as a bullet whizzes by us, burrowing into the rocks at my feet. I throw Avery into the car and dive in after her, covering her body with my own. We're moving before I have the chance to close the door and another shot rings out.

I grunt when a stinging sensation hits my lower leg. I yell, pulling my feet inside and the door slams shut as the driver careens around the circle driveway. Panting, I heave my body off Avery's, checking her for injuries. She's wide-eyed, but unhurt, thank fuck. Groaning, I sit up, pulling Avery with me.

"Are you hurt?" Jag bellows from the passenger seat, practically trying to crawl into the back.

Avery shoves him back, tears coursing down her cheeks.

"Stop it. I'm fine," she snaps, then turns to me. "Go back. You have to go back."

I shake my head, silently apologizing, but she buries her face in her hands and sobs. Everything in me screams to do exactly what she wants—to rush headlong into danger and find Aelia.

Jag's furious face glares at me. "Where the fuck is Aelia?"

I swallow hard, glancing behind at the rapidly dwindling lights of the Guild headquarters.

"They took her. The Guild took her."

"Then go get her back," he bellows, slamming his hands into the dash.

I glance at Avery, still falling apart next to me. Jag continues to yell, but I ignore his lectures. If I go back now, it'll only end up with me dead and no one left to save her. I've had a lot of practice biding my time lately.

"What the fuck is wrong with you? I thought you fucking love her?" Jag sneers. "You don't fucking deserve that woman."

He's right, but I won't admit that to him. Ever since I realized how I felt about her, my goals shifted. If I got her out, I'd have succeeded. I failed her. I broke every fucking promise I made. I can only hope she holds on long enough for me to make it up to her.

I glance back once more as the night swallows the last of the bright lights of Rima.

Hold on, angel. Please hold on.

Thank You

Thank you so much for reading the first installment of Dante and Aelia's
story!
Ready for the next adventure?
Dive into the final book in the Ruins of Rima duology by pre-ordering
Charmed by Darkness.
Out December 1, 2023.

If you'd like to hear about the other stories that have been living in my
head, sign up for my newsletter (including extra scenes & a novella), visit
my website, or follow me on social media visit:

https://emiliaabraham.com

Special Thanks:
K.B. Barrett Designs-Cover Artist and Formatter
Emily Michel-Editor
Emily Renee-Beta Reader

Also by the Author

Shadows of Synd:
Under the Shadows - Book 1
Running From Shadows – Book 2
Becoming Shadows – Book 3
Shadows Within Us – Book 4

Ruins of Rima: *Spin-off Series*
Chasing Darkness – Book 1
Charmed by Darkness (December 5th, 2023)

Available on Newsletter:
Extra Scenes
Epilogues
Holiday Novella
Bridging Epilogues (Shadows of Synd-Book 1 & 2)

Also by Emilia Abraham:
Stuck at Sundown

EMILIA ABRAHAM

After many years of dreaming of becoming a full-time writer, Emilia Abraham took the leap, bringing her words to print. From sweet contemporary romance to spicy why choose and everything in between, she focuses on the happily ever after.

Emilia lives in the Upper Midwest with her husband (who's probably sick of listening to her expound on fictional men) and three kids (who try to steal her post-it notes). When she's not writing, she enjoys reading, playing video games, and consuming copious amounts of energy drinks.